522 889 38 4

Deep

Kylie Scott is a long-time fan of erotic love stories and B-grade horror films. Based in Queensland, Australia with her two children and one delightful husband, she reads, writes and never dithers around on the internet.

www.kylie-scott.com

@KylieScottbooks

By Kylie Scott

The Stage Dive Series

Deep

Kylie Scott

PAN BOOKS

First published 2015 by St Martin's Press, New York

First published in the UK 2015 by Pan Books

This paperback edition published 2015 by Pan Books
an imprint of Pan Macmillan,
20 New Wharf Road, London N1 9RR
Associated companies throughout the world
www.panmacmillan.com

ISBN 978-1-4472-6058-5

1 3 5 7 9 8 6 4 2

A CIP catalogue record for this book is available from the British Library.

Printed and bound by CPI Group (UK) Ltd, Croydon, CR0 4YY

Visit www.panmacmillan.com to read more about all our books
and to buy them. You will also find features, author interviews and
news of any author events, and you can sign up for e-newsletters
so that you're always first to hear about our new releases.

As always, for Hugh

ACKNOWLEDGMENTS

With thanks to all of the readers, reviewers, bloggers, crit-partners, beta readers, friends, family, publishers, editors, assistant editors, copy editors, formatters, artists, models, photographers, promotions people, receptionists, booksellers, sales assistants, mail workers, librarians, and any assorted pets any of you might have, for taking the Stage Dive journey with me. I couldn't have done it without you. You rock.

Deep

PROLOGUE

Positive.

I reread the instructions, doing my best to flatten out the creases in the piece of paper one-handed. Two lines meant positive. Two lines sat on the test. No, not possible. My gaze darted back and forth between the two, willing one of them to change. I shook the test and turned it this way and that. I stared and stared, but just like with the first one sitting rejected beside the sink, the answer remained the same.

Positive.

I was pregnant.

"Fuck."

The word echoed around and around the small bathroom, bouncing off the white-tiled walls and beating at my head. This shit shouldn't be happening to me. I didn't break laws or do drugs. Not since that blip after Dad left. I was studying hard for my degree in psychology and I behaved. Mostly. But those definite neat pink lines stood loud and proud in the pregnancy test's little window, taunting me, the evidence irrefutable even when I squinted or crossed my eyes.

"Fuck."

Me as someone's mom. No.

What the hell was I going to do?

I sat on the edge of the bathtub in my plain black underwear, covered in goose bumps. Outside, a barren limb swayed in and out of view, buffeted by the wind. Beyond it lay the endless gray of a February Portland sky. Screw it all. All of my plans and dreams, my whole life, changed at the say of a stupid plastic stick. I was only twenty-one, for goodness sake, not even in a relationship.

Ben.

Ah, man. We'd barely talked in months, what with me doing my best to avoid any situation where he might be present. Things had been a little awkward ever since I threw him out of my hotel room in Vegas minus his pants. I'd been done with him. Finished. Kaput.

My uterus apparently did not agree.

We'd had sex once. *Once.* A secret that I'd long since decided to take to my grave. Him never telling anyone was a given. But still, his penis went in my vagina one time only, and I'd watched him roll the condom on, god damn it. Me lying spread out on the California king–size, trembling with excitement, and he'd just kind of smiled. There'd been this warmth in his eyes, a gentleness. Given the obvious tension running through his big body, it'd seemed so strange and yet wondrous. No one had ever looked at me that way, as if I meant everything.

An unwelcome warmth filled my chest at the memory. It'd been so long since I'd thought of him with anything other than *ugh*.

At any rate, apparently someone had diddled away their shift at the prophylactics factory and here we were. Pregnant. I stared unseeing at my skinny jeans, lying discarded on the floor. Sure, they'd fit. As in, I could wiggle up the zip halfway and the button was out of the question. The pressure they inflicted upon my belly was a definite no go.

Things were changing so fast. I was changing.

Normally, I had more going on in the back than up front. But for the first time in my life, I actually had the makings of a rack. Not enough boobage to get me a job at Hooters or anything, but still. And as much as I'd like to believe that god had finally answered my teenage prayers, when you added up all the evidence, it wasn't likely. I had a person growing inside of me. A little baby bean-shaped thing made from equal parts of me and him.

Mind-boggling.

What I'd wear tonight was, however, the least of my worries. If only I could get out of going. He'd be there, all six foot five—worth of rugged rock star. Just the thought of seeing him turned me inside out, filling me with nerves. My stomach dived, nausea rolling through me. Puke rushed up, filling my throat and making me gag. I only just made it to the toilet in time to lose what little I'd had for lunch. Two Oreos and half a banana, going, going . . . gone in a hot rush.

Yuck.

I groaned loudly and wiped my mouth with the back of my hand, flushed the toilet and staggered over to the sink. Whoa. The girl in the mirror looked spectacularly crappy, face too pale and long blond hair hanging in straggly wet strands. What a hot mess. I couldn't even bring myself to meet my own eyes.

That I'd dropped the pregnancy test didn't even occur to me until I stood on it. My heel pressed down, grinding of its own accord. Plastic cracked and splintered, the noise strangely satisfying. I just stamped on it, over and over, trampling the bastard, pounding it into the scuffed wooden floor. God yeah, the good vibes just flowed. The first test soon met the same fate. I didn't stop until I was panting and only wreckage remained on the floor. That felt so much better.

So I'd been knocked up by a rock star.

Big deal.

Deep breath. Okay.

I would handle this like an adult, pull myself together and go talk to Ben. We'd been friends at one time. Sort of. I could still talk to him about stuff. Specifically, stuff relating to our progeny arriving in, oh . . . seven or so months.

Yes, I could, and I would.

Just as soon as I'd finished throwing my tantrum.

"You're late. Get in here," said my sister, Anne, grabbing my hand and dragging me through the doorway. Not that I'd been lurking outside, skulking and hesitating. Much.

"Sorry."

"I thought you were going to bail on me. Again." She gave me a quick, affectionate squeeze, then stole my coat off my shoulders. It got thrown onto a nearby chair already overflowing with other jackets. "Everyone else is already here."

"Great," I mumbled.

True enough, there was a goodly amount of noise happening within the multimillion-dollar Pearl District loft. Anne and I didn't come from money. Quite the contrary. If it hadn't been for her encouraging me to go for scholarships and supporting me financially by paying for books, etcetera, I'd never have made it to college. Last year, however, my normally sensible and subdued sister had somehow found herself shacked up with rock 'n' roll royalty.

I know, right? How it all happened still confused me, somewhat. Between the two of us, I'd always played the role of the bubbly one. Whenever Anne got down, I'd pick her back up again, fill the spaces in the conversations and keep right on smiling through the rain. Yet here she was, high on life and crazy in love, truly happy for the first time in just about forever. It was wonderful.

Details regarding their whirlwind romance ranged from vague to none. But just before Christmas, she and Malcolm Ericson, the drummer for Stage Dive (about the biggest rock band ever), had tied the knot. I was now counted as part of the band's extended entourage. To be fair, they'd embraced me wholeheartedly from the start. They were good people. It was just the thought of seeing *him* reducing me to a jittering, nervous wreck with super enhanced puking abilities.

"You'll never guess what happened." Anne linked her arm with mine, towing me toward the crowded dinner table.

Toward my doom.

A crowd of about seven sat around it with drinks in hand, laughing and chatting. I think it was The National playing quietly on the sound system. Candles flickered and small twinkling party lights hung overhead. My mouth watered despite my queasy stomach, what with all the delicious foodie scents filling the air. Wow, Anne and Mal had really gone all out for the occasion of their two-month wedding anniversary. Suddenly, my black tights and pale blue tunic (a loose-knit fabric which in no way hugged or hindered the waistline) seemed insufficient. Though it was hard to go for glamour with a plastic bag in your pocket just in case you needed to hurl.

"What happened?" I asked, dragging my feet ever so slightly.

She leaned in and whisper-hissed theatrically, "Ben brought a date."

Everything stopped. And I do mean everything. My lungs, my feet . . . everything.

A flicker of a frown crossed Anne's face. "Liz?"

I blinked, slowly coming back to life. "Yeah?"

"You okay?"

"Sure. So, um, Ben brought a date?"

"Can you believe it?"

"No." I really couldn't. My brain had stalled, same as everything else. There'd been no date in my plans for speaking with Ben tonight.

"I know. First time for everything I guess. Everyone's slightly weirded out, though she seems nice enough."

"But Ben doesn't date," I said, my voice sounding hollow somehow, as if it were an echo coming from far away. "He doesn't even believe in relationships."

Anne cocked her head, smiling ever so slightly. "Lizzy, you don't still have a crush on him, do you?"

"No." I barked out a laugh. As if. He'd disabused me of such idiotic notions, in Vegas. "So much no my cup is overflowing and the no is spilling onto the floor."

"Good." She sighed happily.

"Lizzy!" A booming loud voice rang out.

"Hey, Mal."

"Say hello to your Aunt Elizabeth, son." My new brother-in-law thrust a black-and-white puppy straight at me. A wet little tongue swiped my lips, and warm panting puppy breath, ripe with the scent of dog biscuits, filled my face. Not good.

"Whoa." I leaned way the hell back, trying to breathe through the urge to yet again heave. Pregnancy was the best. "Hi, Killer."

"Give him to me," said Anne. "Not everybody wants to French kiss the dog, Mal."

The blond, heavily tattooed man grinned, handing the fur baby over. "But he's a great kisser. I taught him myself."

"Unfortunately, that's true." Anne tucked the pup under an arm, giving him a scratch on the head. "How are you? You said you'd been feeling sick, the other day on the phone."

"All better," I lied. Or partly lied. After all, I definitely wasn't sick.

"Did you go to the doctor?"

"No need."

"Why don't I make an appointment tomorrow, just in case?"

"Not necessary."

"But—"

"Anne, relax. I'm telling you I'm not sick." I gave her my brightest smile. "I promise, I'm fine."

"All right." She placed the pup on the ground and pulled out a chair in the middle of the table. "I saved you a place next to me."

"Thanks."

And so it was (with me trying not to barf while wiping dog spit off my face) that I saw him again. Ben, sitting opposite, staring straight at me. Those dark eyes . . . I immediately looked down. He didn't affect me. He didn't. I just wasn't ready to face up to this. Wherein this equaled him and me and that room and Vegas and the consequences that were currently growing in my belly.

I couldn't do it, not yet.

"Hey, Liz," he said, deep voice calm, casual.

"Hey."

Yeah. I was so over him. The date thing had thrown me, but now I was back on track. I just had to compartmentalize any unhelpful lingering feelings, file them away for never.

I took a step closer, daring a peek only to find him watching me warily. He threw back some beer then set the bottle down, swiping his thumb across his mouth to catch a stray drop. In Vegas, he'd first tasted of beer, lust, and need. The most dizzying mix. He had beautiful lips, perfectly framed by his short beard. His hair had grown out of the shaved on the sides and longish on top cool hipster cut, and honestly, he looked kind of shaggy, wild.

And big, though he always looked big.

A silver ring pierced one side of his nose and he had on a green plaid shirt, top button open to showcase his thick neck and the edge of a black rose tattoo. Any money blue jeans and black boots were below. Apart from Vegas at the wedding, and then later that night in my room, I'd never seen him out of jeans. Let me assure you, there's nothing bad about the man naked. Everything was as it should be and then some. In fact, he'd looked a lot like a dream come true.

My dream.

I swallowed hard, ignoring my perky nipples while firmly pushing the memory back down where it belonged. Buried among the Hannah Montana song lyrics, *Vampire Diary* character histories, and other useless and potentially damaging information collected over the years. None of it mattered anymore.

The room had gone quiet. How awkward.

Ben tugged at the collar of his shirt, shifting in his seat.

Why the hell was he staring at me? Maybe because I was still staring at him. Shit. My knees gave out and I collapsed into the chair with an ever so dainty thud. I kept my eyes cast down because down was safe. So long as I didn't look at him or this date of his, I'd be fine and dandy. Dinner couldn't last for more than three, four hours max. No worries.

I half raised a hand in greeting. "Hi, everyone."

Heys and hi's and variations of both floated back.

"How have you been, Liz?" asked Ev, from further down the table. She was seated beside her husband, David Ferris, Stage Dive's lead guitarist and songwriter.

"Great." Crap. "You?"

"Good."

I sucked in a deep breath and smiled. "Excellent."

"You been busy with school?" She pulled out a hair tie and bundled her blond hair up into a rough ponytail. God bless the girl. At least it wasn't just me keeping it casual. "We haven't seen you since Christmas."

"Yeah, busy." Puking and sleeping mostly. Gestating. "School and stuff, you know."

Normally I'd have an interesting story to tell from my psych studies. Today, nada.

"Right." Her husband slipped an arm around her shoulders and she turned to smile at him, eyes all lovelorn and our conversation forgotten.

Which worked for me.

I rubbed the toe of my boot back and forth against the floor, looking left and right and anywhere but straight ahead. I toyed with the hem of my tunic, winding a loose thread tight around my finger until it turned purple. Then I loosened it. It probably wasn't good for the bean, somehow. As of tomorrow, I needed to start studying up on this baby stuff. Get the facts, because getting rid of the bean . . . it just wasn't for me.

The date tittered at something he said and I felt a stab of pain inside. Probably gas.

"Here." Anne filled the glass in front of me with white wine.

"Oh. Thanks."

"Try it," she said with a smile. "It's sweet and kind of crisp. I think you'll like it."

My stomach tipped upside down just at the thought. "Later maybe. I drank some water right before I arrived. So . . . yeah, I'm not really thirsty just yet."

"All right." Her eyes narrowed as she gave me a that-was-weird smile. All too soon it morphed into a flat, unhappy line. "You look a little pale. Are you okay?"

"Absolutely!" I nodded, smiled, and turned to the woman on my other side before Anne could grill me further on the subject. "Hi, Lena."

"Lizzy. How you been?" The curvy brunette held hands with her partner, Jimmy Ferris, the lead singer of Stage Dive. He sat at the head of the table, resplendent in an undoubtedly handmade suit. When he saw me he gave me one of the chin tips the guys seemed to specialize in. It said it all. Or at least it said it all when all they wanted to say was *Hey*.

I nodded back at him. And all the while I could feel Anne hovering at my side, bottle of wine still in hand and big-sisterly concern growing by the moment, pawing at the ground and getting ready to pounce. I was so screwed. Anne had pretty much raised me from the age of fourteen, when our dad left and our mom checked out on us—one day just went to bed and didn't get up again. Now and then Anne's need to nurture still got a little out of control. What she'd have to say about the bean didn't bear thinking about. It wouldn't be pretty.

But one problem at a time.

"All good, Lena," I said. "You?"

Lena opened her mouth. Whatever she'd been about to say, however, was lost beneath the sudden thrashing of drums and insanely loud wailing of guitars. It basically sounded like hell was spilling forth all around us. Armageddon had come a-knocking.

"Babe," Anne hollered at her husband. "No death metal during dinner! We talked about this."

Said "babe," Malcolm Ericson, paused his head banging at the top of the table. "But, Pumpkin—"

"Please."

The drummer rolled his eyes and, with the flick of a finger, silenced the storm raging through the sound system.

My ears rang on in the quiet.

"Christ," muttered Jimmy. "Time and a place for shit like that. Try never when I'm around, yeah?"

Mal looked down the length of his nose at the dapper man. "Don't be so judgy, Jim. I think Hemorrhaging Otter would make a wonderful warm-up act."

"Are you fucking serious? That's their name?" asked David.

"Delightfully inventive, no?"

"One way to put it," said David, nose wrinkled in distaste. "And Ben already picked a warm-up act."

"I didn't even get a vote," grumped Mal.

"Dude." Ben shoved an irritated hand through his hair. "You'll all want to hang with your women. I'll need some people around after the show I can chill and have a beer with, so I went ahead and chose. Suck it up."

Bitter grumbling from Mal.

Ev just shook her head. "Wow. Hemorrhaging Otter. That's certainly unique."

"What do you think, babe?" Jimmy turned to Lena.

"That's disgusting. I think I'm going to throw up." The woman swallowed hard, her face going gray. "I mean, I think I really am."

Huh. And also, ugh, I knew that feeling.

"Shit." Jimmy started rubbing her back with frantic motions.

Without a word, I pressed my spare plastic puke bag into her hand. Solidarity among sisters, etcetera.

"Thanks," she said, happily too preoccupied to ask why I'd had it in my pocket in the first place.

"She had some stomach bug before Christmas." With his spare hand, Jimmy filled Lena's glass with water and passed it to her. "Keeps messing with her."

I froze.

"I thought it had gone," said Lena.

"You're going to have to go to the doctor. Enough excuses, we're not that busy." Jimmy planted a soft kiss on the side of her face. "Tomorrow, yeah?"

"Okay."

"Sounds wise," said Anne, patting my rigid shoulder.

Holy hell.

"You've been sick too, Lizzy?" asked Lena.

"You should both try some green tea with ginger in it," a voice reported from the other side of the table.

Female.

Damn, it was her. His date.

"Ginger creates warmth and helps to settle an upset stomach. What other symptoms did you have?" she asked, causing me to immediately sink down in my seat.

Ben cleared his throat. "Sasha's a naturopath."

"I thought you said she was a dancer," said Anne, her face screwing up ever so slightly.

"A burlesque performer," the woman corrected. "I do both."

Yeah, I had nothing.

A chair scraped against the floor, and then Sasha was standing, peering down at me. Any hopes of avoiding and/or ignoring her presence fled the scene. Bettie Page hair done a vibrant blue, very cool. Christ, did she have to look like she actually had a clue? A bimbo I could handle, but not this. The woman was beautiful and smart, and I was just a dumb kid who'd gone and gotten herself knocked up. Cue the violins.

I smiled grimly. "Hi."

"Any other symptoms?" she repeated, gaze moving between me and Lena.

"She's been tired a lot too," said Jimmy. "Passes out in front of the TV all the time."

"True." Lena frowned.

"Lizzy, you said you'd missed some school, didn't you?" asked Anne.

"Some," I admitted, not liking the direction this grilling was taking. Time for a smooth segue. "Anyway, how are the plans for the tour going? You guys must all be so excited. I'd be excited. Have you started packing yet, Anne?"

My sister just blinked at me.

"No?" Maybe a sudden outburst of verbal diarrhea wasn't the answer.

"Hold up. Have you been sick, Liz?" Ben asked, his deep voice softening ever so slightly. Though maybe that was just my imagination.

"Um . . ."

"Maybe you got the same bug Lena's got," he said. "How much school have you missed?"

My throat closed tight. I couldn't do it. Not here and now in front of everyone. I should have fled for the Yukon rather than come here tonight. No way was I ready for this.

"Liz?"

"No, I'm fine," I wheezed. "All good."

"Um, hello," said Anne. "You said you'd been nauseous for the last few weeks. If I hadn't been away I'd have dragged you to the doctor's way back."

And thank god she'd been on her second honeymoon with Mal in Hawaii. To have found out about the bean with Anne in attendance would have been up there with watching the four horseman of the apocalypse riding into town. Terror, tears, chaos—all of these things and more. Definitely not my idea of a good time.

The date, Sasha, fixed her inquiring gaze to the ever so subtly still gagging Lena.

"Did anyone else get this?" she asked.

"I don't think so." Anne looked up and down the table, taking in the various shaking of heads. "Just Lena and Lizzy."

"We've been fine," said Ev.

"Weird," said Anne. "Liz and Lena haven't been around each other since the wedding. That's over two months ago now."

Murmurs of agreement.

My heartbeat raced. Mine and the bean's both.

"Well, I think they should both take a pregnancy test," announced Sasha, retaking her seat.

A moment's stunned silence.

"What?" I spluttered, panic coursing through me. Not here, not now, and sure as fuck not this way. Bile burned my throat, but I swallowed it back down, fumbling for the second puke bag.

Ben's brow wrinkled and there were startled coughs and gasps from others.

But before anyone could comment, a strange screechy noise came from Lena.

"No," she cried, voice very high and very determined. "No, I am not. You take that back."

The back-rubbing by Jimmy went berserk. "Baby, calm down."

She didn't. Instead, she pointed a shaking finger at the now very unwelcome stranger in our midst. "You have no idea what the fuck you're talking about. I don't know, maybe you've taken a hit to the head from one of those big fancy dancing fans lately or something. Whatever. But you . . . you couldn't be more wrong."

"Okay, let's calm down a little." Ben raised his hands in protest. Sasha kept quiet.

"Lizzy?" My sister's fingers dug into my shoulder, bruisingly tight. "There's no chance, right? I mean, you know better than that. You wouldn't be so stupid."

My mouth opened, but nothing came out.

Suddenly, Lena clutched at her belly. "Jimmy, in your car outside my sister's wedding. We didn't use anything."

"I know," he said quietly, perfect face white as snow. "Time we fucked against the door, night before you left. We forgot then too."

"Yeah."

"Your tits have been really sensitive." With one hand, Jimmy scrubbed at his mouth. "And you were complaining your dress wouldn't do up the other day."

"I thought it was just pie."

They both stared at one another while everyone looked on. I was pretty damn certain they'd long since forgotten they had an audience for all these intimate details. As dinner entertainment went, this had turned into one hell of a drama, and oh god, the horror of it. My head started to turn in dizzy circles.

"Lizzy?" Anne asked again.

Okay, this wasn't good. I really and truly shouldn't have come. But how the hell was I to know Ben would bring along a gynecological psychic? The edges of my vision blurred, my lungs working overtime. I couldn't get enough air. Not to sound paranoid, but I bet that Sasha bitch had stolen it all. Never mind. The important thing was not to panic.

Maybe I should jump out a window.

"Liz," a voice said. A different one this time, deep and strong.

However I'd imagined me and Ben having this talk, it was nothing like this. Not tonight, before I'd even processed it myself. Time to go.

"Lizzy?"

Also, wow, if this was the result of having great sex then I was so never going there again. Not even for mediocre sex. Nothing. I might even rule out masturbation, just in case. You couldn't be too careful. Random attack sperm could be anywhere, just waiting to get a girl into trouble.

I stumbled to my feet, sweaty hands on the table to steady myself. "I should go."

"Hey." A big hand cupped my chin. Lines had appeared between Ben's brows, beside his mouth. But you could only see the hint of them behind his beard, the implication. The man was not happy, and fair enough. "It's okay, Liz. We'll get this sorted—"

"I'm pregnant."

A pause. "What?"

"I'm pregnant, Ben."

The ensuing silence echoed in my ears, an endless gray noise like something out of a horror movie.

Ben stood bent over the table, breathing heavy. I guess I'd

looked to him for strength, but now he seemed every bit as strung out as me.

"You're pregnant?" Anne's voice cut the silence. "Lizzy, look at me."

I did, though it wasn't easy. My chin didn't seem inclined to go in the desired direction, and who could blame it?

"Yes," I said. "I am."

She went horribly still.

"I'm sorry."

"How could you? Oh god." For a moment she squeezed her eyes shut, then opened them again. "And why were you telling *him*?"

"Good question." Ever so slowly, Mal rose from his seat and started walking down the other side of the table. "Why'd she tell you, Benny?"

"Liz and I need to talk." Ben's gaze skipped to Mal, his hand falling from my face. "Man."

"You didn't," said Mal, his voice low and lethal as the tension in the room took an entirely new turn for the worse.

"Calm down."

"Told you stay away from her. Didn't I? She's my girl's kid sister for Christ's sake."

Ben stood tall. "I can explain."

"Shit," muttered David.

"No. No, you can't, Benny. I fucking asked you to leave her alone, bro. You promised me she'd be off-limits."

Past Ben, David Ferris got to his feet, as did Jimmy at the end of the table. It was all happening so fast.

Ben's date, Sasha, the burlesque dancer with the blue hair, seemed to finally understand the shit storm she'd unleashed with her most excellent announcement. Perhaps she wasn't so psychic after all. "We should leave. Ben?"

He didn't even look at her, his gaze glued to Mal.

"You're like a brother to me, Benny. One of my closest friends. But she's my little sister now. Tell me you didn't go there."

"Mal, man—"

"Not after you gave me your word. You wouldn't do that, not to me."

"Dude, calm down," said David, moving up to try and get between the two. "Let's talk about this."

Ben was almost a head taller than Mal, definitely bigger, stronger. It didn't matter. With a battle cry, Mal launched himself at the man. They fell together onto the floor, rolling and wrestling, fists flying. It was a mess. I jumped to my feet, mouth hanging open. Someone screamed, a woman. The rich copper scent of blood hit the air and the urge to hurl was almost overwhelming, but there wasn't time for that.

"No!" I yelled. "Don't, please."

I'd done this, so it was up to me to fix it. I got a knee up on the table before hands grasped my arms, holding me back no matter how I fought.

"Mal, no!"

David and Jimmy tore Mal off of Ben, dragging the struggling man back across the room.

"I'm going to fucking kill you," Mal hollered, his face a mixture of reds from fury and blood. "Let me go!"

More blood dripped from beneath Ben's nose, trailing down his chin. But he made no move to stop it. Slowly, the big man got to his feet, and the look on his face tore me in two.

"You said you wouldn't chase after her."

"He didn't," I shouted, still standing on one foot with a knee on the table and Anne's hand on my arm. "He didn't want anything to do with me. I chased after him. It was all me. I'm sorry."

Silence fell and I was surrounded by stunned faces. And a couple of still-bleeding ones.

"I practically stalked him. He never stood a chance."

"What?" Mal scowled, one eyelid swelling at an alarming rate.

"It's my fault, not Ben's. I'm the one who did it."

"Liz." With a heavy sigh, Ben hung his head.

The fingers on my arm gave a small tug. I turned to face my sister.

"Explain this to me."

CHAPTER ONE

Good girls don't fall for rock stars. It just isn't done.

"Pumpkin! PUUUMP-KIN!"

"Oh god." My sister, the aforementioned Pumpkin, giggled.

I just gaped. It seemed to be my go-to look of the day.

Lord knows, I'd been wearing it ever since letting myself into Anne's apartment this morning. Because I lived on campus, we'd starting doing brunch every Sunday morning since moving to Portland a few years back. It was our sisterly thing. But instead of standing ready to serve the bacon and eggs this morning, I'd found, Anne was fast asleep on top of a tattooed stud on the sofa. Both of them mostly clothed, thank god.

But, wow, what a revelation. I mean, I didn't even know Anne dated. I'd thought me dragging her along to the occasional party on campus was the sum total of her social life.

"C'mon, woman," said Mal, her brand-spanking-new boyfriend. "We can't be late to practice or Davie'll get his panties in a wad. You have no idea what drama queens guitarists can be. I swear, last week he threw a total hissy fit just 'cause he broke a string. Started screaming and throwing shit at people. True story."

"That is not a true story," admonished Anne, shaking her head. "David is a perfectly nice guy. Stop trying to scare Lizzy."

"No-o-o." Mal gave her big innocent puppy eyes, even going so far as to bat his eyelashes. "You think I would lie to Lizzy, my sweet little future sister-in-law?"

Anne just shook her head. "Are we going in or what?"

"Can't believe you doubted me, Pumpkin."

We followed the manic blond drummer into a big old building down by the river. As good a place for a loud rock band to practice as any. The only neighbors were industrial buildings, abandoned for the weekend. Inside wasn't any warmer, but at least we were out of the bone-chilling October wind. I stuffed my hands into the pockets of my gray woolen coat, nervous now that we were actually about to meet them. My sole interactions with the rich and famous started this morning with Mal. If the rest of the band was anything like him, I'd never keep up.

"As if anyone could doubt me. That hurt bad," he said. "Apologize."

"Sorry."

Mal smacked a noisy kiss on her cheek. "You're forgiven. Later."

Stretching his fingers and rotating his wrists, the man bounded off toward the stage assembled at one end. Instruments, amps, and other sound gear covered it and the surrounding area, with roadies and sound techs busy amid it all.

It was fascinating, this, him, and my whole damn morning. Mal and Anne seemed so in tune with each other. Perhaps Anne and I had been a touch too hasty in our dismissal of romantic love and affection. So it hadn't worked out for our parents. Hell, those two had pretty much made a mockery of commitment and marriage. Mal and Anne might yet make a far better case study.

Fascinating.

"He's borderline insane by the way," I said quietly. "So manic."

"Yeah. Isn't he great?" She grinned.

I nodded, because anyone who could make her smile so bright

clearly must be. The light of hope in her eyes, the happiness, it was beautiful.

And the man in question? None other than Malcolm Ericson, drummer for worldwide renowned rock group Stage Dive, had somehow shacked up with my sister. My quiet, calm, color-within-the-lines-or-else sister. Anne was being vague about the details, but the facts remained the same. Her new boyfriend stunned me stupid. Perhaps someone had slipped something into my coffee back on campus. It would certainly explain all of the crazy.

"Can't believe you told him about me crushing on him when I was a kid." Ever so gently, Anne elbowed me in the side.

I grunted in pain.

"Thanks for that," she said.

"You're welcome. What else are sisters for?"

We wandered toward the couple of women sitting on storage boxes at the back of the hall. So cool, getting to see the band practice. Anne had truly been the psycho fan, plastering her bedroom wall with posters of Stage Dive. Mostly of Mal, making today's dating revelation all the more holy hell. But if anyone deserved some amazing, mind-blowing good to come their way, it was my sister. I couldn't begin to tell you how much she'd given up to get us this far.

The blond woman smiled in greeting as we got closer, but the curvy brunette just kept playing with her cell.

"Hello, fellow Stage Dive groupies and hanger-onners. How is your Sunday morning?" the blonde asked.

"Good," said Anne. "How are you feeling, Mrs. Ferris?"

"I am feeling very, very married, thank you for asking. How are you and Mal doing?"

"Ah, good. All good." Anne joined them, sitting on one of the boxes. "This is my sister, Lizzy. She goes to school at PSU. Lizzy this is Ev, David's wife, and Lena, Jimmy's . . ."

"Assistant. Hi." Lena gave me a small smile and chin tip.

"Hi." I waved.

"Nice to meet you," said Ev. "Anne, quickly before they start playing. Tell me the story of you and Malcolm. I still haven't heard how you got together, exactly. But Lauren mentioned he basically invaded your apartment."

Back at her apartment, I'd overheard an odd argument between her and Mal. Something about them having an "agreement." When I questioned her she'd basically told me to butt out, in her own sweet way. I could only take her word that all was well, and try not to worry. Still, the question and Anne's reaction to it interested me greatly. I ever so subtly shuffled a little closer.

The whites of Anne's eyes flashed. "Ah, well, we met at your place the other night and hit it off."

"That's it?" asked Ev.

"Yes, that's pretty much it." Anne's smile wavered only slightly. "What is this, Ev, a grilling?"

"Yes, this is a grilling. Give me more information, please?"

"He's really great and yes, he kind of moved himself in with me. But I love having him there. He's wonderful, you know?"

So they weren't going to get any more out of her than I had. No big surprise. Anne tended to be tight lipped, a private person.

The girls kept on talking.

Up on the stage only the band members now remained, the rest moving off to the side to play with various bits of equipment. They stood gathered around Mal and his drum kit, deep in conversation. So this must be the band. Jeans and T-shirts seemed to be the go-to, scruffy cool hairdos and lots of tats. One of them stood a good half a head taller than the rest, and the rest were not tiny. This guy must be a giant. And it'll sound crazy, but there was just something about the way he stood, the solidity of him. Mountains had never seemed so strong and imposing. Big boots several feet apart and a hand wrapped high around the neck of his bass guitar as if he might swing it club style at any moment to subdue some stray bear. The thick width of his shoulders and the ink on his muscular arms made my fingers itch with the need to explore. It couldn't have been healthy, but I'm pretty damn sure my heart skipped a beat. Every inch of me vibrated with some sort of hyper, crazy sexual tension courtesy of his presence. Never before had just the sight of a man made me go so gaga.

I couldn't look away.

The band meeting broke apart and he took several steps backward. Someone counted them in and *boom!* The first deep, heavy notes of his bass guitar slammed into me, rattling my bones. It left no corner of me unaffected. The song he played was like a spell, sinking deep, taking me over. My belief in love or lust or whatever this feeling was suddenly became assured. The sense of connection seemed so real. I hadn't had many definites in my life. But him, us, whatever this was, it was one. It had to be.

Finally, he turned in my direction, his gaze on his instrument, a short beard hiding half his face. Wonder if he'd be willing to shave it? He wore a faded red tee and dark blue jeans, as per the band uniform. As he played he'd rock back and forth on his heels, nodding or smiling every now and then at the singer, guitarist, or whoever.

And I'm certain each and every one of them performed like the prime specimens of rock 'n' roll musicianship that they were. None of them mattered, though. Just him.

Of course, I knew who he was. Ben Nicholson, the bass player for Stage Dive. But his presence in music videos or Anne's extensive collection of posters had never affected me like this. To be here, seeing him in the flesh, was a different experience altogether. My blood ran hot and my mind emptied. My body, though—it was as if it went on red alert, tuned in to every little move he made.

The man was magic. He made me feel.

Maybe love, marriage, and commitment weren't all some archaic social construct designed to give our young the best chance of survival. Maybe there was more to it. I don't know. Whatever this emotion was, however, I wanted him more than I'd ever wanted anything.

The music went on and on, and I stood staring, lost.

Hours later they finally stopped playing. Roadies flooded the stage, relieving the guys of their instruments, slapping them on the back and chatting. Everyone knew their jobs to perfection and it was fascinating to watch. Soon the four men approached us, looking thoroughly bedraggled. Sweat dripped off their hair, running down their tired but smiling faces. My walking male fantasy had an energy drink attached to his lips, the liquid in the bottle disappearing at lightning speed as he chugged it down. The closer he got and the more I saw, the more my body wanted. The way his T-shirt clung to him, dark from perspiration, made me start panting. The salty scent of sweat coming from his body got me sky-high. I'd sincerely love to explore what else he enjoyed doing that involved getting overheated.

Hells yes, sign me up for some of that.

Up this close, I could see the start of little lines beside his dark eyes. So he was a bit older than me. He couldn't be more than thirty or so, surely, and what was ten years between soul mates? And yes, I knew I was getting a bit overexcited. I just couldn't help it; the way he made me feel didn't come in halves. There could be no moderation.

I didn't tune in to the talk, just him. The rest of the world could disappear for good. I'd happily stand and stare at Ben Nicholson for hours. Days. Weeks.

One of those big hands ran over his short hair and I swear my sex wept in gratitude at the sight. I was out of control. If he fondled his beard I might faint.

"I'm starving," he said, his deep voice in every way a perfect, wonderful thing. "We finding somewhere to eat and drink?"

"*Yes.*"

Dark eyes turned my way, looking down, noticing me for the first time. Oh lord, it was like an epiphany, being held in his gaze. It was starlight and moonbeams and all that fantastical ridiculous stuff I'd spent the last seven years mocking care of my parent's example. This man's existence gave it all back to me—hope, love, things like that. He made me a true believer once more.

Then he gave me a slow looking over. I stood still, grinning, waiting, and inviting his perusal. Fair was fair, I'd been ogling him for hours. And while I might not be putting any supermodels out of a job anytime soon (average height, not much up front, but curvy in the back—just like my sister), he'd be hard pressed to find a girl who could beat me for open and eager enthusiasm. I might only come up to his shoulder, but god damn would I make bending down worth his while.

Slowly, a smile curved his lips, making my heart jump with glee. The man reduced me to the state of a starstruck teenager. Yes to anything and everything that might possibly cross his mind.

"Well, okay then," he said.

"Don't you have to get back to school, Liz?" someone asked. Anne. Right. Whatever.

Man, he was divine. Maybe god existed after all. There might be a few more topics besides love that I'd need to reassess. What a day of revelations.

"No, I'm fine."

"I thought you had an assignment to do?" My sister's voice

tightened in a way which normally sent red sirens screaming through me. But try as she might, I would not be swayed.

"Nope."

"Lizzy," she grated out.

"Ladies, ladies," said Mal. "We got a problem here?"

There were no problems anywhere. Not so long as Ben's gaze stayed fixed on me, making my world turn round. My smile grew shaky as our lustful staring contest continued. Then the man smirked playfully and butterflies went berserk in my belly. Damn him, I would not look away. I could and would win.

But suddenly there was a distinct disturbance in the happy. Some woman was wound around Mal, giggling and cooing and carrying on. And the problem was, that woman was not my sister. Instead, Anne stood watching the scene with her face pale and her mouth set in a grim, resigned line.

Like fuck.

All thoughts of Ben faded from my mind like I was waking from a dream. Sisterly duties called to me loud and proud.

"Hey, Mal," I said, trying for happy-go-lucky and probably failing miserably. "Should we invite Anne's friend Reece along to eat? He often does stuff with us on Sundays."

Reece was her boss and sometime crush. At least until Mal had come along. I most certainly wasn't above using petty jealousy to further the cause.

Anne's brows drew tight. "I think Reece said he'd be busy."

I gave her my best guileless look. "No. Really? Why don't you give him a call and check, Anne?"

"Maybe another—"

"Fuck no, Lizzy. I mean, I don't think there'll be room." The moron rock star looked around, finally noticing the assorted embarrassed faces (his friends') and the outright murderous face (mine) of those assembled.

The ho batted her eyelashes at him. "Is something wrong?"

"It's cool," said Anne. "Why don't you go for a drink with your friend and catch up?"

"I thought we were gonna do something." And Mal might be beyond pretty, but he sure as hell wasn't the smartest drumstick.

"Yeah, but . . ."

"I'm sorry, you are?" the ho asked in her high girly voice.

Ev cleared her throat and announced in a no-nonsense manner, "Ainslie, this is Mal's new girlfriend, Anne. Anne, this is Ainslie."

"Girlfriend?" Ainslie laughed, and I pretty much definitely really now did want to kill her. Slowly. Painfully. You get the gist.

"I was just saying hi to a friend," said Mal, carrying on with the male obliviousness. "What's the big deal?"

"There isn't one. It's fine."

"Yeah, there obviously is or you wouldn't be looking at me like that."

"You need to not talk to me in that tone of voice," Anne bit out. "Especially not in front of other people. Go out with your friend, have a nice time. We can discuss this later."

"We can, huh?"

"Yes."

His mouth curled into a farce of a smile. "Fuck it."

Everyone kind of looked at everyone else, but Anne just stood there. Her fingers clenched and unclenched at her sides, same as mine. God damn it, this couldn't be happening, not to Anne, not now. Just for once let the world play fair.

Soon enough the angry crashing of drums filled the hall, however. It was over. Let the animal pound on his skins.

It seemed no one had anything more to say.

Almost.

"Crap, I forgot!" Rather dramatically, Ev grabbed at her head. "We women all have to go meet Lauren. Girls' night out."

Her husband, the guitarist, just gave her a blank look. "You do?"

"Yep. We're starting early."

And hallelujah.

Anything to get Anne out of this god-awful situation with some of her pride intact sounded good to me. I ignored any inner conflict. Yes, the thought of giving up my chance with Ben hurt. I'm pretty sure my heart and vagina would never forgive me. But Anne looked devastated, her hands trembling. I grabbed her arm and towed her toward the door. A muscle-bound dude done out in all black, who just had to be security, met us beside a shiny new Escalade. We all bundled in with minimal small talk. Everything inside was leather. Seriously, the car was one sweet ride. Not sweet enough to get the sour out of my mouth over Mal's defection, however.

"I don't understand." I turned to face Anne, sitting so eerily still in the backseat. Every inch of her was wound tight and inward, her shoulders rounded and hands clasped in her lap. It was like she was just waiting for another attack, for more hurt. I hated that. If Mal Ericson had kicked a puppy I couldn't be more pissed.

"This," I said, waving a hand at her. "He makes you happier than I've ever seen. It's like you're a different person. He looks at you like you invented whipped cream. Now this. I don't understand."

She shrugged. "Whirlwind romance. Easy come, easy go."

My mouth opened to call bullshit, but I couldn't. I knew Anne too well. We stared at each other for a long moment until the luxury car started rolling forward. The past seven years had bound us tightly together. Tighter than either of us might have liked, truth be told. Love and hope equaled pain. They fucked you over and left you high and dry.

Stupid to believe otherwise. Those were our home truths and we'd learned them the hard way when Dad up and left. Love sucked, and men . . . well, it seemed they were as dependable as they'd ever been.

Still, I couldn't get the memory of Ben out of my head. The way his dark brown eyes had fixed on mine and never wavered. In all honesty, it could have meant anything.

Nothing, or everything, or something in between.

I just didn't know.

"I do not need him," Anne announced from atop the coffee table, her chocolate martini held high in the air.

A round of applause from Lauren.

"I really don't!"

"Right on, sister. Amen."

"In fact, I don't need any man! I'm a . . . I'm a . . ." She clicked her fingers impatiently, face deep in thought. "What's the word I'm looking for?"

"You're a modern woman."

"Yes-s-s," my sister hissed. "Thank you. I'm a modern woman. And penises are just weird anyway. I mean seriously, who the fuck even thought that shit up?"

On the floor, Lauren started laughing so hard she had to clutch at her belly. Me, not so much. Why Anne couldn't give her speeches with her feet safely on the floor was beyond me.

"No, really. Think about it. They're fine when they're hard, but when they're soft . . ." With a faint frown, my sister crooked her pinkie finger and then wiggled it. "So wrinkly and weird looking. Vaginas make much more sense."

"Oh god." I squeezed my eyes shut for a moment.

We'd finally arrived at my sister's apartment late afternoon, due to Ev needing to make a couple of stops. First there was a liquor store. Next, Voodoo Doughnuts. And last but not least, a pizza shop in the Pearl. The big burly security guy driving us had taken it all in his stride. He'd lugged the myriad bags, boxes, and bottles required up the stairs into Anne's small two bedroom apartment. When it came to throwing an impromptu man-hate party, Evelyn Ferris clearly had all bases covered.

My rage toward the drummer in question, Malcolm Ericson, had dropped from boiling to a simmer. The precarious way Anne was swaying atop her high perch worried me more. "Please don't fall off the coffee table and break something."

"Ohmyfuckinggod." Dark liquid sloshed over the edge of her glass, splattering onto the scuffed wooden floor below, only narrowly missing a red-faced Lauren. "Stop being such an adult, Lizzy. I'm the older sister here. You're the kid. Act like it."

I opened my mouth to tell her what I thought of that bright idea, but a hand swiftly covered my lips.

"Do not engage," Ev whispered in my ear, her arm draped over my shoulders and palm still silencing me. "She is drunk off her ever-loving ass and arguing with her will get you nowhere."

The hand withdrew, though the arm remained.

"That's what I'm worried about," I said.

It probably should have felt weird, being so friendly with her on Anne's impressively soft new velvet love seat. I'd only just met Ev. There was something about her, though. Her and Lauren both (I'd met Lauren once before, briefly). You had to appreciate women who exuded an air of no nonsense. Whatever happened with dickhead Mal, I hoped they stuck with Anne. She needed real friends, not the money-, time-, and energy-sucking leeches she'd attracted over the years with her momma bear ways.

"Tell me if I'm wrong, but I don't think your sister lets herself blow off steam very often. She might just need this."

I frowned. "Perhaps."

Up on the table, Anne hummed along with the music playing softly over the stereo. Lost in her own little world. At least the sad face was gone. I'd seen enough of it to last me a lifetime. Just the same, I made a mental note to beat Mal Ericson bloody if I ever saw him again. About the billionth thought of its type for the day.

"Did you enjoy seeing them practice before it all went south?" asked Ev.

"Yeah. I really did." I gave the woman discreet side eyes. "The bass player . . . what was his name?"

"Ben?"

"Hmm." I nodded, feeling my way through the conversation ever so carefully. "He seemed interesting. Pity we didn't get to head out for a meal."

"It was a pity. Couldn't help but notice you noticing him at practice," said Ev, ending any charade of subtlety.

Awesome.

"Relax. I'm not going to say anything to your sister." The woman sighed. "Ben, Ben, Ben. How to describe him? He's a great guy, very laid back."

I said nothing.

"Be warned, though, he's not known for actually dating."

I gave her side eyes.

She gave me a small grin. "Of course, neither was David until we got married. Anyhoo . . . Ben. How serious are you about him?"

"Are you asking about my intentions?"

A startled laugh flew out of her. "Huh. Yeah, I guess I am. I've got a man now, so I have to meddle and play matchmaker. Apparently it's what women do. But seriously, it's not *him* getting hurt that I'm necessarily worried about."

"You going to tell me I'm too young for him?"

"That would be hypocritical of me, considering I got hitched at twenty-one. And you're what?"

"Nearly twenty-one." I shifted in my seat.

"Well he's nearly twenty-nine, just so you know."

Eight years. Not so bad.

I stared into the murky dregs of my second martini as if somewhere in the muck lay a clue. You need tea leaves, though, to tell the future. Vodka, cream, and chocolate liqueur didn't quite cut it. "I probably won't get to see him again anyway, so . . ."

"You give up that easy?" she asked. "The way you were looking at him, I thought you were more determined than that."

"He's a rock star. Are you saying I should stalk him?"

She shrugged. "Rock stars are just people too. I don't think standing outside his hotel in the rain would be a lot of fun, though."

"No. Probably not." I could just see myself doing it, however, sad but true. The idea wasn't entirely stupid. Maybe it would work. He'd definitely been interested. At least, I'm pretty sure he had been, what with the staring and vague smiling. . . .

Yeah, okay, I needed to find out. "Which hotel, just out of curiosity?"

A certain twinkle came into Ev's eyes.

"Yo," a voice hollered. It took about a year, but with movements painfully slow and deliberate, Lauren eventually got to her feet. "Let me grab you another drink there, kiddo."

"I'm fi—" My glass was torn from my hand and the night's self-appointed bartender stumbled off toward the kitchen.

"I better help her out with that or you'll be served straight vodka." Ev sat forward, withdrawing her cell phone from her back jeans pocket. Her fingers moved over the screen, then she tossed it onto the seat at her side, giving me a meaningful look. "I'll just leave that there. I'm sure I can trust you not to look up any bass player's number while I'm in the kitchen, right?"

"Absolutely. I have no intention of searching *N* for *Nicholson* in your contacts index."

"Try *B* for *Ben* instead." She winked at me.

"Thank you," I said quietly.

"No problem. I've seen that wide-eyed crazytown blown-away-by-a-rock-star look before." She climbed to her feet. "On my own face as it so happens. Use that number wisely."

"Oh, trust me. I will."

CHAPTER TWO

Lizzy: Hi, it's Lizzy. Anne's sister. We met at band practice the other day, remember?

Ben: Hey. I remember. How u doing?

Lizzy: Good. U?

Ben: Good. How'd u get my number?

Lizzy: Mutual acquaintance.

Ben: Ur sister & Mal don't want us being friends.

Lizzy: U've friend zoned me already? Ouch. I haven't even made a clumsy inappropriate pass at u yet.

Ben: Ha. U know what I mean. Didn't realize u were only 20 or connected to Mal. Us talking isn't a good idea.

Lizzy: Lucky we're only texting then.

Ben: Bye Liz

Ben: Did u just send me a pic of ur lunch?

Lizzy: No. It's an artistic representation rendered in fries and ketchup of my immense sadness over u ignoring my texts. See the face in the middle?

Ben: What's the green stuff?

Lizzy: Those are pickle tears. Stole them off a friend's burger.

Ben: Cute.

Lizzy: Are u moved?

Ben: Absolutely.

Lizzy: Are u going to talk to me now?

Lizzy: Haha. You're having pizza for lunch?

Ben: Does it look sad or happy?

Lizzy: It looks lewd. How dare you send such explicit pepperoni. I'm not that kind of girl.

Ben: Ha. Got to work. Later, sweetheart.

Ben: Got no one to jam with & your town's music scene is crap on Mondays.

Lizzy: Never. Try The Pigeon. A friend goes to their open sessions.

Ben: I'm there. :)

Lizzy: How'd you go last night?

Ben: Good. Thanks for the info. Not Nashville but not bad. Might head up to Seattle for a few days. Friend's playing up there. Anyway, TY

Lizzy: You're welcome. Busy day?

Ben: Mal's walked in. Can't talk.

Lizzy: Ok. Later.

Ben: Feel shit going behind his back.

Lizzy: Let's talk later.

Lizzy: Hi! How'd ur day go?

Ben: Busy right now.

Lizzy: Ok

Lizzy: I'm going to assume by radio silence that you're not comfortable with us being text buddies. Didn't mean to put u in a bad position with Mal. I'll delete ur number.

Ben: Don't.

Lizzy: ?

Ben: I want to know if u need something u can call me.

Lizzy: Thanks. But I don't want to complicate things for u.

Ben: Problem is I like talking to u. Maybe if we keep it on the down low?

Lizzy: Ok. I'd like that.

Ben: Me too.

Ben: Attached pic is sunset out at Red Rock.

Lizzy: Amazing. What are you doing out there?

Ben: Filling in on keyboard for a friend. His guy broke hand.

Lizzy: Crap. Didn't know you played piano.

Ben: Grandma taught me. But Dave wanted bass so I learned.

Lizzy: Wow. Play for me sometime?

Ben: How about now?

Lizzy: Over the phone? That would be awesome.

Ben: Calling.

Ben: In the studio in LA for a few. How u going?

Lizzy: Studying for a test. Wish me luck.

Ben: You got this, sweetheart. Won't distract u. Later.

Lizzy: :) Later

Lizzy: Roses are red, violets are blue, I like u Ben, do u like me to?

Ben: Ur a terrible poet.

Lizzy: True. I think I might stick w psychology. How's ur day going?

Ben: Slow. Had a business meeting. Boring as shit.

Lizzy: U just want to play music?

Ben: Got me on that. How u doing?

Lizzy: Had an awesome prac. Off to work at book store next. Then got an assignment due.

Ben: Work all u do?

Lizzy: Pretty much. But I enjoy it. Texting u just made my day, tho.

Ben: Fuck ur sweet. Tell me something bad about u. Make it easier for me to stay away.

Lizzy: I see no benefit to me in doing this . . .

Ben: Go on. I'm waiting.

Lizzy: I suck at sports and I'm messy.

Ben: Can't imagine you messy.

Lizzy: My apartment looks like a war zone. Anne always tidied. Gave me bad habits. What about u?

Ben: I flirt with girl's I'm not supposed to. Otherwise I'm perfect.

Lizzy: All that fame and fortune and not an ego in sight.

Ben: Exactly.

Lizzy: :)

Ben: Gotta go, Jim's waiting. Later sweetheart.

Lizzy: Later Ben

Ben: WTF is that pic?

Lizzy: U tell me.

Ben: A mash up of a lion, a beer, & a girl's eyes (yours?)

Lizzy: Right on all counts!

Ben: What's it mean?

Lizzy: I am using my psych studies to mess with your mind. Studies show association with fear encourages romantic thoughts.

Ben: Sly. U uncovered my fear of beer?

Lizzy: Haha. The fear is the lion.

Ben: Ok. So what's the beer?

Lizzy: You know the phenomenon of beer-goggles?

Ben: Chicks look hot when you're drunk?

Lizzy: Right. But turns out the beer-goggler doesn't need to be drunk. Just an association with beer will do. Even a picture.

Ben: Me looking at a pic of beer will make u seem hotter?

Lizzy: You can't argue with science. You poor hapless male. You never stood a chance.

Ben: Liz, I think ur gorgeous. Save the beer pics for someone who needs em.

Lizzy: Damn ur smooth

Ben: U like that?

Lizzy: Very much

Ben: Good. U poor hapless female. U never stood a chance.

Lizzy: :)

Ben: What do you think?

Lizzy: I think that's a pic of a banjo. Yours?

Ben: Deering Black Diamond. Thinking of buying it.

Lizzy: U play banjo too? Whoa.

Ben: Want to learn.

Lizzy: And I want to hear you play. You're a musical virtuoso. Do you sing?

Ben: Ha. U do not want to hear me sing. Trust me. Think I should buy it?

Lizzy: Do it. :)

Ben: Done. :)

Lizzy: ===v=^=={@}
Ben: This another psych test?
Lizzy: No. It's a rose. I worked on it all morning.
Lizzy: Well . . . a couple of minutes between classes.
Ben: Beautiful.
Lizzy: :) Why don't we have coffee?
Lizzy: Is the lack of a response a no or are u shy?
Ben: Shy of Mal shooting me. We better just stick 2 text.
Lizzy: Fair enough.
Ben: Been thinking about u. Talk to me.
Lizzy: I'd love to. Calling.

Ben: U ok? Haven't heard from u lately.
Lizzy: I didn't want to seem too obvious. The stalker hand-
   book said play it cool.
Ben: I know ur not a stalker. Ur dangerous in another way.
Lizzy: I love that u said that.

Lizzy: So do u actually have real stalkers?
Lizzy: Apart from me, I mean.
Ben: You're not a real stalker. They camp across the street
   with binoculars.
Lizzy: That's crazy. U get a much better resolution with a
   telescope.
Ben: You're a goose.
Lizzy: Our honesty is beautiful.
Lizzy: Psychologically speaking, most relationships fail due
   to lack of constructive criticism. Obvious we're made
   for each other.
Ben: You're a total goose. Seriously.
Lizzy: See what I mean?

Lizzy: But we were talking about stalkers.

Ben: Not really for me. I'm lucky. The other guys can't walk down the street without getting hassled. I'm less in the limelight. Not so recognizable.

Lizzy: U kidding? You're built like King Kong.

Ben: Ha. Jimmy had stalkers that got creepy. One broke into his place a few years back stole some shit.

Ben: Mal had one that ended in a restraining order.

Lizzy: Wow. What did the stalker do?

Ben: No, the stalker had to get a restraining order against Mal. He kept showing up at the guys work, trying to hug him and leaving weird phone messages etc.

Lizzy: Lol.

Ben: Gotta go. Music breaks over.

Lizzy: I make killer cheesy cornbread.

Ben: Do u?

Lizzy: I do. & I just so happen 2 be making some right now. My plans tonight r cheesy cornbread & bad zombie films. Tempted?

Ben: Like u wouldn't believe.

Lizzy: But ur busy w the guys?

Ben: No. Guys with their girlfriends. I'm busy killing people.

Lizzy: Online I trust?

Ben: Ha. Yes.

Lizzy: I'd better leave u 2 it then.

Ben: I can torpedo & talk to u. How was ur day?

Lizzy: Not bad. Classes mostly. How about u?

Ben: Recording. Fucking frustrating. Jim was in a mood. This is just between us, yeah?

Lizzy: Absolutely.

Ben: Good. Boring night. Portland is no LA.

Lizzy: Come over. We can throw cornbread at the undead on tv. I'll judge you on your aim.

Ben: Fuck I wish I could.

Lizzy: Me too

Ben: One day

Lizzy: U awake? I can't sleep.

Ben: Count sheep like a good girl.

Lizzy: Can't. Too busy thinking about u.

Ben: Shit, Liz. No.

Lizzy: No, what?

Ben: Don't tell me ur in bed at 2 in the morning thinking about me. OK? U cannot tell me that. Too fucking tempting.

Ben: What are you wearing?

Lizzy: U really want me to answer that?

Ben: Yes.

Ben: No.

Ben: Shit. You're killing me. You know that right?

Lizzy: You say the nicest things. Night, Ben.

Ben: Night, sweetheart.

Lizzy: Sorry I missed your call earlier. Good luck with ur date with Lena tonight.

Lizzy: Actually, that was a lie. I didn't mean that at all.

Lizzy: About ur date. Not about missing ur call.

Lizzy: Now I feel guilty because Lena is so damn nice. I'm going to stop acting crazy & go meet a friend at Steel. Over & out.

Ben: The dive bar downtown? It's a fucking meat market.

Lizzy: Just arrived. Guess I'll see for myself.

Ben: That place is a pit. Get ur ass in a cab & go home. Ur not old enough to b drinking.

Lizzy: I have fake ID. Don't worry. I'll be fine.

Ben: I'm fucking serious. U are not going in there. Full of fucking creeps.

Lizzy: Have a nice night w Lena. U deserve someone great like her. Really.

Still no answer from Ben on my last text.

Emo indie music wailed out of the speakers, as Christy, my ex-roommate, bopped as best she could on the spot beside me.

"Great place, huh?" she yelled.

"Yeah. Great."

The place sucked. I mean literally—my shoes stuck to the floor. The bar was grossly lacking in hygiene. Also, it was overcrowded and reeked of decades of spilled drinks, questionable hookups, and broken hearts. Pretty much in that order. My clothes were going to stink for days. And if one more person trod on my toes, exposed care of my sweet '50s-style black heels, I'd scream. When I'd chosen them I'd needed a pick-me-up, I'd wanted to feel pretty. But now all around us people pressed in. Sweat raced down my spine, dampening the back of my black T-shirt and the band of my jeans.

Yuck.

I pretty much wanted to call in one of those toxic hazard teams to hose me down, decontaminate me from this pit of beer and despair. Ben might have had a point about the place being shit. Damned if I'd ever admit it to him, though. Nope, I was going to have fun if it killed me. I slid my cell out of my pocket just for fun, taking a peek at the glowing green screen. Nothing. What a surprise. Time to saddle up ye olde horse of hopelessness and move on.

"He answer yet?" asked Christy, leaning in and yelling to be heard over the music.

I shook my head.

My former dorm roommate sucked back some beer. "Fuck him."

"I'm trying."

"What?"

"Yes," I hollered, giving her a brave smile. "Fuck him."

"You can do better." Little lines appeared between her brows. "You can."

"Thank you." I highly doubted that. Nice of her to say so, though. I drank a hefty mouthful of my third Moscow Mule. Vodka was the only way I'd get through this. My feelings for Ben were just a weird obsessive-compulsive disorder or something. Or no, posttraumatic stress from meeting manic Mal. I'd inadvertently attached my affections to the first sane and single hot bearded man in the room. A totally plausible analysis. Freud with his own hairy face would be impressed.

Not that I'd be volunteering that analysis for my finals.

Actually, my psych books had been less than helpful in working out exactly what this love thing was about. To be fair, I did learn some fun facts. Turns out a boy rat and a girl rat, both virgins meeting for the first time, can fornicate immediately in a proficient fashion. No messing around working out the mechanics, they're just into it. But not so with the higher primates like monkeys. They bumble and fumble their way through initial attempts, working out the relationship and requirements. So it was a relief to know it wasn't just me. Or even just humans. Apes screw up first dates too. And they don't even have condoms or bra straps to deal with.

Anyhoo, the point is, the books were big on weird facts about animals getting it on but short on the particulars regarding the type of love or lust at first sight that was plaguing my every waking moment—and a good majority of my nonwaking moments too.

Christy's new roommate, Imelda, glared at me over the edge of her bright blue drink. Lord knows what was in there to make it that color. I'd only moved into Anne's old apartment two weeks ago. Apparently, however, these two had already bonded to the point of creepy possessiveness.

The bar had been Imelda's choice.

"Chris says you know the guys from Stage Dive," she said.

My ex-roommate shifted nervously.

I just shrugged. Photos of Anne and Mal together had done the rounds of the Internet a couple of times. It was pretty much an open secret in Portland these days. Though me talking about my sister's business didn't need to happen. Ever. And Christy was well aware of that policy.

"I think it's bullshit," the girl continued, standing so close her hot breath hit my ear.

I resisted the urge to recoil. "Think what you like."

Her eyes narrowed.

"Why don't we dance?" Christy suggested, sounding as fake peppy as could be. "Quick, drink up!"

We did as told. Then, all of a sudden, Imelda was all hands up in the air waving them about without a care. She snagged Christy's hand and started dragging her through the crowd. Christy in turn caught my wrist, towing me along. Alrighty then. Our progression through the throng was not gentle. Elbows and assorted other body bits bumped into me, sending me reeling this way and that. A hand grabbed my ass.

"Hey!" I growled, spinning around. In the dark sea of people surrounding us it could have been anyone. "Asshole."

When I turned back, Christy and her new BF had disappeared. Strobe lights blinded me. I could barely see for shit. Crowds have always made me nervy, and this place was a crush. It wasn't a phobia, exactly, just a distinct dislike I'd been working hard on overcoming.

Surely Christy would realize she'd lost me and come back. Surely. Waiting. Still waiting. Some chick trod good and hard on my toe, bringing actual tears to my eyes. I tried to hop on one foot to give the other a rub and almost landed on my butt in the process. Yeah, Christy wasn't coming back. Furthermore, I might have never loved crowds, but right now I was deep in the land of hate.

God, screw this.

It was ridiculous. I was a hairsbreadth away from being twenty-one and over the whole scene already. Guess I'd just go back to my lonely girl apartment. As nice as it was to have some space, I'd never actually lived on my own before. I wasn't lonely, exactly, it was just that the absence of other people made for a definite adjustment. Bet Ben and Lena were getting on like a house on fire. How could they not, what with Lena being all funny and gorgeous and Ben being Ben.

Another body in the near-dark knocked into me, sending me staggering sideways. Since when did you need to wear full body armor to be in a bar? Perhaps I should head back to the bar, where we'd been standing before. But surely I was better staying here, where Christy last saw me. I looked back and forth in indecision. Neither option appealed. Hell, being here no longer appealed.

I blinked furiously. Not crying, just . . . you know, my toe stung.

It might be time to go catch a cab. I'm pretty sure at home I had all of the ingredients required for emergency mood-enhancing nachos. The bonus being not having to share it with anyone. Call me greedy, I don't care, and bring on the melted cheese, baby.

Suddenly, two huge hands descended upon my shoulders and I was forcibly turned around. Some sort of mountain stood before me. A man mountain.

"Ben!" I cried happily, throwing myself at him (which of course didn't move the man an inch). His big hot body felt divine, heavenly. I wrapped my arms tight around his waist and clung ever so slightly. "I'm so glad to see you."

His hands tensed on my shoulders, fingers rubbing. "I told you not to come in here."

"I know." I sniffed, then set my chin on his chest and gazed up adoringly at him. "But have you noticed how I actually make my own choices like a real live adult?"

"You don't say?" He gave me a dour look and tucked an errant strand of hair behind my ear. Such a simple, sweet move; it worked for me big-time. Of course, anything involving him touching me would.

"How was your date with Lena?"

No reply.

"That good, huh? Oh well."

"I can see you're real cut up about it," he said with a smile.

"Yeah. The pain goes deep. It's really good to see you."

He looked at me for a long moment. "Yeah, you too. Still, kinda pissed you came in here, though."

What a silly statement. I gave him both brows up and *Oh really* in the eyes. Start out as you mean to go on and all that. Because at no stage would I be answering to the man for where I went and what I did. Trust and respect, etcetera.

He shrugged, unimpressed. "You didn't like me going out with Lena. I didn't like you coming here."

"Both of these things are true," I said, relenting just a little. "What are we going to do about them, though? That's the question."

"Hmm." He grabbed hold of my hand, giving it a squeeze. "C'mon, I'll drive you home."

"I'd like that."

Without another word he led me through the crowd, clearing the way with his body. In his plain jeans and plaid shirt, no one seemed to recognize him. In Portland, he was just one more bearded, tattooed dude among many. Attached to Ben, no one messed with me. I was neither bumped nor groped, thank god. Ah, togetherness. What a rare and beautiful thing. No wonder Anne was so wacky about Mal if this was how he made her feel. Walking beside Ben, my heart seemed so light I might hit my head on the ceiling.

"Later," the very pierced bouncer said, opening the door to let us through.

"Thanks, Marc."

Outside, the air was crisp, decidedly cool. I bundled myself up in my coat. Ben didn't seem to have brought one. He just shoved his hands in his pockets and hunched his shoulders. A beaten-up Chevy truck, from the '80s at best, sat at the corner. It might once have been pale blue. With all the fading and the couple of spots of rust, it was hard to say.

"This is your ride?" I asked, surprised.

In lieu of a response, Ben unlocked the passenger side door, holding it open.

"Huh."

I climbed up and in, sitting carefully on the cold, cracked vinyl seating. Cassettes spilled out of the glove box. Actual cassettes. "Stunned" kind of fit the situation. The man had money, lots of it.

He swung the door shut, then strode around to the driver's side. Soon enough the engine was roaring to life with minimal splutter. Clearly the car was kept in good condition.

"Expecting a Porsche?" he asked.

"No. Just something slightly less older than me."

He snorted.

We pulled out into the traffic, the low hum of some old Pearl Jam song playing. Cassettes. Christ.

"It belonged to my grandfather," he said. "He taught me how to fix it, handed over the keys when I got my license."

"Nice."

He gave me side eyes.

"I mean it, Ben. I didn't have much in the way of family myself. So I get that's nice."

A faint smile. "Yeah. We didn't have a lot of money so . . . I thought so."

The shadows of his face were frankly fascinating beneath the passing street lights, the sudden brightness of oncoming traffic, everything. He had perfect cheekbones. You could almost miss them above the beard, but the lines of his face were both sharp and beautiful. His lips, for instance. I could have stared at them for hours.

"Will you tell me about your home?" I asked.

"Not much to tell," he said, eventually. "Mom and Dad owned a cleaning business so they were gone most of the time. They were real hard workers. The business was everything to 'em. My grandparents lived next door and they fed us and kept an eye on things."

"Must have been wonderful to have them around. A stable influence like that can mean all the difference to a kid."

"You diagnosing me or something, Miss Psychology Student?"

"No. Sorry." I groaned. "Please continue. You mentioned an 'us'?"

"Me and my sister."

"You have a sister? What's she like?"

He squinted, little lines appearing beside his eyes. "Martha's . . . Martha. She's living over in New York these days, enjoys the party scene."

"That's pretty far." I couldn't imagine being on the opposite side of the country from Anne, living without my last bit of real family close by. "You must miss her."

"It's probably for the best," he said. "She caused some shit a while back. I didn't help much either."

I stayed silent, waiting for him to go on. People usually would feel compelled to fill a silence, you just had to be patient.

"Martha and David went out all through high school, and after,

when the band started to take off. Then she did something stupid."
He shook his head. "So fucking dumb."

"What did she do?"

He raised a brow. "You haven't heard?"

"No."

"Huh. Thought Ev might have talked about it."

"I've only met her a couple of times."

"Yeah, I guess." His fingers tapped out a beat against the steering wheel. "Martha didn't like Dave being away so much. We were working hard, touring when we weren't recording. Thought she understood. . . ."

A fire engine roared past with sirens blazing, distracting us for a moment.

"We were finally getting somewhere, really starting to make it, playing to bigger crowds, and getting some decent publicity." He exhaled noisily. "Anyway, she must have figured with him being on the road all the time that he had to be messing around on her. She got pissed one night and cheated on him."

"Oh."

"Guy couldn't have been more crazy in love with her if he tried. Never even saw him look at another woman. They'd been so tight for years. I tried to tell her, but she got this stupid idea into her head, and . . . yeah." His low laugh was bitter, horrible to hear. "She took something beautiful and shit on it. Everything went to hell after that."

"I'm sorry."

"Me too. Really thought they'd make it, get married, have kids and everything. Live the dream. She worked as an assistant for the band for a while, but when Dave and Ev got married she didn't take it too well."

"That's when she moved?"

"That's when she moved." He said nothing for a moment. "Tried one last time to get him back, and I was stupid enough to help. It didn't turn out so well. Things were tense between me and Dave for a while, and it wasn't good for the band."

"I'm sorry." I took a big breath, choosing my words with care. This had obviously hurt him. It was in the tone of his voice, the shadows on his face. Also, I didn't want to treat him like a patient or a subject. He mattered to me much deeper than that.

"It seems you guys are closer to brothers than friends, even though he and your sister didn't wind up staying together," I said. "But I'm sorry you got caught in the middle of it. That must have been hard."

"Yeah. Don't know why I'm telling you all this." He gave me a look out of the corner of his eye. "You're too easy to talk to, you know?"

I smiled. "So are you."

"You haven't told me anything yet."

"Ah, all right." I rubbed my palms against the sides of my jeans, warming them up. What to tell him? His honesty and openness meant I could give him no less. Might as well just lay it all out. "My parents divorced when I was fourteen. It messed me up for a while. But Anne helped me get back on track, helped me graduate and get into college."

"Pretty good sister."

"She's an amazing sister."

His gaze switched back and forth between me and the road. "You work hard too, though."

"Yes. But college is expensive and she sacrificed a lot to get me there, so she deserves the bulk of the credit."

"Sounds like you both hauled ass to get out of a bad situation."

"Hmm." I rested my head against the back of the car seat. The man was far too easy to talk to. I liked it. "That's it really. I work part time at the same bookstore as Anne."

He half smiled, and sadly even that made me giddy. God, he

was beautiful. I never wanted this car ride to end. We could drive to Wisconsin for all I cared. Just point the hood east and keep going until we ran out of gas.

"Messed you up in what way?" he asked.

That stopped the happy. "Not a topic I like to talk about."

He just waited, drawing me out, playing me at my own game. Sneaky.

"I hung out with some losers. Drank, did drugs. Speed and pot, nothing too hard-core. I ditched school and did things I shouldn't have. Dangerous things. Dated the wrong guy for a while." My fingernails dug into me through the fabric of my jeans. All of those memories were ugly. I'd been so young and idiotic. "Then I got busted stealing. The guy who owned the shop kept saying he was going to call the police, but Anne managed to talk him out of it. That scared the shit out of me. Plus, seeing how upset Anne got about it. It finally got through to me that I wasn't the only one hurting. I stopped sneaking out at night and messing around, started going to school again. I was just so angry that they couldn't keep their shit together and be like a normal mom and dad."

"I bet."

"Though what even is normal? Seems like everyone's parents are divorced these days."

"Yeah. Just about."

"Doesn't make for much of an example, does it?"

He made a humming noise of agreement.

"So that's why I'm into psychology. One day I hope to be able to help other kids ride out the rough patches."

He smiled.

"Anyway, enough of me and my early-teen angst." I crossed my legs, turning toward him in the seat. "When did you start playing bass?"

"Fourteen or so. Dave was always crazy about guitars, and then

Mal's mom got him the kit. Jimmy'd already decided he was gonna be the singer. I had an uncle who owned an old bass guitar. Grandpa talked him into giving it to me."

"The same Grandpa who gave you the truck? He sounds awesome."

"He was, Lizzy. He really was."

We pulled up outside my apartment building. Funny, I'd never hated the sight of it before, but I didn't want the trip to end. Time alone with Ben, talking, was special. I clasped my hands in my lap, studying the lines of his face. A moment later, he turned off the engine.

"Thank you for the lift home," I said.

"Any time. I mean that." He rested a hand on the steering wheel, shifting slightly to look my way.

Happy chemicals stirred inside of me. Lustful, crazy things telling me to jump him, to climb all over him and cover his gorgeous face in kisses. To rub my jaw against his beard and see if it felt soft or not. To let him see exactly how he affected me, how adored he could be.

"Kills me when you look at me like that," he murmured.

I just smiled. My tongue was too tangled for any attempt at wit. Thing was, I couldn't *not* look at him like that. It just wasn't in me to be any other way, not with him.

He exhaled hard, staring out the windshield. "I go to that club a couple of times a week to pick up. Place like that? Easy as hell. Pretty much the only reason people go there is to get drunk and get laid."

"I see."

"I'm serious."

"Okay, Ben. You're not a virgin. Duly noted. Me neither, by the way."

Dreamy dark eyes pinned me in place, owning me. He licked

his lips. Every time he did that my hormones erupted into the song of joy, a full orchestra plus heavenly choir accompanying. The whole shebang. It was ridiculous.

"Fuck, you're pretty," he sighed. "Make me wish for all sorts of shit I shouldn't."

"Who says you shouldn't?" I asked, leaning closer.

"Mal. Your sister."

"This isn't about them. It's about you and me."

"Sweetheart. Liz . . ." The deep, dirty way he said my name, holy shit. His voice rumbled through me, lighting fires and causing chaos everywhere it went. I'd never be the same.

"Yeah?" I leaned closer, and then closer still, heart thundering and lips at the ready. Never in my life had kissing someone seemed so important. I needed his mouth on mine. His breath and his body, all of him.

Nothing else mattered.

I turned, propping a knee beneath me to help with the height difference. Hesitant but hopeful smile in place, I put my hand on his shoulder, getting closer. Fuck waiting on him to make the first move. Time to go after what I wanted.

"Liz."

"Yeah?"

That's when it registered. Ben's body language was all wrong. The man wasn't moving into me, wanting me back. I was alone in this.

"You don't . . ." Words caught in my dry throat, sticking. I withdrew my hand.

"I can't."

"What?"

He stared straight ahead. "You should go in."

Whatever face I had on, it wasn't happy. "You want me to go?"

"It's for the best."

"It's for the best," I parroted, staring perplexed at the dogged shadows on his face.

"I can't do this, Liz. I can't do it to the band."

"And you answer to the band for who you date?"

"We're not dating."

I cleared my throat. "No, we're not dating. But god, we spent hours talking and texting to each other."

The look he gave me was tortured. "I'm sorry. I can't."

"Right." All of the emotion inside me felt huge, overwhelming. Still my mind worked, turning all of the evidence over, trying to figure out where I'd lost the track. How the fuck I came to be flailing in the woods. "I think you were a little bored, a little lonely maybe, so you played with me."

With a grimace he turned away.

"Tell me I'm wrong."

Nothing.

At least now I knew where I stood. As if that was any real consolation. I pushed open the passenger's side door, climbing down.

"Liz—"

I slammed the truck door shut, cold metal stinging the palms of my hands. Done with him. I was so damn done with him. The bitter night air slapped me in the face, waking me right the hell up. How fucking embarrassing. I'd felt so much and been so sure. Went to show you how much I knew.

Nothing.

Not a single fucking thing.

Time to put my heart and hopes back on ice.

CHAPTER THREE

Ben: Hey, how you going?
Ben: You doing okay? Studies all good and everything?
Ben: C'mon, Liz. Talk to me. I'm still your friend.
Ben: So I guess you'll be at the wedding?

"He's not really going to wear one of those white satin Elvis jump-suits, is he?"

My sister shrugged. "Whatever makes him happy."

"Yeah, but this is your wedding."

"*Our* wedding," she corrected, applying a final coat of lipstick then blotting it carefully on a tissue.

"God, Anne. You look amazing."

She really did. The vintage lace dress was divine. With her bright-red hair artfully drawn back from her face, she looked so elegant. I had to blink a time or two, my eyes actually getting a little misty. Given how long the makeup artist had labored over my face, I didn't dare mess up her hard work.

"Thank you." She reached out, giving my hand a squeeze. "You're looking pretty awesome yourself, birthday girl."

My birthday had actually been yesterday. Anne had insisted on waiting until I was old enough to legally join in the wedding celebrations in Vegas. Rather an unexpected delight, since treating me like a full-fledged grown-up wasn't really her thing.

Ev, Lena, Anne, and I had spent my birthday hanging out in this Bellagio villa's personal hot tub, nibbling yummy things and sipping cocktails while being waited on hand and foot. Because of course the villa came with a personal butler. Oh, and the outdoor fireplace had been roaring because during December in the desert it actually does cool right down at night. Last but not least, we had cake pops, because nothing could possibly be better than cake on a stick covered in candy.

That shit owned my soul.

I smoothed down the skirt of my own vintage dress, a knee-length ink-blue Dior number we'd found during a Saturday market hunt a few weeks back. It was beautiful. Feminine without being froufrou. My hair too had been pulled back into a simple but classy style.

Wonder what Ben would think.

Not that it mattered. I felt good about how I looked and that was that. My world didn't stop or spin based purely on his or any other male's validation. Until my feelings for Ben simmered down some, however, I'd just keep doing my best to avoid him—or at least eye contact with him. Even a stubborn heart like mine had to give up eventually. School had been busy and work much the same. What with Anne occupied with wedding arrangements, Rhys had given me extra hours in the bookstore, so there'd been plenty to keep me occupied. Ben Nicholson had been little more than a stray thought. Mostly. It would be nice later tonight to get out and let my hair down a little. See what Vegas was all about.

Sam stood, giving me a nod. It was time. Any lingering thoughts about the man gave way to squeeful excitement. Muted conversation could be heard coming from the living room, the faint sounds of music.

"Okay, future Mrs. Ericson. Everyone's arrived so—"

"Pumpkin!" an overly familiar voice wailed. "Pumpkin, where are you?"

A picture of perfect calm, Anne turned to face the doorway and hollered back, "In here."

The doors crashed inward and Mal appeared, turned out in a truly amazing slick black suit with matching Converse on his feet. What a sight. His golden hair shone, falling over his shoulders. Left undone at the bride's request. Already he felt more like a brother. But even I had to admit, the man had it going on and then some.

"You're not meant to see me before the ceremony," said Anne.

"I don't like rules."

"I noticed."

He ambled up to Anne with a faint smile on his face. "You know, I look pretty fucking awesome. But, Pumpkin, you look even better."

My sister smiled back at him. "Thank you."

"Gonna marry me?"

"You better believe it."

He buried his face in her neck. A moment later Anne squeaked and beat him on the back. "Do not give me a hickey before the wedding, Mal, or I will kill you."

Maniacal laughter filled the room.

"I'm serious!"

"I love you. Let's wed it on." Like something out of a movie, he swooped her up into his arms and carried her out, pausing briefly at the door. "You don't look too bad either, Lizzy. C'mon, let's do this!"

I picked up both mine and Anne's bouquets and followed with a smile. This was going to be awesome.

Out in the super fancy living room, the furniture had been set aside, leaving plenty of space for the ceremony. And the Santa Elvis performing it. The big bewigged guy wore a belt bearing so many sparkly stones it was a wonder his pants stayed up. That thing had to weigh a ton. Vases full of red roses covered every available surface, the heady scent filling the room. A roaring fire burned in the corner. It was perfect, beautiful, and there were so many happy, familiar faces all gathered around, waiting to share the moment. Anne finally had the family she deserved.

In the corner, a string quartet started playing, and Santa Elvis opened his mouth. His rendition of "Love Me Tender" was wonderful. Or so I was later told.

Ben stood to the side with Jimmy and David, all of them dressed in similar dark suits. Only Ben had actually ditched his jacket and tie. He'd rolled up the sleeves of his white dress shirt, leaving the ink on his thick arms exposed. God, he was glorious. So . . . manly, for want of a better word. Everyone else faded into the background. He looked so damn fine. It hurt, and angry or not I'd have told him as much, had I been able to find my tongue.

He looked up and found me staring. There was no censure in his eyes. Just the same, embarrassment threatened to flood me, turning my face to red. But he stopped and stared at me too. If our breathing and hearts were beating in exactly the same rhythm, it wouldn't have surprised me. It was crazy. I should have known better by now.

There was just me and him.

Things were said and I heard my sister's laughter.

His gaze strayed down over my dress then back up again. Little lines appeared beside his eyes, his face tensing. As for me, my jaw ached from all the things I was holding in, all the words left unsaid. Or maybe it was just more of the same, the urge to convince him that there was something real between us that was worth the risk.

Some jumble of sex and friendship and I don't know what. The fabled connection.

In all likelihood, he still wouldn't want to hear it. The man made my head and my heart hurt.

"No, you're not doing it right." The pronouncement split my focus, my gaze darting to the front of the room. Something was wrong in wedding town.

"*I'll* do it," Mal told Santa Elvis.

The King just shrugged. Guess he got paid either way.

"Of course you, Anne, take me, Mal," he proceeded, my sister still held high in his arms. "You're my Pumpkin, my whole damn world. You get my music and all my weird moods, and you think I'm funny when other people are just shaking their heads wondering what the fuck I'm on about. I think it's cute when you have your little hissy fits, but if you need me to listen and take shit serious, I promise I will. Good times or bad, you're with me and I'm with you. No matter what, we'll always work stuff out together, okay?"

"Okay," said my sister, raising a hand to wipe a tear from her face.

"You're the only woman I want or need, and no way are you into any other guy, 'cause you got me and I'm awesome. We good?"

"We're good."

"Right," said Mal. "We're married."

"They're married!" shouted Santa Elvis, throwing in a hip swivel just for fun.

Music started up again and the room filled with the sounds of clapping and cheering. Mal's and Anne's mouths were melded together. I wanted that, what they had together, and without a doubt it would be worth waiting for. After spending seven years believing love had to be just so much bullshit, I couldn't give up on it again now. That was the truth. One day I'd find someone else who made me feel like Ben did.

I just had to wait it out.

Santa Elvis started beating out "Viva Las Vegas" while those assembled went wild. Everyone apart from me and Ben. Shit. I'd pretty much missed the entire ceremony. Thank goodness, Mal's dad appeared to be taping it. Worst sister ever. I went to start clapping, like everyone else, then remembered the posies of flowers still gripped tight in my hands. Whoops, better not.

So many happy smiling faces—except for one. Oh great, my mom was here. From the other side of the room, her mouth wrinkled, brows drawn in tight. Seemed my initial lack of attention on the bride and groom hadn't escaped everyone's notice. Her gaze darted between me and Ben, her frown deepening. Might be best if I avoided dear mama for the rest of the night. Possibly the next decade too, just to be safe. The last thing I needed was for Jan to decide to start sticking her nose back into my life now.

No, thank you.

"Little sister," Mal cried, bearing down on me with arms wide open.

He'd obviously finally set Anne down, because she was busy being tag-team squeezed by David and Ev. My new brother-in-law basically tackle-hugged me, picking me up around the waist and squeezing me crazytown tight. Breathing . . . so passé.

"This is going to be great. I always wanted a little sister," he said. "Older sisters are okay, I mean, don't get me wrong. But little sisters are way more fun, right?"

I just kind of wheezed.

"And you wait until you see what I got you for your birthday. Best. Present. Ever."

"Dude, put her down before you fucking break her," said Ben with some urgency.

"What?" Mal deposited me back on my feet. Thank god.

I gave my sore ribs a rub, taking nice deep breaths. "There was a touch too much love in that hug."

"Oops. Sorry, little sis."

"All good." I grinned, still catching my breath. "Congratulations."

"Yeah. Congrats, man," said Ben. They shook hands vigorously, followed by some shoulder slapping.

"Thanks, dude."

Without missing a beat, the drummer moved on to his next love hug victim. Which left me and Ben staring at each other again. Not awkward at all.

"You look great, Lizzy."

"You too." I couldn't meet his dark eyes any longer, so instead I studied his shoes. A nice safe target. The big black boots made for quite a dramatic contrast against the cream marble floor.

He said nothing.

And yeah, okay, I was done. "Have a nice night."

"Liz, wait—"

"Must mingle."

His hand hooked my arm. "Wait. I want to talk to you."

"I don't think that's a good idea." I pulled my elbow free.

"Please."

That one simple word did it, made me hesitate. Stupid soft me. "Okay. Maybe later."

"Later."

It was good to want things in life. Didn't mean you were necessarily going to get them. Already, the thought of hearing whatever he had to say brought anxiety rushing to the surface. Bridesmaids are busy people; I had shit to do. Ben Nicholson could just wait. Tonight wasn't about me or him or the lingering mess between us. Not even a little. There were about twenty-five or so people present, excluding Santa Elvis and the string quartet. Mal's family, his dad and sisters, husbands and kids. Mine and Anne's mom (henceforth known as She Who Must Be Avoided). The Stage Dive members and their partners, plus Lauren and Nate, of course. Lots of people to meet and greet and mingle up a storm with.

But first I wanted to hug my sister. To hold her tight and know that good things happened to good people, and that she was every bit as happy as she'd always deserved to be.

So that's what I did.

After I spent almost five hours chatting and being the best brides-maid possible, the wedding reception finally began to wind down. Hand to god, I'd more than earned my night out on the town. I'd avoided both Ben and my mom by never standing still for long. My attempts to keep Mal's clutter of nephews and nieces under control went a long way toward helping.

Mental note to never, ever have children. Working with them would be fine, but I wanted to be able to clock out at the end of the day, thank you very much. They might be cute, but they could also be total maniacs. I was pretty damn certain Mal would be getting hit up for the replacement of at least one of the fancy jacquard-covered chairs. I'd tried to get the pâté finger art out, but with little luck. The perpetrator of that particular crime remained hidden under a hallway table.

Couples were beginning to get overly amorous, what with the late hour, rich food, and expensive booze. As for me, I was ready to par-tay!

"We're about to slip away," reported Anne, hooking my elbow with a hand. Her other arm was occupied resting around her hus-band's neck.

"I guessed." I nodded. "The dude attached to the side of your head kind of gave it away."

Mal didn't bother coming up for air. Instead, he kept right on nibbling at Anne's ear. But he did say something. Some muttered string of words I didn't have a hope in hell of understanding.

"What did he say?" I asked.

"He said we have to go consummate our marriage," said Anne.

"Of course he did. Have fun with that."

"We will."

More incoherent mumbling from the guy attached to her ear.

"I thought that was meant to be a surprise for when she got back?" replied Anne.

Mal finally surfaced. "But it's just so cool. I am just so cool. I think she deserves to know this."

"It's your present, it's up to you. Tell her if you like." Anne laughed.

The smile Mal gave me was megawatt, blinding. "I got you a baby blue 1967 Mustang GT for your birthday."

"You did?" I shrieked in glee.

"Exactly. Aren't I just the best? Ohmigod I'm fucking amazing! My own mind is just blown by me. Put it there, little sis." He held up his hand for a high five.

I slapped palms with him with much zest. "That's awesome, Mal!"

"I know, right?"

"Thank you so much."

"It's nothing." A careless hand waved my gratitude away. "Sheesh."

Only Anne seemed unenthused. "You got Liz a muscle car? You bought me a Prius."

With pouty lips, Mal framed her face with his hands. "Because you're my Pumpkin Prius princess. Girls like you don't drive muscle cars."

"Girls like me?"

"Beautiful, clever, good girls with lots of respect for traffic lights and shit like that. Besides, you've got me. You don't need any more muscle in your life."

I wouldn't say Anne looked appeased, exactly. But she did drop the subject after yet another lingering kiss.

"What are you up to tonight?" she asked me eventually.

"I thought I might go dancing or something," I said, rocking back on my heels in excitement. Vegas, here I come. "Put my legal ID to good use."

Anne's grin faltered. "Right, yeah. Listen, Sam was thinking of going around to a couple of clubs too. You mind if he tags along?"

Ruh-roh. "Sam the security man?"

"Yeah." Her gaze wandered around the room for a moment, avoiding mine. "He won't get in the way, I promise. He's a really great guy and going out on your own in Vegas isn't the smartest idea. You don't mind do you? I promise he won't get in your way or anything."

"No, I guess not."

"Good." She visibly relaxed, leaning against Mal. "I think they took your stuff up to the penthouse suite already, by the way. You've got the key, right?"

"Yep. All set."

"And if you go anywhere on your own, don't get lost in the hotel. That place is huge."

"I'll be fine. Go make merry with your husband." I smacked a light kiss on her cheek. "Congratulations. It was a wonderful night. You looked beautiful."

"What 'bout me?" came from Mal.

"Very pretty." I gave him a pat on the head. "Later!"

I had a man to forget and a town to explore.

CHAPTER FOUR

"What'd you say your name was again?"

"Liz."

"Lisa?"

"Close enough." I gave the drunken blond a smile and took another sip of my margarita. He might be cute, but cute didn't make up for rampant stupidity or a blood alcohol level sky-high, such as he had to have. He gave me his version of a pantie-wetting grin and I had no doubt it worked when the dude was sober. Or when the object of his lustful affections was in the same state of inebriation.

Sadly, my two-and-a-half-margarita happy buzz didn't even begin to qualify.

We'd been dancing for an hour or so, having fun. There'd been no real touching or grinding or anything to lead him on.

Because I knew limits, didn't I? Yes I did.

The hotel had a large selection of bars and nightclubs. Not to mention the plethora of nearby ones. We'd started at a place across the road before heading back closer to home. Good music, lots of dancing, and a couple of drinks. My fun had been found, my hair let down.

Anyway, a pity he had to go and wreck it now by trying to

score. Over my shoulder, Sam the security man (who most definitely didn't dance) kept the same position he had for the past three hours, holding up the bar with a glass of whiskey in hand. He'd wanted to check out a couple of clubs, my ass. The man had been sicced onto me for certain. For not the first time tonight, he narrowed his eyes at my dance partner and shook his head in disbelief. I just smiled back at him. Tonight wasn't about serious. It was about laughing, dancing, having a few drinks, and celebrating being young and single.

My drunken companion slipped an arm around my waist, licking his lips. "So, Lila."

"Yeah, Mike?"

A frown. "Mark. My name's Mark."

"Oh, gosh, sorry, Mark. My bad."

"No worries, babe." A hazy grin slipped across his face once more as he leaned forward, moving in for the kill.

I think not.

I turned my face away and took a hasty side step, escaping his attempt at any mouth-on-mouth behavior. Once my last half of salty, tequila-infused heaven on ice was finished, I was out of there. Sam and I could find somewhere else to hang. If it wasn't guaranteed to give me a brain freeze I'd have just downed it. "Well, this has been great."

"Party's just starting," he slurred.

In what was no doubt planned to be a smooth move, the douche stumbled into me, knocking my back into the bar. Worse yet, my god damn drink spilled all over the floor. Those things were not cheap, and I sure as hell hadn't been willing to let Mark buy me any. He'd started getting enough ideas as it was. Idiot.

"Shit." I shoved at the drunken twit's chest, trying to get him off of me. "Move it."

Like my words had suddenly grown superpowers, the dickhead flew backward into the crowd, landing sprawled on his ass several yards away. Whoa. How about that. I gazed in slack-jawed surprise. Then, into the wide-open space in front of me stepped Ben.

Crap.

"Hey," I said, setting my now empty glass on the bar. "Hi."

His forehead was furrowed, his mouth a severely straight, unimpressed line. Goodness, did he look angry. Between the beard and the expression on his face, he looked downright barbaric. He might as well be dressed in furs and carrying a spear, presenting me with the boar he'd caught for dinner. Ah, good old-fashioned Stone Age romance.

"How you doing?" I asked.

Still nothing from him.

"Did you want something to drink? I was just about to move on to another club, but if you'd like to hang here for a while, that's fine with me."

He set a hand on the bar either side of me, fencing me in. Huh.

"Having a good night?" I asked.

"Not really. Been looking for you."

"That's sweet. But you didn't need to do that."

"You knew I wanted to talk to you."

"Yes, I knew."

"You said we'd talk later."

"I know. But here's the thing: maybe I didn't want to talk to you after all, Ben. Maybe I just want to forget what happened and move on with my life."

Behind him, two of the bar's bulky security guys ever so gently escorted my former drunken dance partner from the premises.

"Bye, Mike." I finger waved.

"And what the fuck were you doing with that guy?" he growled.

"Dancing, until he got a wee bit too inebriated. My safety isn't the issue here. I have my friend Sam with me, should I run into any trouble." I nodded to where the man stood by the bar.

If anything, his presence just seemed to make Ben crankier. "Then why wasn't he doing something about that idiot crawling all over you?"

"Probably because he knew I had it covered."

He cocked his head. "You had it covered?"

"Yep."

"Funny, sweetheart. Cause I could have sworn I walked in here to find some *drunken asshole trying to maul you*." The man, he fumed, his cheeks turning red and eyes blazing. It was kind of impressive.

"I realize it looked bad, but I had it under control."

"You did, huh?" His laughter, it didn't really sound the smallest bit amused. "Christ. You're done here."

"Ah, no. I'm actually not. Now see, this is where we have a problem." I folded my arms. Then unfolded them because like fuck I'd look defensive. He was the one in the wrong, not me. "You're not prepared to take me, or my feelings, seriously. What you want is to hide away in Mr. Too Cool for Commitment land and just play with my affections when it suits you. Okay, I've accepted that. But none of that means it's okay for you to come in here and act like you're the boss of me. None of it."

"That so?" he asked, leaning down so that we were almost nose to nose.

"That's so, baby." I play-punched him in the shoulder, which it should be noted, I barely came up to. Okay, so maybe the alcohol on a mostly empty stomach had made me slightly/lots braver/sillier. "So why don't you take your little caveman jealous tantrum bullshit somewhere else. See, I do this funny thing I like to refer to as whatever the fuck I want. Understand?"

He just stared.

"And as pretty as you are with your beard and your muscles, you are too damn tricky and . . . complicated and shit for me."

"I am?"

"Yes, you are. Are you finally seeing my point here?"

"You bet."

"Excellent. So take your hotness elsewhere, kind sir. I want no part of it!" Huh. I had so told him. Drunken bravado was the best.

He nodded once, not so much at my words but as if he'd decided something. It didn't take me long to find out what. The man grabbed my hips tight and bent, setting his shoulder to my middle.

"Don't—"

And up I went. Then down went the front half of me. Down, over his shoulder in a fireman's hold.

"Ben, put me down."

His arm went around my knees, a hand holding onto the back of one thigh. Almost at a not cool height. Though not a single little damn thing about this actually was cool. Then the ground started moving beneath us.

"Ben!"

He didn't even slow down.

"I take it you're finished for the night, Miss Rollins," asked Sam.

"Make him put me down," I screeched.

"I'm afraid I can't interfere. You see, Mr. Nicholson also contributes to my wages."

"You have to be kidding me."

"Puts me in kind of a difficult situation. You understand."

I had nothing.

"To be fair, he texted me asking where you were, hours ago," said Sam. "I didn't tell him."

"Oh yeah, you're a peach."

Sam grinned. The jerk.

"I've got this," grumbled the prehistoric asshole carrying me.

"Right," said the incredibly useless security man. "Might go lose some money on a card game, then. Night-night."

Ben just grunted.

So I smacked him on the ass. "You're being absolutely ridiculous. Put me down."

"Nope."

"Do you have any idea how insane this must look?"

"Don't care."

"I do. God, Ben. You drive me nuts."

Another grunt. How original.

My laughter came out slightly too high-pitched, too crazy. What a night.

So tempting to lose my shit, but no. Conflict resolution. I was a professional to the last. "Ben, why don't you put me down and we can talk about whatever you want over a drink. You've obviously got my attention now."

"I don't think so."

"Look, I'm sorry I didn't take your request to talk seriously before. Let me make it up to you."

He ignored me.

Pity those around us didn't. They giggled and pointed and carried on like we were a damn comedy act. But did anyone think to try and help me? No.

People.

"I'm trying to be reasonable here!"

"I know."

"Which is pretty fucking mature of me, given I'm upside down talking to your ass, Ben!" I growled in frustration, slapping at his rear one more time just for fun. Had ever a man been born so bone of head and firm of butt? I think not.

"Keep that up, I'm going to start giving it back to you," he warned. "And my hands are a hell of a lot bigger than yours, Liz."

"You are such an asshole."

"You know, you act all cute, but you've got a mouth on you when you get riled up."

"Bite me."

"It's late, Lizzy. Time for bad girls to go to bed," he said.

"Aw, Ben. If you were having trouble scoring, you should have just said so. We could have worked something out."

His laughter was low-down and dirty. "That's real accommodating of you, sweetheart."

"No worries. I think it's a damn shame a big strong hairy rock star such as yourself has to take to kidnapping women out of bars to get any."

Cool air hit the back of my thighs as the skirt of my dress was raised. Teeth grazed over my soft skin in warning, his breath coming dangerously close to warming pertinent areas. Or maybe that was just my imagination. Either way, time to freak right out.

"Don't you fucking dare," I screeched, wriggling around.

Arms tightened around me and the sharp teeth were replaced with his lips. "Stop squirming."

"Stop being such a bastard and put me down."

"You said to bite you." The idiot tittered.

Whatever. Simple people are often easily amused.

Hell I was a long way up. It was a little scary. Down a fancy hallway we ventured, the sound of slot machines and the faint stink of cigarettes indicating the massive gaming room had to be somewhere near. Next, a glossy elevator with an ad for some show, playing on repeat. The foolish man had left his wallet sitting in his back pocket. At last, some entertainment. Why not, since I was along for the ride?

"Who's Meli? And . . ." I held the next scrawled-on piece of paper up to my face. "Crap. I think it says Karen. I don't think you should call Karen for a good time. The poor girl can barely spell her own name. Hey, mind if I borrow your credit card?"

The Neanderthal dipped and my feet once more met the ground. He held onto my elbow with a strong hand. A good thing because, whoa, my head spun around and around as the world slowly righted itself.

"Give me that," he growled, snatching the wallet out of my hands and stuffing it back into his pocket. "Stop acting like a brat."

"I'm acting like a brat? Are you serious?"

"Saying you'll talk to me later, then disappearing."

I snorted. "Because hearing more of your excuses sounds like such a good time."

"It's not like that."

"Bullshit," I said, hands on hips. "Go find someone who wants to play your games, Ben."

"Fuck." He turned away, mouth all scrunched up. "I wanted to apologize, okay?"

I watched and waited.

"I miss you, Liz. I didn't mean to hurt you." He seemed sincere, eyes all tortured. "I'm sorry."

"Okay. But I still can't do it."

His gaze searched my face. "You can't what?"

"Be friends with you."

He said nothing.

"I'm sorry. I know you're lonely and you miss L.A., but I can't. I have feelings for you and I can't just put them away because you're not prepared to go there."

He pressed his lips tight together, hard enough to turn them white. Then he turned his back on me.

"Ben?"

Silence.

"For what it's worth, I missed you too."

The elevator pinged and the doors slid smoothly open.

"Thanks for the lift." I wandered out, fishing my room key out of my bra ever so subtly. He'd been right. It probably was time to call it a night. At least I'd gotten some dancing and a drink or two in. I'd seen some of Vegas for myself and Anne and Mal were happily married. All in all, a highly successful trip. So why did it feel like I was being broken open because of him one more time?

Ben trudged along behind me, saying nothing. He could do as he pleased. Obviously. It was around midnight, give or take. Today had been long, with all the wedding preparations, and last night had been a late one, with my birthday celebration. Fact was, bed sounded like a damn fine idea actually.

I opened the door to my penthouse suite and stepped inside. Everything was marble and mirrors and splendor. The curtains were drawn back, displaying the Strip all lit up. A thing of beauty.

"Wow."

The moody man mountain leaned his butt against the table, legs spread wide and muscular arms crossed over his chest. What he did to me. I never stood a chance. My heart went *boom* and my body woke right the hell up. The temptation to go climb him, to touch him and taste him, was too strong. He needed to leave.

"Shouldn't you be off hitting up Karen or Meli or whoever else passed you their number?" I asked.

"You jealous?"

I tried to smile. I'm pretty sure I failed. "What would be the point?"

He just gazed at me, his blank face a mystery. Hell, all of him a mystery. One I would never solve.

"You can leave," I said. "I won't be going out again."

The man crashed down on the couch. "Give me a break. I've been chasing you all over town for the last few hours."

Again and again. Whatever.

Beyond the open living and dining room lay the bedroom. A mother of a bed. You'd pretty much want to pack a lunch if you were going to try and cross the thing. More flower arrangements and fancy furniture. The bathroom was equally huge and majestic.

Two baths, for some reason. Wild. I wandered up to one of the basins, studying the girl in the mirror. Not bad. Pretty enough, if not beautiful. Hopefully the bulk of the time she had half a brain in her head and a promising future ahead of her.

But in the meantime the updo needed dealing with. Then I could get down to scrubbing all the makeup off my face. Maybe I'd even test-drive one of the tubs.

Ben appeared in the doorway with an open beer in his hand. Another of the buttons of his white shirt had been undone. Such a bull of a neck. No god damn idea why that worked for me.

"I take it you've decided you're staying?" I reached back, searching for the first of what would no doubt be many, many hairpins.

"You mind?"

"No, I give up. But what would Mal say?"

"I'll crash on the couch," he said, ignoring my question entirely.

I continued duking it out with the do.

"Let me help." He stepped closer, setting his beer down. Dark brows drew in a ways as he gave my hair a good glaring at. Then, with careful fingers, he gently tugged free his first pin and tossed it onto the counter.

"Thanks."

Without comment, he kept on with the job while I watched. Weird. I barely came up to the guy's shoulder, even in my high heels. The width of him dwarfed me. I wasn't particularly tiny or petite, being basically average everything. But with him standing behind me I looked like some small, dainty thing. The guy could crush me one-handed. Hell, he'd done a pretty good job on my heart from afar.

"Don't know why you do all this," he said. "It looks just as good down."

My eyebrows rose right up. "I didn't know you noticed."

Nothing.

I stole a sip of his beer. A fancy German one in a big shiny green bottle. Hoppy. Nice.

"Don't need all that shit on your face, either." He took the beer off me and had another swig before returning to tending my hair. Our gazes met ever so briefly in the mirror, then his darted away. He took a deep breath, got busy.

"Thanks. I think."

A shrug.

My fingers toyed with the edge of the counter, nails flicking back and forth. A nervous habit. He shifted slightly, moving a little closer. I could feel the heat of him at my back, the solidity of him.

"Maybe I should do this myself," I said.

"You'll be here all fucking night you try to do it by yourself. How many pins did they stick in this thing?"

"I lost count after the first dozen or so."

He worked for a while in silence. Yeah. Awesome. Not awkward at all.

"Happy Birthday for yesterday," he mumbled in a rough low voice. More pins were tossed onto the counter.

"Thanks."

Carefully, he started pulling sections of my hair free, letting them fall down my back. The intent look in his eyes, the absolute focus as he did it, nearly killed me. What the hell was going on here? Talk about mixed signals. Maybe I'd have a cold bath, ice, the whole works. It would take at least that to put out the fire in my pants.

"Happy Twenty-Ninth Birthday for before Christmas," I said, voice wavering. "I, um . . . I know I was there for the dinner, but . . ."

"But you were avoiding me." The edges of his mouth slid into a smile. It seemed self-deprecating somehow. Definitely unfunny.

"Yeah."

He stared at me in the mirror. And then he stared at me some more. God, I wish I could read him. Just for a moment even. I wished I could touch him even more.

"Funny," he said. "We were only texting, but I got used to it."

"Me too."

"What do you want for your birthday?" he asked, changing the topic abruptly.

"Ah, nothing. You don't need to buy me anything."

"I want to get you something. So what do you want? What do you need?"

Him and him with his heart on his sleeve. "The handle on my canvas satchel broke the other day. Guess I could do with a new one of those, if you wanted to get me something. But Ben, it's really not necessary."

"A satchel. Okay. What else?"

"Nothing else. Thank you. Just a new satchel would be great."

He shook his head. "Most women would be asking for diamonds."

"Ben, I don't like you because you have money. I like you because you're you."

His thumb stroked over the back of my neck, there and gone in an instant. Perhaps it was an accident. "Thank you."

I plucked a pin from my hair, taking over the job. "We better get this done. It's late."

"I got it," he said, focusing on my hair once more.

"Okay." God he was beautiful. Why did I have to go nuts every time he came near? Just once it would be nice if I could not play the fool where this man was concerned. "I think maybe you should leave. I think I need you to."

Thick fingers removed another pin, like I hadn't said a word.

"Why are you here?" I reached back behind my head and grabbed his wrists, stilling him. "Ben?"

"Because apparently I'm shit at staying away from you."

"Then I guess we have a problem." Our fingers meshed, holding on tight.

"That's putting it fucking mildly."

My eyelids started blinking like crazy for some reason. "I warned you not to flirt with me again unless you meant it."

He didn't answer, just released my fingers and went back to playing with my hair, running it over the back of his hand, laying it over my shoulder. Such a stern look on his face, the frown embedded on his sharp features. My hands fell back to my sides.

And call me a blundering fool, but I was going there again. Apparently I would never learn. Hair half up, half down, and the buzz from the margaritas fading much too fast to help fuel such bravery. Damn it. I looked crazy—and hell, I probably was. Who are we kidding?

"Hey." I turned, cupping his cheek with my hand. The bristle of his beard felt amazing, sort of soft and yet not quite. Even more amazing, he wasn't stopping me or drawing back.

"Talk to me," I repeated.

"Fucking hated seeing that guy all over you."

"What? In the bar?"

A jut of the chin and he went back to examining my hair, carefully extracting another pin.

My hand slipped down, fingers skating over the side of his warm neck. The skin was so soft and smooth. "If it makes you feel any better, I pretty much want to scratch Karen and Meli's eyes out with my bare hands. But that doesn't change the situation here."

The edges of his mouth turned down.

Fuck it. I edged forward, getting closer, leaning into his broad chest.

No.

No.

Apparently the dude seriously liked my hair. Because something in his pants was definitely making its presence felt against my stomach. The fire in my pants turned into a blazing inferno. I'm surprised we weren't both incinerated on the spot. Everything low in me tensed, my thighs getting weak and strung out all at once. So this was what being really and truly fuck-me-now-or-I'll-die turned on felt like. And yet, leaning into the heat and strength of him, I also felt perfectly safe.

Just not from rejection.

"Ben?"

"Hmm?"

"What is this? Do you know what you're doing?"

"What I shouldn't be doing."

He slid his hand down my back, drawing me in firmly against his erection. Oh yeah. I dug my fingers nails into his neck, holding on tight. If he tried to ditch me now, I'd kill him. No joke. Death by hairpins. It would be messy but highly necessary.

Lucky for him, he didn't.

"I mean it," he said, voice devastatingly low but certain. So beautifully, perfectly certain.

"Okay."

He covered my hand with his, holding it against his skin. The small acceptance of me touching him turned me on almost as much as the heat of his body. I rocked against him, rubbing myself against his erection.

The man swore up a storm. "Fuck, Lizzy."

"What a good idea." My heavy head lolled to the side and his hot mouth was there, sucking, licking, and biting. My blood ran hot, racing through me at the speed of light. His teeth sunk just a little into my skin, making me moan. Then his hand slid down, cupping my ass through the silk of my dress, fingers digging in. And this was all nice, really nice. But I wanted to kiss him so bad.

"Let me . . ." I stretched up, looping my arms around his neck, dragging his mouth down to mine. Once, twice, he grazed my lips with his. The fucking tease. And I had no control over him at all because, "You're too tall!"

He laughed deep and dirty, hands sliding over my ass to lift me up. Genius. The man was a fucking gorgeous, bearded, bass-playing, oversize genius. My legs went around his waist and the smile on his face—shit. It was a total smirk. Just this once, he could have it, and for the record, it looked damn good on him too.

"Better?" he asked.

"Yes." I attached my lips to his and shoved my tongue into his mouth and kissed the man stupid. Just like I'd been dying to do for so long.

He groaned, one hand cupping my ass, the other rubbing and caressing the back of my neck. Encouraging me or holding me in place, I don't know. Either way, it felt sublime. What was going on between my legs, meanwhile, the hard length of his cock rubbing just so, pretty much drove me out of my mind. When had sex gotten so good? My six-or-so-year abstinence had a lot to answer for, and yet I was damn glad I'd waited.

I kissed him deep, tasting and exploring. The feel of his beard brushing against my face, the soft slip of his hair through my hands. In lieu of actual fucking, I'd done a lot of making out over the years. No one kissed like Ben, though. Though I'd started out in charge of the mouth-to-mouth, the battle was more of a draw now. His tongue slipped into my mouth, teasing and tantalizing me, turning me on even more.

I hadn't even realized we were moving until my back hit the wall. The bathroom wall. We wouldn't be making it to the bedroom this time, and all right, fair enough. His hand moved from my neck to fumble with his zipper, knuckles brushing against the damp crotch of my panties. Ratcheting up my excitement levels just that much more. Then his finger hooked the satin material of my panties aside and his cock was rubbing against me there. Right fucking there. Yes, yes, yes.

"Ben."

"Lizzy. Shit. Stay still."

"I'm trying."

He pressed into me, the lips of my pussy giving, opening to take him. And there was a lot of him. His hips flexed and I squeaked in surprise. But it wasn't long before we were both groaning, in both the good and the bad ways. The thick head of his cock was lodged inside of me, but going no further. Not without some serious pain, at least on my part. How damn wide was the guy?

Ben rested his damp forehead against mine, panting. "This isn't working."

"I'm not a virgin, it's just been a while. It should fit!" I clung to him tighter, hiding my face in his neck. No way would I burst into tears, despite the current uncertainty of the situation within my actual tear ducts, fueled by both pain and need. How ridiculous. A hand rubbed my back in big, soothing circles.

"Shouldn't have rushed," he said.

I sniffed.

"Easy." He lifted me off of him, and even that did not feel good. "'s okay."

"I really wanted this." I confessed into his neck. "You."

"And you'll have me. Shh."

We moved again, this time into the bedroom.

"I had no fucking business being inside you without protection anyway."

"It felt good. Until it felt bad."

"I know."

A hand searched for the zip on the back of my dress, tugging it down. The air-conditioning hit my skin, sending a shiver down

my spine. Or maybe it was just the way he looked at me, all aggressive and tender at once. I was laid out on the mattress, Ben working busily to get me bare.

"We're really not stopping?" I asked, lust burning bright once again. Not that it had ever really disappeared. How could it, with him around? My girl parts were sadly predictable like that.

"Fuck no."

I smiled, wiggling and rolling this way and that, according to what would be most helpful. No hesitation. Off came my bra, the slick pointy-toed heels and thigh-high stockings, then he hovered over my fancy silk panties.

"What?" I asked, panting just a little.

Fingers stroked over the curves of my hips, my thighs. The man was probably used to models and starlets, women in no way normal. Of all times to get an attack of the nerves. I crossed my arms demurely over my bare breasts, biting at the inside of my cheek.

"Ben, what's the problem?"

"No problem." His gaze met mine. Then he noticed the crossed arms, covering my chest. "Don't."

My hands fluttered, unsure what to do.

He took hold of both wrists, bending over me to press them into the bed above my head.

"Keep 'em there," he said, voice gruff, clipped, and eyes deadly serious. "'kay?"

"Okay."

His hands traced down the length of my arms, over my armpits, then down my sides. The tension inside me seemed unbearable. My mind was whirling in circles, befuddled and aroused both. What was he going to do?

Thumbs hooked into the sides of my sole remaining piece of clothing and slowly dragged them down my legs. While his tickly bearded chin trailed down over my breastbone, between my pert

breasts, and over my belly. Softly, he placed a kiss on my belly button, then dropped my underwear onto the floor.

"All good?" he asked.

"Y-yes."

The man sank to his knees by the side of the bed, the palms of his hands stroking over my thighs. "Good."

Without further preamble, he grabbed my hips, dragging me to the edge of the mattress to meet his waiting mouth. And yes, my legs were spread, they were wide open. With his head in the way, they had few other options. The feeling of his hot, eager mouth on my pussy . . . there were no words. Or at least, none sufficient to sum this up.

"Fuck. Ben."

My back bowed, head pushing into the mattress. The pleasure was bigger than my body could contain. Every ounce of my consciousness was focused on the fast-building buzz between my legs. My heels pressed against his back through the fine material of his fancy dress shirt. He wrapped his arms around my thighs, holding me to him. As if I wanted to get away. His tongue dragged through my sex, lips sucking and teeth almost biting. Everywhere he went his facial hair followed, making my nerve endings tingle and my tummy tighten. Too much and not enough and give me more. Every now and then he'd give me a warning nip somewhere, such as the sensitive join of body and thigh, like I needed a reminder regarding who was in charge.

Who was doing what to whom.

He ground his face into me, eating me, going wild, and it felt fucking amazing. Mind-blowing, breath-stealing. Everything. I got it now. Beards were the best. His tongue was like a lick of heat, his lips silken smooth and so damn strong. That beard, however. Holy shit. Too many sensations, too much, and all I could do was take it. The man was damn skilled, but I didn't want to think about

how many women he'd practiced on. Forget that. Only now mattered.

I was so damn wet. He slid two thick fingers into me, working me inside and out. My whole body tensed unbearably tight, until it seemed like I might shatter. Just explode into chaos and lovestruck confusion. Then he flicked his tongue back and forth across my clit, stopping to suck at it every other time, lips encasing my swollen, completely overexcited sex.

I couldn't take it any longer. My whole body went *boom*.

I came with a shout, eyes open wide but unseeing. He'd colored my world in sparkles. Multitudes of little flashy lights, filling my mind and lighting me up. I just floated, lost in the feel-good chemical haze he'd induced. The mediocre to bad sex I'd had during my juvenile, idiotic, wild phase didn't even begin to compare. Nothing in common with how Ben worked my body. The pleasure he gave me. Damn he was good at oral. Scarily so.

When the haze of blinky lights faded, he was busy pulling his shirt off over his head. Apparently undoing the buttons would have taken too long. He wiped off his mouth, dark gaze glued to me all the while. Next he toed off his boots and ripped into the pants—belt, button, and zip. Plain black boxer briefs outlined a monster of a hard-on. No wonder it wouldn't fit. And the way he looked at me, like he wasn't sure if he wanted to take a bite out of me or what. I don't know. But his gaze slipped over me so warmly, belying the hunger in his eyes.

Then the boxers went down and he was climbing over me, hooking an arm around my waist to drag me back into the middle of the bed.

"Are we going to—"

"Yeah," he said, then tore open a condom wrapper with his teeth. One-handed he rolled it on, the slippery, smooth latex rubbing against me between my legs.

"Good. That's . . . that's good."

His moist lips covered mine, kissing me hard.

"Trust me," he said, positioning the broad blunt head of his cock against my opening.

I nodded.

"Legs and arms around me."

"Yes." I did as told, wrapping him up tight.

"That's it, sweetheart," he murmured, flexing his hips.

His lips played with mine, tongue licking my jaw, my neck, as he worked his cock inside of me. Arms encircled my head and his beautiful face was so close, bristly cheek resting against mine, teeth nipping my ear. Now that I was plenty wet, things went smoother. But still, he was not a small man. He felt good, but . . . substantial. Thick. It might take me a while to get used to him.

And there weren't enough words to explain how I wanted to get used to him, in all the ways.

"Wait." I squirmed beneath him, tilting my hips to take him deeper. "Oh god, yeah. Like that."

"There?" He surged forward, filling me, his hips pressing me deep into the mattress. I sighed and he moaned, his pelvis shifting restlessly against me.

"Yeah."

"Fuck you feel good," he said, face buried in my hair. "So fucking good."

I flexed my thigh muscles, tightening my hold on him. Given half a chance, I'd never let him go. In return, he groaned, easing back to thrust forward again, slow and easy. The motion smooth and precise. Ben fucked me so sweetly, working himself deep into me in sure, steady strokes. Accustoming me to his presence. His body trembled with the effort, sweat dripping off his brow. I'd never experienced anything more perfect than being in bed with him. Being the focus of all his attention.

It was like we were each other's whole world. Nothing else existed beyond the bed.

His mouth took mine, his hand slipping down between us to explore where we were joined. Fingers caressing the stretched lips of my sex, just above my still sensitive clit. I gasped and he smiled, adjusting his angle slightly so he rubbed against it. He fucked me harder then, pushing me up and up toward climax once more.

"Ben," I panted.

His arms tightened, caging me in, keeping me safe. A hand slipped beneath my ass cheek then traveled up my leg, sliding over my sweaty skin. He grabbed ahold of my thigh, hard, fingers digging in. The familiar ecstatic tension spread through me, completing me. It was out of control. Everything about sex with Ben was out of control. The way his hard chest rubbed against my breasts and the single-mindedness in the way he watched me, gauging every response. His big body covered me, his cock filling me. Pleasure was the only possible response.

I came, shuddering, biting into his shoulder. I shook and shook, and he held onto me even tighter. He drove himself deep and came, one hand in my hair and the other still wrapped around my thigh.

Nothing could ever compare.

Ben collapsed beside me. He hit the mattress so hard I bounced into his side and stayed there, curling up against him. It took a while for the world to stop spinning, for us both to catch our breath.

My insides buzzed. Hell, my whole body buzzed. I hid my face in his skin, grinning like a fool. How incredible for me and him to be in the same bed doing the postcoital bliss thing. I'd been this happy, this certain of something, precisely never in my life. It wouldn't be easy but it would be worth it. Mal and Anne would adjust, because eight years was nothing, really.

I rolled onto my side and snuggled into him. The dude had more than enough body warmth for both of us in the cool air-conditioning. Then, from somewhere close, came a buzzing.

Ben stirred, reaching down to snag his cell from the pocket of his jeans before tossing them aside. When he saw the name on the screen his whole body stiffened. The buzzing went on. His thumb slid across the front of the cell and he held it to his ear.

"Hey."

A faint voice from the phone.

"No, no. I dropped her back at her room."

More from the caller.

"For fuck's sake, man. When will you get it through your head nothing's going on? Girl's not my kind."

My heart stuttered. It hurt.

"Ha-ha. Yeah, fuck off. Go back to your bride. I'm heading to a bar uptown. Shilly's playing. Said I'd join for a while."

More talk.

"Yeah, I'll tell him you said hi. Later."

Above me, the ceiling swam blurrily, my vision wavering. Silly me, always so surprised. When would I learn?

"Were you ever going to tell him?" I asked quietly.

"What?" Ben sat at the side of the bed, head in his hands. He was just having a moment, the sex had been intense and so on. All of us processed emotional moments in our own sweet way. "You want a drink or something?"

"No. I want the truth." Strangely calm, I sat up, tugging the sheet with me. All of a sudden being naked didn't seem like such a smart idea. "Were you ever planning on telling Mal about us?"

"We only just finished having sex. The man's on his honeymoon. It's his wedding night. You really want me to get into it with him right now?"

"No. What I'm asking is if you're planning on getting into it with him ever."

Ben looked away, wiping his face with a hand. "It's complicated."

"Yeah. But I'm not sure you lying to him helps."

"And I'm not sure me telling him I just banged his little-sister-in-law would help, either," he snapped. "Shit. Liz, I didn't mean it like that."

"I know. It's complicated." My voice seemed so small.

He looked back over his shoulder at me, face guarded. "Wait . . ."

"It was an accident. You got jealous when you saw that guy with me in the bar, overheated. I get it."

"I didn't mean—"

"You never do." Without further ado I rolled off the bed, taking the sheet with me. "I'd like you to leave."

"Lizzy." It was right there on his face and in his eyes. The set of his shoulders shouted it, and those curled fingers just reinforced everything. Regret.

"Leave, please. You know you want to."

Jeans lay abandoned just inside the bathroom door. I halfheartedly kicked them aside, locking myself in.

"Sweetheart." A timid knock or two. "C'mon, open up."

My back to the door, I slumped down, not stopping until the hard marble chilled my ass. Egyptian cotton didn't have such great thermal properties, apparently. Tears fell, but I just ignored them. Whatever.

"Let me explain."

I don't think so.

"I just . . . I panicked when I saw it was him. Fuck, Lizzy." An angry thump on the door. "You don't get how hard this is. I like you, but . . ."

But. But me no buts. Fuck.

"I'm not saying I wouldn't have told him in time."

Huh. Nor was he saying he would have.

"Christ, can I at least have my pants?" he grumbled.

No, actually. No he couldn't. From me, he couldn't have a single thing more. I'd given all I would.

More tears fell unchecked. My body still buzzing but my heart breaking open. How confusing. So much good with the bad. It really was complicated. Everything went quiet out there; he said no more. I guess, at the end of the day, I just wasn't the kind of girl that "complicated" worked for. I wasn't in search of drama. I wasn't only happy when it rained. So instead I sat on the cold bathroom floor and cried and cried.

Eventually, dimly, I heard the front door slam shut.

Over and out.

CHAPTER FIVE

NOW

"No."

"What do you mean, no?" asked Anne, face incredulous.

"No. I'm not going to explain what went on between me and Ben to you."

She just blinked.

"It's personal." I stood tall, despite feeling about two inches off the floor. "I just wanted you to know that I chased him, not the other way around. I had feelings for him and I acted on them. End of story."

So I guess I would explain what happened between us. At least a little of one side of the sorry tale. Hopefully enough to save the band. Good god, did my pride lay in tatters on the floor.

Mal wouldn't meet my eyes, and Ben's nose was still bleeding. Awesome. What a mess. The entire dinner party had denigrated into some blood-splattered, rock 'n' roll wrestling, multiple-surprise-baby-announcement mess. My fault. I should have handled it differently. Not that I had any idea how I could have done better just yet, but whatever. Doubtless some genius ideas would taunt me at two in the morning.

There were a lot of judgy eyes in the room. All of my new friends and family gathered around to watch the explosion. Shit.

"I'm sorry," I said and bolted for the door. I grabbed my coat and left.

A banging noise.

I cracked open an eyelid. In the darkness the alarm clock shone 3:18 a.m. in brilliant green. What in the ever-loving hell? The banging continued, followed by the muffled sound of voices. One was loud and belligerent, the other far calmer. I got up and flicked on the living room light, stumbled over to the front door. Whoever it was would just have to take me in socks, old sweatpants, and an oversize T-shirt. Away from the warmth of my bed, goose bumps covered my arms.

"Liz?" a familiar rough voice demanded. "Open up."

I did as asked, yawning and rubbing the sleep from my eyes all the while. "Wow. You look a mess."

"Yeah," said Ben, swaying slightly.

He stood upright mostly due to the aid of David, one big arm thrown over the other man's shoulders. Hair hung in his face, combining with the beard for a cross between a yeti and a Cousin It kind of feel. From between the dark strands, red eyes peered out at me. Oh, and lest I forget, he also stank like he'd recently bathed in a keg of beer, using Scotch-scented soap. Lovely.

"Sorry 'bout this," said the guitarist, half dragging Ben into my apartment. "He insisted on coming over."

"It's fine."

"On the couch?" David asked, face lined with strain.

"Ah, have to be the bed, please. He's too big to fit on the couch."

"Serve his stupid ass right if he woke up on the floor." David sighed.

"Let me help." I slid beneath Ben's other arm, trying to take some of the weight. Christ, the man could put a bear to shame in the sheer bulk department.

"Hey, sweetheart," said the giant drunken sod.

"Hey there, Ben." I grabbed hold of his hand, hanging on tight. "How you feeling?"

"Great." He chuckled.

"I'll go first," said David, directing the three of us sideways so we'd fit through my bedroom door.

"Okay. Go slow."

"Yep."

Operation Haul the Drunken Baby Daddy into Bed was going well. Except when Ben kind of stumbled halfway through. He surged forward, his forehead cracking into the doorjamb. I swear I felt the building shudder. There was definitely an indent in the wooden frame.

"Ow," he said, sort of contemplatively.

David just laughed.

"Crap. Are you all right?" I asked, trying to push the hair back from his face to see, while keeping him upright and hopefully safe from further harm. "Ben?"

"He's fine. Dude has the hardest head I've ever seen. One time when we were kids we got stoned up on the roof of my house. Ben walked straight off the edge. We were all freaking out, but by the time we got down there he'd already gotten on his bike and headed home. The big idiot's basically indestructible." David directed us toward the side of the bed. "Okay, let him go."

I did so, and the father of my unborn child toppled face-first onto the mattress. At least that had to be a soft landing. Still, he lay there completely unmoving, apart from the rebound of the springs. God, I hoped we hadn't accidentally killed him. If we had, at least the neglect wasn't willful.

I grabbed one of his sneakers and gave it a shake. "Ben, are you still breathing?"

A groan from the man on the bed. Not too bad, as signs of life went.

"Don't worry," said David. "He's fine. Just let him sleep it off."

I nodded, still frowning just the same.

"You right with him?" asked David, hands on his hips. "I can send Sam over if you like. He's finished babysitting Mal from what I hear."

"No need, thanks. Is he all right? Mal?"

He gaze softened. "Passed out just like this one, apparently."

Seriously, such a mess. Anne and Mal would probably never talk to me again. Well, Anne would, but she was my sister, so she had to forgive me eventually. Mal was another situation entirely. The thought of losing his high opinion and easy affection bit deep. Consequences were a bitch. Realistically, however, I couldn't imagine myself having done any differently even if I'd known Mal and Anne would be pissed. I mean, I'd already known that and it didn't even make me pause. Fewer star-crossed lovers and more adults should be allowed to date who they wanted.

Maybe if I'd known the night would result in the bean . . . I don't know. There was only one thing I was sure of: sex equaled nothing but chaos and confusion. It was official.

I squeezed my eyes shut. "You must hate me."

David's brow wrinkled up. "What? Why?"

"For causing all this trouble." The urge to flail was huge, but I restrained it. For now. Instead, I got busy wriggling Ben's shoes off his feet. No way were they making contact with my sheets.

"I'm assuming you didn't have to hold a gun to Ben's head to get him to fuck you?" The guy watched me unblinking, face dead serious.

"Um, no."

David shrugged. "There you go."

"Isn't that taking a slightly overly simplistic view of the situation?"

He smiled. "In my experience, shit usually is pretty simple when you get right down to it. When it comes to matters of the heart, you decide where you belong and you go be there. Simple. Ben wanted to be here. Don't think I didn't try to talk him out of it, either. The bastard insisted."

Maybe. "Wonder what his new girlfriend would make of your theory."

"Yeah." He winced, his mouth widening in imagined pain. "I'll leave that one up to you two to sort out. But try not to stress. Can't be good for Ben junior."

"Right." I rolled my eyes and dropped Ben's shoe on the floor. "But how is this going to affect the band, the two of them fighting?"

It took him a long time to answer. "I honestly don't know."

Fuck.

"Night. I'll lock the door on my way out." He raised a hand in salute. "Call Ev if you need anything."

"Thanks, David."

The front door clicked closed behind him, leaving me alone with Ben. He lay passed out sideways across my queen-size bed. Ben was in my actual bed. Holy hell. I didn't quite know what to do with that information. A pity there was nothing but boxes and junk in the spare room. Not that I didn't want him near. My heart wasn't so sensible. It was just time for me to start taking the safer option when it came to him. Past time even.

"Hey." I leaned over the mattress, giving his leg a shake. "Roll over."

A moan.

"Come on, big boy. Move it. You're taking up all the bed."

Incoherent muttering.

This was not working, and like hell I'd be sleeping on the love seat. I pulled off a sock and tugged on his big toe. "Ben. Wake up."

In slow motion, he stirred, lifting his shaggy head and looking around.

"Roll over."

"Wha—" He turned, easing himself up and over, as requested. He blinked and grimaced and looked generally displeased with the world. A lumpy red line bisected his forehead. Whatever David said, that had to hurt. "Lizzy?"

"Got it in one."

"How'd I get here?"

"David just dropped you off, remember?"

He scratched at his beard. "Uh. Okay."

"You need to move, you're taking up all of the room."

Bewildered, he rose up on his elbows and took a look around. "This your bed?"

"Yes."

"Did we . . ." He raised an eyebrow suggestively.

"No, I already learned my lesson, thank you very much."

"You sure?" He gave me a wonky smile. "It could be fun."

"Yeah, you look like you've had enough fun for the both of us for one night, buddy."

"Maybe." He contemplated the thin cotton of my shirt for a good long while, one corner of his mouth moving upward. "Hey, you're not wearing a bra."

"Shut up and move, Ben."

A groan. "All right."

It took him about forever to wriggle and roll and finally get his big fat head up on the pillow. On my favored side, damn it. Whatever. I lie down on my back beside him, keeping a nice, fun, celibate distance between our two bodies just in case he decided to try and get some. More sleep would be so great. To grow the bean, I really needed rest. My limbs were weighed down with lethargy, my head full of blergh.

"We could cuddle," he suggested, the words slurred, blurring together into one dumb drunken idea. Man, if he'd been even one inch sober I'd be all over him. A hug right now, letting me know everything would be okay, sounded sublime. A silly, childish wish, I know. Things were complicated enough. "I wouldn't try nothing, swear."

"Nice double negative. No, Ben."

A grunt of dismay.

"Go to sleep."

The world seemed still, almost perfectly quiet. A car passed by outside and the wind blew around the building. Everyone else would be fast asleep at this hour. I studied the water mark on the ceiling, the shadows cast by the dodgy old lamp on my bedside table. For some reason, being alone with him in the dark seemed too danger-ous. The light could stay on.

"I'm gonna be a father," he said, eyes closed.

My whole body tensed instantly. "So I heard."

"Wasn't planning on having kids."

"You weren't?"

"No."

Drunk or not, he sounded so definite, so sure. It was like a dag-ger to my heart, the pain overwhelming. It hurt to breathe. "Not even when you were a little older?"

A sharp shake of the head in the negative.

Well.

I didn't know what to say. My throat constricted and my eyes stung. He'd had little more choice in becoming a parent than I had. We were both being thrown into this, and there were plans more than mine being disrupted. Still, he wasn't the one whose body was being hijacked, for all intents and purposes. Not that I hadn't had the option to end the pregnancy. I did, but I hadn't taken it. My heart had made its decision and there was no going back. Still, it was hard not to be all bitter and betrayed over his announcement. I didn't even have the luxury of being able to get blind rotten drunk. And believe me, dealing with all this sober sucked. My rational mind coughed up so many plausible, reasonable excuses for him—he was surprised, he was drunk, give him a chance to think things over, blah blah blah.

But fuck them all. Fuck him.

I'd kind of already been expecting the worst, to be in this alone. Now I knew. Twice he'd disappointed me; this couldn't be a surprise. Nothing had changed, not really. I slid a hand over my stomach, spread my fingers over the ever so slight bulge there. It might have just been my imagination, but I could feel her already getting busy in there, growing away. We'd be fine. We'd manage.

"Didn't want to settle down," he continued. "And kids, they need stability and shit. Time, energy, all those things."

"True." My voice sounded hollow, an emotionless echo.

At least I had the apartment paid up for the foreseeable future. Reece could no doubt use me more in the shop. I was fortunate there. Probably be best if I dropped out of school and started saving. Given how many days I'd been missing due to the puke-o-rama of morning sickness, my grades wouldn't be rocking this term anyway.

I swallowed hard.

"Like my life the way it is," he said, voice slurring at the edges.

"Yeah, I did too." I gave my stomach a pat. "Sorry, Bean."

"Like my freedom. Being able to jump on a plane and go jam with a friend or play on their album. Things were perfect the way they were."

"Hmm."

"Couldn't stay away from you."

"Why not?" I asked, honestly curious.

"Don't know. You just . . . you stayed on my mind."

"And other women didn't?"

"Not like you."

"No?" Perhaps booze boy was back to wanting sex. Given my heart got stupid the minute he appeared, it was hard to tell.

He exhaled hard. "Wanted you, but . . . you were my friend too. I mean, really my friend. You didn't want nothing but me. To talk to me, to spend time . . ."

Silence.

"I knew you wanted more, but you didn't push. Missed you when you were gone and I couldn't tell you shit, talk to you about stuff."

My turn to sigh.

"Liz?"

"Yeah?"

"What are we gonna do?" He sounded almost afraid.

I gave in and rolled onto my side, all the better to watch him. If only he looked worse in profile. Instead, the dominant nose and plush lips seemed almost majestic somehow. The bastard. I inched closer, studying him. Eyelids closed, lips sealed shut. His forehead had smoothed out in repose, the curve of his cheekbones so obvious. I'd never really gotten to stare at him to my heart's content. All the same old feelings rushed up inside, only now there was more. So much more. A tiny bit of him and me was growing inside my body, making a permanent connection between us. It was kind of terrifying. I wondered if she'd have his mouth or his eyes.

The room stayed silent.

"Ben?"

I waited, but he said no more, his breathing falling into a deep, even pattern. Then the snoring started. I reared back in surprise. Holy fucking hell. He had to be kidding me. I covered my head with the pillow, resisting the urge to smother him with his. A chain saw duel to the death would be quieter than the commotion currently going down in his nasal region.

"Ben," I cried into the pillow, throwing in a scream or two of frustration for good measure, and more than a couple of tears.

This guy and me, we were doomed from the start.

"Time to wake up." I ever so gently kicked the bed.

The man sprawled out spread-eagle across it didn't even move. Sadly for him, Sleeping Beauty's time had come.

"Ben!"

His head shot up, eyes dazed and confused. "Huh?"

"Wake up. It's nearly eleven."

I set his coffee on the bedside table, then wandered over to the other side of the room to sip my own. Also to throw back the curtains, because I'm mean on broken dreams and limited sleep.

He blinked, yawned, and shied back from the light of day like a vampire. The dude definitely didn't sparkle, however. Nor did he smell particularly fresh.

Out of all the many fantasies I'd had about him, his waking up in my room looking like roadkill hadn't featured strongly. Yet, even with his clothes and hair all askew, and stinking of sweat and beer, there was just something about him. Something magnetic, urging me to get closer, and closer still.

Stupid me. Probably just pregnancy hormones or something running rife.

"Lizzy."

"Yeah?"

"Ah, shit," he groaned. "Davie listened to me. He should have just dumped me back at my hotel."

No comment. "Coffee's there beside you."

"Thanks." Slowly, he sat up, rubbing at his head. Then he looked around the room, taking it all in as if for the first time. Which it pretty much was. His eyes lingered on the cheap Japanese woodblock prints I'd picked up at the markets, and my stuffed bookcase. The stack of laundry waiting for a day when I wasn't busy feeling like I was about to start yet again puking my guts up. No doubt the scene was a dramatic comedown compared to what he had to be used to. I'd imagine chandeliers, marble, lots of splendor. Glamorous models in the place of one pasty-faced girl with wet hair and old jeans and an equally worn sweater that'd shrunk in the wash.

Whatever.

"We need to talk," I said.

He froze, and fair enough. Honestly, those four words had to be the most loathed between two people, ever. They were basically a death knell, right up there with *we can still be friends*. Except he and I had never gotten that far.

"Yeah, we do." He took a gulp of hot coffee, watching me over the rim of his cup the entire time. "Why you hiding over there? Scared I'm going to get physical or something?"

"No." I sat on the edge of the bed. "Just wanted to keep out of your way in case you felt the need to bolt again."

He coughed out a laugh. "Ouch."

I shrugged. Then I felt guilty. Then I remembered the snoring and stood tall once more.

"Look," he said, turning his head my way. "Whatever you need from me, okay?"

My mouth opened, shut. "Thank you."

His fingers flexed around the cup of coffee. "You want to keep it, right?"

"Yes."

A nod.

I took a deep breath, reaching deep inside for some strength. Time to get on with the business of letting him off the hook and out of my life. No tears or tantrums. We were beyond that now. "I know you didn't want to have children, Ben. That you like your life as it is. So if you—"

"I never said that," he bit out.

"Yes, you did. Last night."

"Lizzy." Dark eyes pinned me in place. "Hold up. What I say when I'm drunk off my ass doesn't mean a damn thing, all right?"

Given how many interesting things he'd said, I wasn't so sure about that. "All right."

"Do not use that against me." His nostrils flared as he took a big breath. "Last night . . . you kind of caught me off guard with this."

"It kind of caught me off guard too," I said, struggling to keep my voice from going all fishwife on his ass. "I didn't want to tell you under those conditions, Ben. It just happened. You can thank your new girlfriend for being so discreet."

He flinched. Direct hit, ten points.

"Look, what I'm trying to say here is that it's my decision to have this baby. And if you decide that you don't want us impacting on your life, then I understand." I curled an arm around my middle, hunching in on myself. "That's all."

Slowly, Ben rose to his feet, setting the coffee cup aside. "You think I would do that to you?"

"In this situation, I honestly have no idea how you're going to react."

"You're just expecting the worst."

"Last night—"

His hand cut through the air. "Do not repeat what I said last night."

I said nothing.

Then he must have realized how bad it all looked and sounded.

The anger in his eyes calmed, his stance relaxing. "Shit. Sorry. I didn't mean to raise my voice."

"What do you want me to do here, Ben?" I threw my hands in the air. "Give me a clue. I'm pregnant. Neither of us planned it. We've barely even talked since that night in Vegas, and now you're seeing someone new. What do I do?"

"Give me a chance to catch up."

I just stared at him, trying to keep my cool. Took two to tango, yada yada.

"I'm serious." His shoulders heaved up and down. "Just give me a chance to catch up and I promise, Lizzy, I will have your back."

It sounded so promising. Honest to god, it really did. "What about your girlfriend?"

"She's got nothing to do with this." He didn't even hesitate. "This is just between you and me."

"Right." Any issues I had with the woman and her place in his life were mine. Sucked to be me. "Okay."

He picked up his coffee, his Adam's apple bobbing as he drank deep. "I'll, ah, get the lawyers to start drawing up some papers."

"Lawyers?"

A sharp nod.

"You're going to need money—living expenses, whatever. They'll get that all sorted out. Make sure you're looked after."

"Oh." I stared at the rumpled bed, my mind in a whirl.

"That okay?"

"I guess I was hoping we could keep this just between you and me. But you're right. You need to protect yourself."

"Lizzy, I don't mean I think you're going to try and rip me off or something."

"I'd hope not, considering I haven't asked you for a single thing."

Wow. Talk about looking uncomfortable. His tongue worked

behind his cheek as he glared at the view out my bedroom window. Guess the tree out there really had done him wrong.

"The rent on this place is paid and I have a job, so I'm fine for now. But you get your lawyers to do whatever." I rubbed at the sudden pain between my eyes. This conversation was enough to give anyone a headache. "Guess I better get one too."

He pushed his hands into the back pockets of his jeans. Then he changed his mind, sat, and started putting on his shoes. "It's best if we get all that official stuff sorted up front, you know?"

No, in all honesty, I really didn't know. He'd just clearly demonstrated as much. My stomach performed a particularly nauseating somersault maneuver and I swallowed hard, fighting back the urge to puke. Gah. What I needed was a cracker. A cracker would solve everything. With all due haste, I hustled ass into the tiny kitchen and got busy feeding my face. This at least I had under control. Nothing I could do about Ben and his lawyers and whatever. But fetching a cracker? Now that was within my command.

Bean and I would be fine.

Fuck the world and all the rest.

"I gotta go," he said, now avoiding my eyes from the all-new position of the living room. Awesome. Once he left, he'd have to get a new hobby. Maybe he could work at forgetting my name or something. "There's a practice session I need to get to. Tour kicks off soon, so things are really busy right now. Thanks for being cool about me crashing here. It won't happen again."

"Sure," I said.

"And don't worry about money or working extra hours. I'll get that all sorted out."

"Great." And it was great, but it was also cold and businesslike. "Thanks."

He mumbled some other stuff, but I just kind of tuned out. It was nothing I wanted to hear. How depressing this day had turned.

I hated everything and everyone and anything else I could possibly think of. Apart from Bean. She was the innocent one in all of this mess.

God, sex sucked.

Never, ever would I do it again. Not even a little.

Also, there was a sad lack of cake at this pity party. Enough. I needed to shake this shit off. Get my mojo back. I'm positive pregnant women are supposed to glow or something. I just needed to find my light. Perhaps I'd go for a drive, get some fresh air. A solid idea. Right now, getting as far away from here as I possibly could sounded delightful, and my car was something special. It'd been waiting for me at the airport upon our return from Vegas. Mal had, as promised, gotten me a baby blue 1967 Mustang GT for my birthday. Best present ever. It was the prettiest heavy metal beast on the block. Ben looked vaguely panicked every time he laid eyes on the vehicle.

But yeah, my car was awesome.

A pity it wouldn't be suitable for transporting a baby around in, having only two doors. I'd just have to make the most of my beauty while I still could. Given that I had a whole day to myself, that meant driving out to the coast.

"Later, Liz."

"Later." I raised a cracker in salute, but he was already gone. And, for once, my heart couldn't quite bring itself to care.

CHAPTER SIX

Voices hit me as soon as I stepped through the apartment building's front door. Loud voices, and lots of them. Odd. Lauren hadn't mentioned anything about throwing a party tonight. Wait. My mistake. Those weren't party time voices. No, these were pissed in the nonalcoholic way.

I jogged up the steps, unbuttoning my coat. For a car that predated me, the Mustang ran spectacularly well. Its heating could be a little iffy, however, especially if you liked to crack open the window now and then to feel the ice-cold wind on your face. Silly, I know. It was just something I felt the need to indulge in every once in a while.

The hallway was brighter than usual, a light from the second floor shining out. I hastened up my steps.

Holy shit. My front door had been smashed off its hinges.

". . . expect a twenty-one-year-old girl to manage with a baby—" That was my sister's voice.

"Like I said before, she won't be doing it alone." And that was Ben's.

"Because you'll get your shit sorted and get married to her. Right, baby daddy?" Crap. That was Mal, and he sounded even angrier than he'd been the night before. "You'll do the right thing and give up the single lifestyle with a different woman every night, won't you? 'Cause you're so fucking known for seeing shit through."

"Man, we've been over this already—"

"Yeah. And you're still not saying the right things. Do you get that?"

The living room was certainly crowded, that's for sure. Ben, Anne, and Mal were facing off in the middle. Clearly, two against one. While Sam the security guy and Lauren watched on from the sidelines, for some reason.

"Guys," I said.

They argued on.

"Guys!"

Still nothing.

Finally, I put two fingers in my mouth and let loose with an ear-splitting whistle. A talent I'd perfected in my younger years. Useful for annoying the living shit out of my sister, if nothing else. The noise even rattled my own head.

Nothing but silence followed.

"Hi. How are you all?" I stood in what remained of the splintered frame. "I'd really like to know what happened to my door."

"Lizzy," said Ben, exhaling hard. "Thank fuck. Been worried sick about you."

"Where have you been?" My sister rushed forward, catching me up in a tight hug. "I've been trying to call you all day. We checked everywhere and couldn't find you."

"Sorry. I just needed some alone time." I squeezed her back, unable to stop from smiling. The thought of Anne turning her back on me had scared me more than I liked to admit.

"Well, I get you might want that." She stepped back. "But you could have told someone."

"You can't just disappear like that." And Ben kept right on frowning. "Shit, Liz, you're pregnant."

"Don't upset her," snapped Anne.

Ben ignored her. "I don't know what the hell's going on in your head. But you need to let me know where you are."

My eyebrows went up and my mouth opened, ready to rip him a new one.

"She doesn't answer to you. She'll let you know if and when she decides to let you know," said Mal, laying down the law to his bandmate before turning my way. "You will text your sister next time you decide to go wandering for a day, understood?"

My mouth, it still hung open.

"Christ, man." Over and over, Ben's hands rolled into tight fists before releasing again. "Can you cut the shit and get off my back for a fucking minute?"

"Don't swear at him." My usually sensible and staid sister poked a finger dead center in Ben's broad chest. "You're the one that caused this mess, thank you very much. She might still be a little young and naive, but you're definitely old enough to know better."

"That's right." Standing about as tall as a skyscraper, despite only coming up to Ben's nose, Mal stared him down. Or up. Whatever. "This is a family matter. You can leave, thanks."

The battle for control played out plainly on Ben's face. He forced out, through gritted teeth, "I can leave?"

"Yes."

This was insane.

Someone had to step up and be the voice of reason. Sadly, that someone was me. "Okay. Hold up, everybody. Why don't we all just calm down for a minute."

With all the skill and speed of a seasoned male stripper, Mal turned on his heel. "And you, young lady! You are grounded until further notice."

"I'm grounded?"

"Babe." Anne winced. "That's not going to fly."

"And you are never to talk to Ben again. He is clearly a very bad influence on you." The drummer continued, oblivious, sneering at his former friend. "Is that understood, Elizabeth?"

Lauren snickered.

"Yeah. Okay," I said.

"Good."

"Get out," I said, my voice quite cool, quite calm. A little tired, but hey, it'd been a long day.

"What?" asked Anne.

"I love you both very much," I said. "But I'd like you both to leave now, please."

Her face fell and she took a step closer. "You don't have to handle this on your own. I get that things were stressed last night, but we do need to talk about this. I'm worried about you."

"I know, and we will."

A heavy sigh. "Will you call me tomorrow so we can talk?"

"Yes."

Anne gave me a slow nod. "Okay."

With a faint smile, Sam rose from his position on the couch and squeezed past me, out the door. Or what remained of the door. I still needed a *what the hell* on that count.

"Someone'll be by to fix it shortly, Miss Rollins," Sam said.

"Thank you."

"Holler if you need anything." Lauren left too.

"Thanks."

"But I don't want to leave," hissed Mal. Heated whispers continued on between him and my sister. He even brushed her hand off of his tensed, folded arms. "She doesn't know what's best for her. Not like we do. Me in particular."

More whispers.

"Well, does Ben have to go too? I'm not leaving unless he is."

"Mal," I groaned. "Please? If I promise to come over tomorrow and talk to you both about it all, please will you go for now?"

His eyes and mouth narrowed.

"Pretty please?"

"Fine." He slung an arm around Anne's neck, dragging her in against his body. "We know when we're not wanted. Don't we, Pumpkin?"

"Eventually, yes." My sister gave me a small smile.

"Thank you," I said, giving her free hand a squeeze before turning back to Mal. "And I need to know I haven't broken up the band."

Mal scowled and snarled.

Actions had consequences. I'd learned the lesson well. "Please."

"Fine. But only because you asked so nicely. Outside of band business, he is dead to me," Mal said to Ben, motioning a finger across his throat.

"Dude." Ben sighed.

"I mean it. I'm really pissed at you, bro. You knocked up my new little-sister-in-law. This is way worse than the time you broke my bike trying to take that jump in middle school. And that was *bad*." The newlyweds headed for the door. "See you tomorrow at rehearsal."

"Yep," said Ben, collapsing onto the love seat. His head fell back against the wall and he eyed me tiredly. "You gonna throw me out too?"

"I probably should. Are you what happened to my door?"

He wiped a hand over his face. "Yeah. Sorry about that."

"I couldn't help but notice that it's kind of no longer attached."

"I kind of broke it down."

"Right." I wandered over and planted my butt in the black leather wingback chair opposite him. Mal and Anne had left me some seriously sweet furniture when they vacated the apartment. "Why, may I ask?"

"Anne called, said she couldn't find you and you weren't answering your phone." He set one ankle on the opposite knee, his sneaker jiggling, constantly moving. "I got worried you were in here alone, freaking out about shit after this morning or something and refusing to talk to me."

"Ah."

"I overreacted." He wore his usual blue jeans and a T-shirt. Damn he wore them well. You'd think with my being pregnant that the hormones would settle down a little. But the silly things still burst into a happy dance every time he came near. It was ridiculous. I needed to gird my foolish loins, invest in a chastity belt or something.

Instead, I stuffed my hands between my legs, squeezing my thighs tightly together.

"We've got a problem," he said.

"Yeah."

"No, I mean a new one."

"What?"

He sat up, putting both feet on the floor. "Sasha didn't take my breaking up with her too well. Threatened to go to the media about you."

"You broke up with her?" My heart beat double time.

He paused. "Well, yeah."

"Why?" Oh, hell. My mouth. I blurted out the question before I even stopped to think. "I mean. Okay, none of my business. I don't want to know."

It wasn't hope firing to life in my belly. No way could I be that stupid. Again. It had to be something else. Maybe Bean had taken up water aerobics or something.

Ben just kind of stared at me, stuck on pause for the longest moment. "Anyway."

"Yes?"

"You staying here on your own probably isn't a good idea. Especially now that the door needs fixing."

"True."

"Security is pretty shitty here anyway. So, I was thinking maybe it would be best if . . ."

"If?" I sat perched on the edge of my seat, literally waiting with bated breath. He couldn't be about to ask me to move in with him. Into his actual personal space. No one ever hung out at his hotel room or wherever the hell he lived. I had to admit, I'd been curious. Plus, the thought of living with him made me break out in a cold sweat. "If what?"

"If you moved in with Lena and Jim until we went on tour." His dark eyes never left my face. "I mean, I'm just assuming you'll come on tour now. You might not want to."

"You want me on tour?" But he didn't want me in his place. How confusing and disappointing both. Or maybe he wanted me on tour to keep an eye on me, the old silly-young-Lizzy-can't-look-after-herself standard. Christ, it hit me: I was going to be a mother. Apparently, I was going to be a single parent, no matter what soothing noises he was making. Come what may, I could only depend on myself.

"Figured with Anne planning on going, and Lena being pregnant too, that you might come," he said. "People will pack you up, all you'll have to do is get on and off a private jet every couple of days and then relax. These places have masseuses and whatever. There'll be doctors available to keep a check on you. I'll make sure you're looked after."

"I don't know. . . ."

To stay behind with Anne and the other girls gone wouldn't

make me happy. I guess making friends wasn't really my forte. After the early-teen nutso period, I'd pretty much kept to myself. Anne and I had perfected the art of putting on a normal home front. Anyone looking beyond it would not have been good, because clearly mom wasn't functioning as the responsible adult. When Anne left to go on tour, I'd basically be alone. But there was more than me and my lonely girl ways to consider. There'd been so many dubious tales about what happened on tour. Him and other women. I didn't need to see that. Not this year, or the next. The Sasha thing had hurt enough. Wonder why he'd dumped her?

"I don't want to be in your way," I said, hands twining in my lap. "It might get awkward if we were in each other's faces every day."

I got a caveman grunt. It sounded serious, of the deep thoughts variety. Didn't clue me into shit, however.

"What do you think?" I asked.

The face he gave me was complicated, brows drawn together but lips slightly apart. It seemed he was on the verge of saying something.

Waiting.

"Speak, Ben."

He tensed. "I want you to come."

"Why?"

"To make sure you're okay, so I can keep an eye on you, so you're not here dealing with all this on your own. Lots of reasons."

As reasons went, they weren't bad ones. But as Mal had pointed out, Ben had issues with follow-through. History dictated he would eventually change his mind and leave me high and dry. What sort of father would he be? Lord help him if he ever pulled that shit with my child. No matter his size, my rage would be epic.

"Come on," he said, voice firmer. "We need to start figuring this out together. How to get along and be parents and everything. I don't want to be the guy Mal's accusing me of being. Give me a chance here, Liz."

"I honestly don't know what's best."

He hung his head. "Look, if you want to stay here, finish up school for the semester, I'll organize security for you. Take care of everything. It's your choice. I don't want to push you into anything."

"Security?"

"Yeah."

"Wow." I patted my stomach, my smile not quite staying in place. "I keep forgetting I'm carrying a famous person's baby. The next-generation Stage Dive."

He spread out his hands, a helpless kind of look in his eyes. At least he was here trying.

It was up to me. "All right, I'll come. I was thinking of dropping out of school. I've missed so much, with morning sickness, and days can still be hit or miss. I don't like my chances of catching up with everything going on."

A nod and a smile. His thick shoulders slumped like he'd finished fighting a war.

"You want me to stay with Lena and Jimmy?"

"I want you and the baby safe and looked after. Not that I'm not willing to be the one looking after you. It's just—"

"It's fine. It's complicated with us not actually being a couple and everything. I get it." I leaned back in my seat, turning it all over inside my head. "Not that I don't appreciate the offer."

His serious gaze revealed nothing. "Liz . . ."

"Mm?"

I waited, but he didn't continue. Thank goodness Bean would be a girl. (I could just feel it. Mother's intuition, etcetera.) Men were such a mystery. Not one I particularly cared to figure out at this point in time. Life had become busy enough. At least there'd been no further mention of lawyers. Baby steps—all puns intended.

"I'll sort things out for myself. I'll go to Mal and Anne's," I said. "It's not long before the tour starts. He shouldn't be able to drive me crazy that fast."

His brow furrowed. "You sure?"

"Yes." I nodded.

"'kay. But you'll let me support you financially, right?"

"Look, I ran some figures through my head today. Given that the rent on this place is paid up, and with my work at the—"

"Wherever you're going with this, the answer is no." The man leveled me with a look. Or tried to.

"Excuse me?"

"No, you can't go it on your own. More important, you don't have to. You've got me."

"But I haven't got you, Ben. That's the whole point." I sat forward in the seat, willing him to understand. He opened his mouth, but mine was faster. "Please, just listen. I'm going to have a baby, and that is huge. It's so big, when I try to think about it I feel like my head is going to explode. But I'll deal with it all because I have to, because this baby is relying on me to. What I can't think about or deal with is you—you and your life and how this all affects it. Because I know, no matter what you say, that having this baby is never going to be your first choice. So then I feel guilty, and then I feel angry because I feel guilty, and then it's just a big ugly mess that I don't know how to deal with."

"Liz." He scrubbed at his face with his hands. "Shit. It doesn't have to be my first choice. Having a baby now wasn't your first choice either—"

"But—"

"No," he said, hands gripping his thighs tight. "My go to talk. Your turn to listen. Please."

I stopped, then nodded because fair enough.

"Okay." His thick shoulders rose and fell on a deep breath. "This is our baby. You and me, we made it together, whether we meant to or not. Those are the facts. No matter how I might have liked my life to play out, this is what's happening. No fucking way am I going to be some douchebag absentee dad missing from my kid's life or letting another man raise him."

"Or her."

"Or her." He gave me a meaningful look. "Yes."

I pretended to zip my lips closed.

"Thank you." Yeah, his tone wasn't sarcastic at all. "And I'm not letting you do this alone, either. No matter what Anne and Mal think of me right now, I am sticking by you however I can. We're not together, but we'll figure it out. The best way I can help you right now is to make sure you don't have to worry about money."

I took a deep breath, turning it all over inside my head. The man had a point. It would be nice to cross monetary concerns off the list. How many strings and complications the funds came with, however, concerned me. But he was Bean's father. If he did mean to be present, as stated, then I had to accept that, embrace it even.

Give him the requested chance.

"Worrying about you today, not knowing where you were or what was going on with you . . . it got me thinking. This'll fuck with your life every bit, if not more, than it will with mine. We don't need to add lawyers to the mix, what with your connection to Mal and everything. We can keep this simple."

"Hmm."

"Stop frowning." He frowned.

"I'm thinking."

"There's nothing to think about. It's already done."

"What?"

He scratched at his beard. "Transferred money into your account today. It's all done."

"How did you get my account number?"

"Anne gave it to me. I think she meant it as a dare."

My eyes felt wide as wide could be. "How much money?"

"Enough that you don't have to worry for a while."

"How long a while?"

He just stared at me.

Oh, whoa. Something told me a millionaire rock star's version of *a while* was a whole lot longer than mine. The thought made me panicky, my fingers twisting together in my lap. Legal documents were scary, but the thought of him giving me masses of his money seemed even worse. "But lawyers and contracts and stuff. What you talked about this morning."

"We'll sort it out between us, like you wanted." He seemed so calm, while I was anything but. "It'll be okay, Liz."

"That's a lot of trust you're putting in me."

"We're having a kid. We gotta start somewhere, right?"

There were scuff marks on my favorite boots. Quite a few of them. At least I wouldn't be growing out of my shoes. My clothes, on the other hand, would probably need replacing before long. Most of my things were a little worn or were bought secondhand. Not as if I'd have been willing to ask Mal or Anne for a handout to fund a flashy new maternity wardrobe. They did so much for me already. It would be bizarre to not have to worry about money. We hadn't grown up with much. I couldn't really remember a time when money hadn't been an issue.

"Right," I mused.

"No big deal."

I wasn't so sure about that.

"I appreciate you being willing to monetarily support us. That's going to make a huge difference." I told the floor, because looking at him seemed too hard just then. "It's a real weight off my shoulders."

"Listen," he said. "I'm sorry about last night. And this morning. I'm just . . . I'm doing the best I can here."

"Of course." I smiled as bright as bright could be. "We'll be friends for Bean's sake."

"Bean?"

My smile grew more genuine. "In the early stages they're kind of bean shaped and sized."

"Oh. Right." His fingers lay laced in front of him, jiggling yet again. For a second, his gaze landed in the region of my belly before darting away again. "Give me a chance to catch up, get used to the idea. Then we'll talk some more."

"Okay."

"And of course we'll be friends," he said. "We *are* friends."

"Of course."

He smiled back at me. But I don't think either of us was feeling anything but fear just yet.

CHAPTER SEVEN

While the guys were down at the Chateau Marmont in L.A. being interviewed by *Rolling Stone* magazine, up in Portland a complete stranger was checking out my girl bits. The fancily framed medical degrees hanging on her office wall did nothing to detract from the awkwardness of where she put her gloved fingers.

Yep, going to the OB/GYN was just the best.

Everything with Bean was fine, by the way. And hearing her heartbeat for the first time rocked my world. She was real. This was real. I was actually going to be a mother. Amazing.

With the band touring and Ben's ban from Mal and Anne's apartment (also, I'm pretty sure he was avoiding me, despite all his fine words), it was a full four weeks after he filled my humble bank account to bursting before we laid eyes on each other again. It took that long for me to stop constantly barfing and to be given the go-ahead to travel. Due to having my head in the toilet, I'd missed out on Vancouver, Seattle, Portland, San Francisco, and L.A. Anne and I met up with the band in Phoenix. We arrived near the end of their concert, having been delayed by a storm.

Sam met us and took us to the side of the stage to watch the encore. It was cool to see Stage Dive play live again. I was sitting on an empty box behind a massive screen that projected the happenings out to the stadium audience. I couldn't see the people, but I could hear them. Roadies, set construction workers, and similar were also hanging out, waiting.

The minute the show was done, Mal attacked Anne. The man was all over her like a rash, rubbing his sweaty self against her and basically dry-humping in public. She didn't seem to mind. We didn't hang around, everyone heading straight to the hotel. Apparently any interviews and meet-and-greets were done before the show.

I got a welcoming chin tip from Ben, but that was it in the rush.

The line of luxury black Lexuses crawled to a stop as we neared the swanky hotel's back entrance. Hands battered at the windows, people struggling to get close enough to press their faces up against the darkened glass.

It was freaky.

Dave and Ev were already inside, having been in the first vehicle. Ben, Lena, and Jimmy jumped out of the vehicle in front of us. Immediately, Lena and Jimmy hurried through the corridor made by security, into the safety of the hotel. But Ben delayed, signing autographs and shaking hands.

There were so many people out there. A veritable sea of women and men both, crying, screaming, and carrying on. I'd known how big the guys were, but knowing it and seeing it were two entirely different things. There were even TV crews among the mix, cameras catching it all.

"Shit," I whispered, hunching down.

"Someone can't keep a secret," said Anne, sitting between Mal and me on the backseat.

Mal just shrugged. "Where we're staying always gets out. This is the norm. Get used to it, ladies."

A black-clad security person opened the door and the clamor hit me. It was staggering. A wall of mindless, maximum-volume, gray noise. Sweat wet my back but my mouth dried to nothing. Anne nudged me gently, nodding toward the door and the batshit-crazy crowd beyond. I swallowed hard and nodded back. Like it or not (*not!*), we were going out there. Generally, agoraphobia wasn't much of an issue (or enochlophobia, if you want to get technical about it). It didn't stop me from doing anything. Get me anywhere near a loud swarming mass of people, however, and I'm rarely at my best.

I cautiously stepped down, feeling my way across the concrete. All of the flashes from the cameras were dazzling my eyes.

Crap.

The crowd surged forward, closing in, and the line of security struggled to hold them back. People were yelling shit, none of it decipherable over the sound of my heartbeat pounding behind my ears. They were chanting a name, and from the shape of their lips, I'm pretty sure it was Mal's.

I stood frozen, gaping, totally immobile. Fuck. Nope. Couldn't do it. What if I somehow tripped or got trod on or misstepped and accidentally hurt Bean?

Before I could turn tail and run back to the car, however, a strong arm wrapped around me, pulling my body in against the safety of his.

"I've gotcha," he said, his breath warming my ear.

I wasn't up to speaking.

Ben hustled me down the narrow corridor formed by security and into the building. Both of his arms were around me, holding me tight until he had to remove one to punch the button for the elevator. Cool air soothed my hot face while I concentrated on getting back my breath. God, what an idiot I was, losing it like that. Some great mother or psychologist I'd make.

Behind us, Mal and Anne were still out there, barely visible among the crowd.

"Let's go." Ben's hand slid down to mine, grabbing hold to tow me into the elevator.

"Aren't they coming? What are they doing?"

The elevator doors slid closed.

"With Mal, it could be anything. Don't worry, they're fine."

I craned my neck, necessary for viewing him at close range. His hair was a little longer, tied back in a tiny man bun, his beard neatly trimmed. Still beautiful, damn it. His T-shirt, plain black with an Arizona postcard printed on the front, fit just right, being neither too big nor too small. The tang of salty sweat lingered in the air around him. I wanted to bury my face in his chest and breathe deep, over and over again, despite the scent of booze. I just wanted to get as close to him as physically possible. One day those feelings would fade. Hopefully one day soon.

He looked down at me with a tight smile, still holding on to my hand. The smile definitely didn't make it to his eyes. If anything, I'd say the man looked nervous.

"Sorry about wigging out," I said.

With a low digital tone, the doors slid open.

"Don't worry about it," he said, and let go of my hand, instead applying gentle pressure low on my back to guide me forward. His motions were sure, his steps steady. However much he'd had to drink, he was clearly still coherent. "C'mon."

Cream carpet shushed our steps, baby chandeliers lighting our way. It wasn't very different from Vegas, with the same pricey, luxurious appearance. Another couple of security guys prowled about up here, keeping an eye on things.

"Doesn't that bother other customers?" I asked, nodding in their direction.

"Band's got this floor. You're two doors down in Mal and Anne's suite." Ben held up a card to the swipe thing. The little light turned green and he pushed the door open. "Might as well come on in for a minute."

"Okay." Not exactly a warm welcome. Man, this was all so hatefully awkward.

Inside, his suite was big, with a nice view and lots of comfy-looking couches in shades of beige. Quite a collection of liquor bottles covered the side table, the only visible trace of any rock 'n' roll lifestyle in the otherwise pristine room.

None of my business what he'd been up to the night before. None at all.

"You okay?" he asked.

"Yes." We sat down opposite each other. "The morning sickness has eased up."

"Great."

"Yeah."

A nod.

"Thanks for the texts," I said. "That was good of you."

"No big deal."

Morning and night, he'd sent me the same brief almost impersonal question: *U ok?* I'd responded in kind: *Fine! Great! Terrific!* A smiley face now and then. It wasn't as if I could tell him I'd spent the morning hurling, feeling three days dead, with my emotions all over the place, my breasts aching, and my brain slowly being pickled by hormones. Things were too weird between us for such brutal honesty. Besides, he had a lot on his mind, with the concert and all. So instead I'd whined to Anne, and she'd been good enough not to tell me it was my own damn fault. The look lingered in her eyes now and then, but I could ignore it. No point feeling sorry for myself. Onward and upward—or outward as the case with my womb might be.

My hand strayed to my tiny baby bump, barely visible beneath my blue tank top, and Ben's gaze followed. He rubbed the side of his hand against his lips, eyes stark. The look he gave my abdomen was one of great fear. I couldn't take it.

"Do you have a juice?" I asked.

"Sure." The man leapt out of his seat, obviously eager to be gone. He moved to the side cabinet where the bar fridge was cunningly concealed. The room was so silent. When he opened the small juice bottle, the pop of the air seal being broken made me jump.

"Maybe I should get going," I said, rising to my feet. "Leave you to it."

"But your juice . . ."

All of a sudden, the front door crashed open and a party walked in. There could be no other description. Laughter, beer, men and women, they all poured into the expensive suite until the room was close to capacity.

"Epic show," yelled a lanky guy with long black hair and a woman attached to his hip.

He and Ben smacked palms. "It was good."

Their talk got drowned out by Metallica. A tall guy covered in tats broke a beer off from his six-pack and thrust it into my hand. I took it out of sheer instinct, the wet can chilling my skin.

"Hey," he said, giving me a grin. Pale red hair sat spiked up, and you really had to give it to him, he had a nice face. "I'm Vaughan."

"Lizzy. Hi."

"Didn't see you here last night. I'd have definitely remembered you."

What a flirt. Must have been the boobs. I'd done okay in the past, but I wouldn't call myself a man magnet. Especially not in a room where half the women looked and dressed like lingerie models.

"Ah, no," I said. "I only got in this evening."

Vaughan opened a beer for himself, setting down the six-pack on the coffee table. "A fan, or attached to the band somehow?"

"Both, I guess."

"Both?" His eyes lit with interest. "Well, you're in Ben's room, so I'll assume you're a friend of his."

I just smiled. "How about you? How do you fit in here?"

"I play bass for the warm-up band, Down Fourth."

"Hey, wow! I've heard of you guys. You're great," I said, clapping my hands all enthused. You'd think I'd never met a famous musician before.

His grin grew broader. Way to be cool, me.

"I really love that song you do . . . Shit . . ."

He laughed while my face slowly started to burn.

"No, I know the name." How embarrassing and frustrating. "I do. I had it on repeat just the other day."

"It's fine."

"Don't tell me." I closed my eyes, searching for the information inside my head. To have my own body rebelling against me, turning me into one big giant, idiotic walking baby-making machine. It wasn't fair. "Just give me a minute."

He laughed at me some more.

"Gah. Stupid pregnancy hormones." I stopped dead.

The whites of Vaughan's eyes suddenly seemed huge and glaringly bright. Yet again I faced down man fear. I don't know why. It's not like there could be any possible chance it was his kid I carried. The irony of a guy who got down to death metal being scared of a pregnant girl was not lost on me.

Way to keep a secret. The minute I said it, I wanted to slap myself silly. Either that or buy myself a muzzle. My pregnancy had been kept under the general populace's radar, and I really wanted to keep it that way.

"I'd prefer that information didn't get repeated," I said, dropping my voice and moving a little closer to the man. "It's just that it's early days, and—"

"Vaughan." Ben stuck his hand out to the man with an excessive amount of male zest. "How you doing?"

"Yeah, good, Ben."

"See you met Liz." He pushed the long since requested juice into my spare hand, liberating the beer from my other. Then he cracked the ale open and drank deep.

"Yeah, we were just talking," said Vaughan, the fear of babies happily gone from his face, replaced once more with his friendly smile. Thank goodness. Maybe he wouldn't say anything. "Turns out she's a fan."

"She is?"

"I am," I confirmed. "I had 'Stop' on repeat all last week."

Nailed it.

"How about that." Ben's smile looked about as natural, and as comfortable, as a polyester pantsuit in June. Whatever he was up to, it wasn't good. Then, just to confirm my thoughts, he slid his arm around my neck, pulling me in close. Only not as you would a girlfriend or a lover. Nope, nothing like that at all. "Liz is Mal's new sister-in-law. Aren't you, sweetheart?"

"Yep." Funny, I'd always loved it when he called me that. This time, however, was different. I took a sip of the apple juice to try to cool myself down.

Brows drawn in, Vaughan looked back and forth between the two of us, obviously confused. "Didn't realize."

"Yeah. Sorry to put the fear of Mal into you, but she's out of bounds. Okay, man?" Ben planted a kiss on top of my head, then went that last irrevocable step too far and actually ruffled my hair like I was snotty-nosed kid. "Word with you in the bedroom, Liz?"

"Sure thing, Ben," I said through gritted teeth.

He ushered me through the crowd, with a hand to the small of my back once more. The door to the main bedroom was closed— probably the only reason it too hadn't filled up with people.

I didn't say a word until he'd closed us in. Then I still didn't say a word.

Instead, I threw my drink in his face.

"What the fuck?!" he roared, wiping apple juice out of his eyes.

"How dare you ruffle my hair like I'm your kid sister or something." I dropped my empty glass onto the carpet. "How dare you?"

"I was doing you a favor."

"Like hell you were."

The man set aside his beer aside and stormed forward, towering over me. "The guy is a fucking man-whore, Liz. Nearly every night on tour he's had a different woman."

"What utter crap."

"I'm not lying to you. He was flirting with you, trying to get into your pants. It's what he does."

"I'm not talking about him."

Ben blinked.

"You and I, we are not together, remember? If I want to flirt with a guy, I will. It is none of your business."

"You're pregnant with my child." The anger in his eyes—a smarter woman would have stepped back. Screw that. I went nose to nose with him. Well, as close as I could get to it, with the height difference. Next time we fought I was definitely bringing a ladder.

"That's right, Ben, I'm carrying *our* child," I said, breathing hard. "And I'm on tour to help us to figure out how to get along and be parents. Something that involves us having mutual respect for one another."

"I got respect for you, Liz. What I haven't got is the ability to stand by while some player tries to chat you up."

"Oh yeah? Tell me you haven't had sex with one of those wonderfully liberated, barely dressed ladies out there. Let me know this isn't just some messed-up double standard you're trying on me."

He couldn't do it. His lips slammed shut and he shifted, edging back, putting room between us. It shouldn't have hurt, but it did. Hearts are dumb like that. At least he didn't try to give me excuses.

"No?" I asked.

Still nothing.

"We're not together. You have no right to try and warn a guy off me. And treating me like you did—like a child, ruffling my hair, calling me 'sweetheart' that way. . . ." My eyes were itchy, turning liquid. Like hell. "How fucking dare you."

I should have stormed out. I wanted to. The thought of losing it in front of the cool party crowd, however, stopped me cold. There had to be an alternative. Just a few minutes and I could pull myself together, go find my room. "I need to use the bathroom."

My dignity was small, about the same size as my bladder since the invention of Bean. I pretty much had to pee constantly, so it wasn't a complete lie, despite the sudden rising damp in my eyes. Dumb hormones. Idiot men and their god damn sperm. I strode into the grandiose bathroom and slammed the door shut. A tear trickled down my cheek, followed fast by another.

And the girl in the mirror, she still wasn't glowing. How fucking unfair.

I went and did my business in the toilet, scrubbed my hands and then my face. All of the emotions inside of me kept building up, threatening to leak out again. This situation with Ben was doing my head in. So I did what any sensible knocked-up twenty-one-year-old college dropout would do and climbed into the massive, empty sunken tub to cool down and reassess my life. It was actually quite comfortable. In the distance I could hear the party carrying on with chatter and music. You'd think an upmarket hotel such as this would have thicker walls.

For a good five, ten minutes I sat in there, calming myself, coming to grips with the situation. Perhaps Ben and I shouldn't talk for a while. We didn't have to be friends to raise a child together, if indeed that's what was going to happen. Him changing his mind on being involved would surprise approximately no one. Harsh but true.

Whatever. Come what may, I'd manage.

"Where's Lizzy?" asked a muffled voice in the next room, male and abrupt. Jimmy Ferris. Why he'd be interested in me I had no idea.

"In the john," said Ben. "What do you want with her?"

"Take it Mal and Anne are busy making up for lost time. Lena thought she might like to come hang with her."

"We're in the middle of something right now. I'll ask her in a few."

Jimmy snorted. "You're having a nice chat, huh? That why you're dripping wet and there's an empty glass on the floor? Try again, Ben."

"None of your fucking business."

"You're right about that. It's not. But oh well . . ."

For a moment there was nothing, during which I strained to hear something, anything.

"Man, you are fucking shit up with her so damn bad," said Jimmy, breaking the silence. "One way or another, this girl's going to be in your life from now on. Way you're playing it, won't be in a good way."

"What do you know about it?" growled Ben.

"What do I know about fucking up things with girls? You serious?"

No reply.

"How many times you talk to Lizzy in the last month?"

"We talk."

"Not face-to-face or I'd have heard about it from Mal. Another fucking mess you've failed to fix."

"I'm working on it," said Ben, his voice full of anger. "I'll smooth shit over with him."

"Believe it when I see it."

"Don't lecture me on messing with the band. Where the fuck were you that last practice session before Seattle, huh?"

Jimmy scoffed. "Taking Lena to see her obstetrician. Do you even know what the hell one of them is?"

"Of course I fucking do."

"Yeah? You taking Liz to her visits? Looking after her? 'Course not. Because if you were, every other member of this band would have a shitload more respect for you than they got right now."

"We were heading on tour," said Ben.

"Some things are more important, man. Take looking after the woman carrying your child, for example."

"Jim—"

"How many times have you even called that girl since we've been on tour?"

"What the fuck? You a relationship counselor now?"

Jimmy laughed. "My woman isn't throwing drinks in my face, so as far as you're concerned, I might as well be."

"She's not my woman."

"She's the girl you put a baby in, asshole. And if she's been going through half the shit Lena's been dealing with, then you are just about the lowest cunt I've come across in a long time for making her do it alone."

Guess Ben had no answer to that.

Have to admit, I felt bad for him. He loved these guys like brothers, and I'd been coping okay on my own, give or take. And yes, I did feel a little guilty for listening in on the conversation. Given that I was the topic, however . . .

"The baby's got her moods bouncing all over the place. One minute she's depressed as hell, worrying how we'll deal with this, sure things are gonna go to shit and I'll leave her. As if. Then the next, everything's great and she's excited again about becoming a mom."

A pause.

"It's hard on her, man, all the changes. And it's scary as hell to be facing, I know."

"Jim—"

"No. Just shut up and listen. I'm nearly finished." Jimmy exhaled roughly. "None of us planned this. But you need to drop out of the running for dickhead of the year and get yourself sorted out before it's too late."

"Okay. I'll talk to her."

"Think, Ben. Just think. How the hell are you going to explain this to your kid in five or ten years' time, hmm? That your baby momma doesn't talk to you because you spent her entire pregnancy hiding behind a bottle and getting blown by groupies?"

My stomach contracted sharply. There we go. I knew he'd been with other women, of course. It still hurt, however.

"It's not like that," yelled Ben.

"It's exactly like that. Give me a fucking break, dude. Just because I don't come to your nightly soirees doesn't mean I don't know what's going on here. Hell, anyone can see it."

Silence again from Ben.

"I don't know if you want her or not. But I'm telling you now, you're gonna lose her, and you're gonna lose your kid, and any shred of self-respect you might still have along with them. Your parents were useless, same as mine, so you know what it's like. Get your shit together."

The bedroom door opened, the noise from the party coming in clearer.

"Lizzy wants to hang with Lena, just bring her on over. She's welcome any time."

Ben didn't reply.

Noise from the party dropped in volume once again as the bedroom door closed. Then there came the *boom*. Once, twice, three times. I stared at the bathroom door in surprise, with just a small dash of fear. It'd been damn loud.

Might be time for me to go.

"Liz, can I come in?"

"It's not locked," I told the door.

Ever so slowly the handle turned. Then Ben stuck his head in as if he was expecting more projectiles, liquid or otherwise, to be lobbed his way.

"It's safe," I said.

"Hey."

"Hi."

He said no more, instead turning to the sink to wash off his face and neck. Guess I'd done a good job of juicing him, because he stripped off the Arizona T-shirt and tossed it aside. Next, he spent some time washing his hands.

Only then did he approach. "Mind if I join you?"

I shrugged. "It's your bath."

With a sigh, he climbed in and sat down opposite me at the other end of the tub. I tucked my legs up, ensuring he had plenty of room without us being required to touch. He stretched out his long legs on either side of mine, gaze glued to my face. What a sight we must have made, me fully dressed in the dry tub and him in his jeans and big black boots. Man, he had a nice chest. I did my best not to notice, but some things are beyond my control. A half-naked Ben was most definitely one of them. The fight with Jim, however, concerned me. As did the raw pink knuckles of his right hand. These guys obviously enjoyed hitting walls when they got testy. I could remember Mal once doing the same. Males. So violent.

Because of course I hadn't thrown anything at anybody lately.

"Take it you heard me and Jim fighting," he said.

"Hard not to."

A nod.

"He was right about one thing: it's been a while since we talked. I mean really talked."

"Yeah."

No one spoke for a moment. I sure as hell wasn't going first. Right in that moment, I just wasn't that brave.

"I, um . . . shit's been busy with the tour." He stretched his arms out around the edge of the tub, obviously getting as comfortable as hard ceramic and the situation would allow. A small line of blood down his right hand, ignored. "Weeks leading up to it, Adrian had us talking to every damn reporter in the country. It was insane."

"Oh."

"The producers think the music just makes itself. Once Dave's written the songs, they think it's a round or two in the studio and we're done. But that's bullshit. Takes hours, sometimes days, to get the sound right." Fervor shone bright in his eyes, beyond the booze and whatever. His passion for the music. "Dave used to be a perfectionist about it too, but all of the guys are distracted now, eyes on the clock, wanting to get home to their women. I'm the one sitting there with Dean and Tyler till four in the fucking morning, getting it perfect."

"Sounds like a lot of work."

"It is. Jimmy and Mal go off onstage and Dave's still the poet writing the songs. In the band, it's all down to me now, though, to work the sound." He scratched at his chin. "Know it makes me sound like a self-congratulating art geek, but it's important, you know? Whatever we put out there, I need to know in my gut it's the best we've got."

"I can understand that."

"Wasn't avoiding you, Liz, but I wasn't putting any effort into seeing you, either. You might have noticed."

"Right."

"Thought I'd let things with Mal and Anne calm down. That's just another excuse, though." Dark eyes bored into me, as if he could see my soul. Who knows, maybe he could. I always felt too open, too exposed, around him. He made me so messy with all these wants and needs. I don't know if it was love that I felt for him or lust. But whatever it was, it sucked.

"I'm sorry, Liz," he said, his soft, deep voice filling the room. "I said I'd have your back and I didn't. I disappeared on you again, and this time you were actually going through shit. Serious shit."

Huh.

"Jimmy was right. You shouldn't have had to go through it alone."

"It wasn't so bad." I turned away. A lot of emotion for one day. "I had Anne."

"Yeah, but this is our baby, and Anne isn't me."

I breathed in through my nose and out through my mouth, nice and slow, trying to calm my racing heart. It was true. His absence had left a bruise, and no amount of go-girl lectures delivered in the bathroom mirror could alter the fact.

"Is she?" he asked.

"No, Ben, she's not."

He slowly nodded, like something had been decided.

"So what now?" I asked.

"Talk to me." The fingers of his left hand flicked and fiddled with the hard upper rim of the bathtub. Nerves or what, I had no idea. At least the blood from the knuckles on his right hand had dried.

"About what?"

"All the stuff I should have been hearing the past month." The man was serious. Very much so. "No more of this useless fucking texting, Liz. Talk to me. Right now, face-to-face. Help me prove Jim wrong."

Give him another chance.

I stared at him, lost, my brain searching for the words. Any easily retrieved information lacked in either dignity or strength. Ah, man. Could I trust him with my weaknesses and issues? That was the question.

"C'mon. How have you been, really? What's been going on with you?" he pushed. I frowned at him and he frowned right back. "Liz, please."

I groaned in defeat. "All right, I suck."

"Why do you suck?"

"So very many reasons." I pushed my hair back from my face—no more hiding. "Pregnancy sucks. It's natural, my ass. I finally stop throwing up, but I'm tired all the time. Giving up coffee was horrendous. None of my clothes fit right because of these stupid breasts, and they ache constantly. I have to pee like every thirty seconds, and then to top it off, I cry every time the Healthy Hound ad comes on. It's ridiculous."

Little wrinkles appeared either side of his nose. "You cry at a dog food ad?"

"Yes. The puppies jump all over each other to get to their mother and it's just so beautiful, with their cute little tails wagging and everything."

He just stared at me.

"I know it's psycho, Ben. Believe me, I'm well aware of this."

"Hey, it's fine." He covered a smile with his hand. Too late, the bastard.

"You try dealing with all these hormones going apeshit. Crap. Apeshoot."

"Apeshoot?"

"I'm trying not to swear," I explained. "You want the first word our child comes out with to be something bad?"

"No. Gotcha." The man was incredibly bad at hiding a grin. "No swearing."

Jerk. I narrowed my eyes on him, holding back my own smile.

"I'm taking you seriously. I am." He flat-out lied. Though it was rather nice to see him smile and to hear his low laugh. At least the bad mood was gone.

"And my ankles are all fat and gross," I said. "It's ridiculous."

"What? Show me." A giant paw grabbed hold of my limb, dragging it onto his lap. Without preamble he pushed up the leg of my jeans and wrestled off my sandal, dropping it out onto the floor. "It looks fine. There's nothing wrong with it."

"I'm retaining fluid. It's disgusting."

One-handed, he flipped back his long, dark fringe, giving me a look most dubious.

"Let go of my foot, please. I don't want you to see it."

He slowly shook his head. "This what you've been doing the last month? Talking yourself into crazy shit and crying at dog food ads?"

"My ankle is distinctly thicker, Ben. And I explained about the dog food ad. Give me my foot back."

"No." He tucked one leg underneath the other and rested my foot atop it before proceeding to rub my toes. Damn, that felt good. The man had incredibly strong fingers. Must have been a result of all that bass playing. Thumbs dug in deep to the arch of my foot and my spine basically melted. Heaven, nirvana—I had it all within my grasp so long as he kept doing his thing.

"God, that's so nice," I happy-sighed, sinking further into the tub.

He made a gruff noise. It could have almost been construed as the word *good*.

"Is your hand all right?" I asked eventually.

He looked up at me from beneath dark brows, lips shut. His magic fingers paused for a moment, then kept right on kneading. "I might have put a hole or two in the wall after Jim left."

"Oh."

"He was right. You've been dealing with this on your own from the start and all I've done is throw money at the problem, hoping it would go away." He moved down to rubbing at my heel, taking care with the swollen ankle. "I didn't want to know, Liz. That's why I kept my distance. I just wanted to go on like normal, pretend none of it was happening."

"Me too. But my body keeps messing things up for me." I laughed, despite the topic being distinctly unfunny. "We're not that different, Ben. This situation has thrown us both for a loop, and that's putting it mildly."

"Don't make excuses for me," he grumped.

"All right, you're an asshole and you let me down. Again. Feel better?"

The smile was much wider this time. "Thought we weren't swearing."

"Oops." It was amazing what a foot rub did for my mood. Right then, I pretty much loved the whole world. Real anger lay beyond my reach. He grasped my other foot, again rolling up my jeans, and tossed aside the sandal. I did not fight him—no sir, no way.

"Can I ask you a question?" I said.

"Shoot."

"Why didn't you ever want children?"

"Because this is me, Liz. What you see is what you get. I like things calm, easy. But you and me, we've never been easy. Minute I saw you, it's been complicated. First with Mal, and you being a little younger, more serious, and now with the pregnancy." He shook his head. "Some women don't give a shit if I come and go. It's all good. But with you and the baby, you need more from me than that. And you deserve more."

"We're messing with your lifestyle."

He looked up at me from beneath drawn brows. "It's more than that. Shit. Never tried to explain this to someone before. When you were a kid, did you ever have some game you played that just rocked your world? And you'd wake up in the morning and realize today was the day you got to do nothing but play that game all day, and it was like life could never get better? That's what my life is like. Every day I get to get up and play music, I get to create something."

I nodded sadly, finally understanding. Ben was a man living his dream. As if anyone could compete with that. Maybe he'd liked the idea of me. Reality was, however, there'd never been room for me in his life.

"When the guys are busy, I can hop on a plane and go mix things up with another band," he continued. "Fill in or be a guest on their album. Even jamming with strangers in some shitty little bar where no one knows my name. That's my life, every day. I get to make something new, learn something. And it's fucking amazing. There's nothing like it."

"Sounds great."

"It is," he said. "And that's why I never thought about kids. Even a girlfriend seemed too much of a distraction. Don't get me wrong, I like women. But it was always easier to find someone for the night than to commit to something that stops me from being who I am, doing what I love."

I nodded. What was there to say? To go into a relationship expecting the other person to change was stupid. Ben and I had been over before we began, I just hadn't known it, understood, until now. No doubt he liked me just fine, but not enough.

"Doesn't mean I'm not going to be there for you and our kid. You said we could be friends," he said. "That offer still available?"

Friends was the right thing to do. I pushed aside my disappointment and put a smile on my face. "Absolutely."

"I'd like that."

It was me and Bean, and Bean and me. Come what may, I'd have my baby girl's back. Her daddy could do what he would. And the truth was, if he kept massaging my feet this way, I'd be his best damn friend, despite the break in my heart.

He kept his face down, his concentration on the task complete. Generally my feet were not that fascinating. Maybe he did have a foot fetish after all. Fingers drew soothing circles over my crappy ankle before digging in once more to the arch of my foot. Total and complete bliss. I could pretty much feel my crazy baby hormones rolling over and offering up their soft underbelly to him, preening and calling him Daddy, the dirty things. What this man's hands could do to me. Every part of me felt floaty and wonderful. Shivery good even.

Wait up. Crap, I was seriously turned on.

A wounded heart was apparently no competition for an over-eager vagina. The urge for sperm made no sense. I already had a baby on board. My tarty, attention-seeking nipples stood out loud and proud beneath my top, just begging for his lips. The situation between my legs wasn't any better. Since when had my feet become such hard-core, triple X–rated erogenous zones? His able hands made sweet pornographic love to my toes, and my muscles turned to jelly. My legs just fell open in invitation. Beyond my control, I swear. It all just felt so impossibly damn good.

Holy god damn hell. No one had warned me pregnancy could send you into heat.

Despite the ecstasy, I couldn't help but notice there was only like three . . . four inches between the pad of my foot and the bulge behind the fly of his jeans. It wouldn't take much to touch. Why, little more than a flex would be more than sufficient. I could just brush my toes against the poor man's crotch and then gasp, pretending it was all some silly (wonderful) accident. Oops, clumsy me, fondling the innocent, unsuspecting man's genitals with my foot. How embarrassing—though really it could happen to anyone.

Not.

And really this is partly why, in my experience, friends don't rub friends' feet unless there's more going on. I got easily enough confused about the man, no need to make it worse.

A small moan slipped my lips, echoing in the tiled room.

"You okay?" he asked.

"Fine."

"You made a noise."

"No, I didn't."

A little line appeared above his nose. "Okay."

"That's great," I said, drawing my now slutty limbs back to the safe side of the tub. "Thanks. Very kind of you. I think we'll make great friends."

He gave me a long look. "Any time. If you need something, I want you to tell me. That's the only way this is going to work."

"Okay." I needed his naked body at my disposal. Now.

"I want total honesty from you, okay?"

"Total honesty." So help me, I'd ride him all the way home and back again.

"From now on, we talk," he said. "All the fucking time. Yap, yap, yap. That's us."

"Got it."

"Great." The way his tongue and lips played with that simple little word, it meant much, much more than it was ever meant to. And it might have been my imagination, but I'm pretty damn sure his pupils were about twice their normal size. They were like twin pools of black rock 'n' roll sexiness and desire just inviting me to jump on in and get all wet and wild and wanton. All of a sudden, breathing seemed to be an issue for me. Same with thinking, clearly.

I don't know what it was about the man that made me attempt to get poetic. But it really needed to stop.

"I better go," I said.

"Fucking crazy . . ." he muttered.

"What?"

"You."

I groaned in embarrassment. "Come on, give me a break. I explained about the dog food ad. And hey, I told you that in confidence too. Don't you dare repeat it."

"Not talking about that," he said, the hint of a curve in the corner of his mouth doing dreadful things to me.

"What then?" I asked, both wanting and dreading knowing.

He hesitated, hiding another smile behind his hurt hand.

"Total honesty. Come on."

"Pretty sure you don't want to hear me talking about my dick."

"Your, um, your dick?"

"Yeah."

"Huh. How much have you had to drink?"

"Not nearly enough for this." The smile he gave me, I nearly came on the spot. The fact that it came framed in his particularly sleek-looking beard almost did me in. I knew exactly how his facial hair felt against me. So stimulating. Never had I wanted to rub my cheek and other pertinent parts against someone's face more. When it came to that night in Vegas, my memory was way too good.

"You asked if I'd had sex since I found out about the baby," he said. "Answer's no."

"Yeah right." I laughed.

"I'm serious. Nothing since that night. Haven't even come close."

Wow. "Why?"

"I don't know. Guess I lost my libido." He scratched at his chin. "Wasn't even interested. Just . . . nothing."

"You couldn't get it up?" I asked, mildly horrified, and much too curious. Ben always seemed so virile.

"I didn't want to get it up," he said. "There's a difference."

"Huh. But Jimmy said—"

"Jimmy doesn't know everything." He cracked his neck, irritation in his gaze. "Wish you hadn't heard all that."

I couldn't truthfully say the same. Their conversation had been most enlightening.

"I couldn't get interested in screwing anyone because I was worried about you and the baby," he said. "Dealing with all this has been big, you know?"

"Yeah. Sex having consequences is kind of a bummer." I smiled. "I guess I've been pretty sheltered, really. Anne always dealt with the serious stuff. But this time she can't. It's all on me."

"And me."

"Yes." Time would tell.

"Anyway," he said. "Just thought you'd find it funny."

"That you were suffering from erectile dysfunction? Ben, there's no way I'd find that funny."

"It's wasn't erectile dysfunction, Liz," he said with a wounded gaze. "Don't say that."

"Okay, okay. Sorry."

"I was just numb. Lost my interest in sex for a while."

"Right. Numb."

"Anyway," he said, still frowning. Male egos. So touchy. "Soon as I'm around you again, my dick decides to come out of hibernation. Thank fuck. Was worried I'd have to wait till you'd had the baby to get it back."

"Yeah. Phew." I thought the information over for a while. Not necessarily good news—for me, at least. The other women of the world would probably benefit greatly by it, however. "Well, we did talk out some of our issues, so it's entirely natural that you'd be feeling better about the situation, I suppose."

He screwed up his face. "Sweetheart, I'm not talking about us being friends, though that's nice and all. I'm talking about the fact that you turn me on. Have since the minute I met you. Physically, you get to me."

"I do?"

"Yeah, you do. I'm just going to have to channel that interest elsewhere."

My mouth worked, though nothing came out for a while. I got to him. God, if only he knew how much he still got to me. Hope was well out of my price range, however. I couldn't afford to get physical with him. My emotions were far too involved, and clearly the man was only out for some fun. Without a doubt, I knew that now.

"Ben, are you sure this isn't some mental block you were having," I asked. "All the worry about the pregnancy and how it was going to affect things, as opposed to me physically?"

He raised a brow.

"Hey, I've seen some of those women out there," I said. "They're stunning. And if they've been hanging around you night after night, then it seems unlikely that me with my beginner's baby bump and fat ankles suddenly lights up your life."

His tongue played behind his cheek and he said nothing. There was definitely laughter in his eyes, however.

"I'm just trying to be rational," I added.

"Problem is, rational doesn't come into it."

Hmm.

"Dicks don't have brains. It's why men get into trouble."

The man had a point. Dicks obviously didn't have emotions, either, the annoying things.

"The point I'm messing up here is, Liz, you're right. I was jealous. I want you. I'm not going to act on that because shit's complicated enough and we're working on being friends here. It's what's best for the baby."

"Right." What he said was no less than the truth. Still, my vagina went into a deep depression. My heart wasn't too happy about it, either.

"The business is hell on relationships—all the separations and everything. Couples don't last. Seen it time and time again. I don't want to put our kid through some messy split and neither do you."

"What?" I cocked my head. "You really mean that. But what about David and Ev?"

"Time'll tell."

My eyes were wide. "I think that's sad, Ben."

"Trust me, Liz. What's best for our kid right now is you and me working on having a long-term relationship we can both live with. That means us being friends and figuring out how to be parents together, right?"

"Right. I guess."

"I know I'm not the psychology student here, but I also think it would really help if you didn't get with any of my friends or people I work with. Ever. I think that would, ah, complicate things."

"Yes. Fair enough."

"And I won't hook up with any of your friends, either. Ever."

"Thanks."

He tipped his chin in acknowledgment.

"Wow, we're really going great, setting up the friendship boundaries," I said.

A smile.

"This should all work perfectly." Heartbreakingly so.

"I hope so," he said.

"Might be best if we didn't talk about your penis and sex between us again in the future, though. Maybe we should tone back the total honesty just a little."

He winced. "You're right. My bad. No need to confuse shit."

"No problem."

He held out his right hand to me, knuckles pink and large fingers calloused. "Friends?"

"You bet. Being friends will be great."

CHAPTER EIGHT

Being friends sucked.

All told, there were thirty-five stops on the tour—seventeen in this first leg, before we headed over to Europe, then back home again to tour the northern states. The band played a new city pretty much every second night without break. Ben had been right, though, everything that could be done for me was done. All I had to worry about was walking on and off private jets and gestating while room service catered to my every whim.

The routine went roughly like this: We arrived in a new place and settled into our hotel while fans screamed and fainted out front. Sometimes the guys got the rest of the day off, usually spending time with their significant others. Or, in Ben's case, jamming with the warm-up act, Down Fourth, and a case or two of beer.

Not to say that the guys didn't hang out together.

It seemed, though, that couples in their first year together spent the bulk of their time bonking. Noisily. Jim and Ben often hit the gym, and they'd all get together for an occasional early or late-night dinner. Since Mal still refused to talk to Ben outside of band business, however, those were difficult, to say the least.

The bulk of their time went toward publicity. TV shows, radio stations, news reporters—you name it, they talked to them. Then there'd be sound checks and rehearsals and meetings. Stage Dive might have toured the country a time or two, but the amount of the country they'd actually gotten to see was likely small. When it wasn't about the sexing, it seemed to be all business, all the time. Gave me plenty of opportunities to catch up on my reading and get a jump start on next year's classes, when I wasn't with Ben, trying to figure out how he and I could be friends. That the mere sight of him set off my horny hormonalness didn't help. The hours I spent amusing myself with my hand after one of our visits was plain sad. Pregnancy was crazy.

In Albuquerque we had a drink together one morning. Herbal tea for me and about a gallon of black coffee for him. Conversation was stilted, largely due to Ben having had only three hours' sleep.

No, I didn't ask for the exact details.

In Oklahoma we attempted lunch in his room. Problem was, an overly zealous fan managed to get onto the floor and handcuff himself to the emergency evacuation stairs door handle, opposite Ben's suite. Between his yelling and the fire alarm he managed to set off, lunch got canceled and the building was temporarily evacuated.

In Wichita we tried going for a walk, but then Ben nearly got mobbed and we had to make a run for it back to the hotel. He might not stick out back home in Portland, but in other cities, on Stage Dive—sighting alert, we weren't so lucky.

I hate to admit it, but by Atlanta I think we were both starting to give up. No plans were made. Plus I had the sniffles.

In Charlotte my cold decided to get more serious and a doctor was called in, doubtless at great expense. I could have told me to rest up and keep taking the prenatal vitamins for a whole lot less. My nose gleamed bright red and flowed like a river. It was beautiful. Anne was the only one permitted to come see me. No one else could afford to share in my germy state. Her having Mal stick his tongue in her mouth every chance he got didn't seem to matter. Adrian, the band's manager, immediately slapped a quarantine order on me. I wasn't permitted to stick my head outside my bedroom door, or else.

Asshole. As if I would.

Ben: U ok? Lena said you can't have visitors.

Lizzy: Fine. Just a cold.

Ben: Shitty. How bad? U c Dr?

Lizzy: Yes. Morning sickness & growing bean got me run down. Gotta drink more juice etc. Keep up the prenatal vitamins. Immune system is looking after her more than me apparently.

Ben: Ok. Need anything?

Lizzy: No thanks. Heard her heart again. Beating strong.

Ben: U can hear her heart already? Fuck. Amazing.

Lizzy: I know right?

Ben: Could be him.

Lizzy: Don't mess with mother's intuition.

Ben: Wouldn't dare.

Lizzy: I never realized there so many different types of juice. Thank you.

Ben: Think of anything u need tell me.

Lizzy: Will do. Thanks again.

Lizzy: Thanks for the flowers.

Ben: No problem. Feeling better?

Lizzy: Nope. All hail the Queen of Phlegm. They put me on antibiotics. Should be better soon.

Ben: Good. Can I get u anything?

Lizzy: No thanks. Have a good concert. Break a leg or whatever.

Ben: Take it easy. Rest.

Lizzy: Did Mal tell u I was staying here?

Ben: Ur not coming to Nashville?

Lizzy: No. They don't want me flying. Mal didn't tell u?

Ben: No.

Lizzy: Crap. Sorry.

Ben: Never mind. Ur still sick? How sick?

Lizzy: Nothing serious. They're just being careful. Plus u guys can't get sick.

Ben: Calling.

Lizzy: Losing voice. Hurts to speak.

Ben: Shit. U sure?

Ben: What did Dr say exactly?

Lizzy: It's common cold. Headaches & blocked nose. No high fevers which might b dangerous. All normal.

Ben: Mayb we should get 2nd opinion.

Lizzy: Don't worry. Anne will b w me. I'll be fine in a few days. C u in Memphis.

Ben: Keep me up to date. Need anything?

Lizzy: Will do. Just sleep. Later.

Ben: How u feeling today?

Lizzy: Nose running less green.

Ben: Good. Been worried about you.

Lizzy: I'm getting there. Sleeping and catching up on lots on day time tv.

Ben: Great. Take it easy.

Lizzy: With Anne in Nurse Ratched mode I have no other choice.

Ben: Haha. Family.

Lizzy: Exactly.

Ben: Can I get u anything?

Lizzy: I'm ok.

Ben: Sorry I missed ur call. What's happening?

Lizzy: Just wanted to wish u luck w the concert. How is Memphis? Any sightings of the King?

Ben: Not yet. But he's here somewhere. How u doing?

Lizzy: Much better. Bored. Want out of bed. Dr said a day or 2. Blood pressure was a little low, made me light headed. But no big deal.

Ben: You fainted? What happened?

Lizzy: No, just felt off. It's fine. Taking extra iron.

Ben: Christ, u sure?

Lizzy: Yes. Please don't worry. It's all getting worked out.

Ben: Shit. Ok. Be good to see you.

Lizzy: You too. So sick of being sick. Meet me in St Louis?

Ben: Deal.

Lizzy: Anne said u rang her. Brave.

Ben: Wanted to make sure u were ok.

Lizzy: I know. But I am telling u everything.

Ben: Yeah. Just worried.

Lizzy: Dr's good. If anything changes I'll let u know straight away. See u soon.

Lizzy: I am now the proud of owner of a wide selection of super comfy pjs and the worlds most extensive collection of zombie films.

Ben: :)

Lizzy: You rock in all the ways.

Ben: Pjs were Lena's idea. Zombies were mine.

Lizzy: They both made my day. Thank you.

Ben: What movie u watching?

Lizzy: Dawn of the Dead.

Ben: Original or remake?

Lizzy: Remake. Love the actors in it.
Ben: Cool. Never seen it.
Lizzy: It's not Romero, but its fun.
Ben: Show it to me sometime.
Lizzy: You got it.

Lizzy: Arrived. Going to sleep.
Ben: Ok?
Lizzy: Yes. Just tired. Have a good concert.
Ben: Thanks. C u in the morning.

Yes, the sad fact was, Ben and I were probably better at texting one another than we'd ever been communicating face-to-face. Apart from that one night in Vegas. Oh, and the time in his truck. And in his hotel suite tub after his argument with Jimmy, though he'd been somewhat under the influence that night.

Anyway, the flight wore me out. I went straight to bed when Anne and I hit Saint Louis. But I didn't exactly get much sleep.

"Fuck off, dude!" was my wake-up call. "You don't come in here."

"Out of my way," said someone in a distinctly deep and pissed off tone.

"Easy." Another male voice. A different one this time.

"Ben, be reasonable. She's still sleeping." That was Anne, her voice placating.

"It's one o'clock in the afternoon. She said she was better, why the fuck is she still sleeping?"

I sure as hell wasn't anymore.

"Anne, he's got a point. Has anyone checked on her lately?" I think that was Lena, but what she was doing here, I had no idea.

"Something's wrong. I want a doctor here now," said Ben.

"Just a minute. We're all worried about her." Ev, perhaps?

Hell, it sounded like everyone was visiting.

"Told you, man," said Mal. "You don't come into my rooms. I may have to work with you. But I don't want a fucking thing to do with you outside of that."

"For Christ's sake . . ."

"You fucked with my trust."

"I know," sighed Ben. "And I'm sorry. Right now, though, I need to know she's okay."

"I'm fine," I said, stepping out of my room. "Hey, you're really all here."

And I do mean everyone. David and Ev, Lena and Jimmy, and of course my sister and Mal, what with me still sharing their suite. Thank goodness I was wearing a pair of the spanking new blue lounge pants and matching striped tank top, tiny bare baby bulge poking out in between.

"Liz." Ben rushed me, engulfing me in his big strong arms.

"Hi." I mumbled into his T-shirt-covered pec. Yeah, I'd kind of frozen. Generally, we didn't do this, but also it felt far too good. My poor, tired body got shivery in the best way. The man was just asking for me to hump his leg or something. Desperate really wasn't pretty.

"Are you okay?" he asked, studying my face.

"I'm fine. I just overslept. Sorry to worry everyone."

He frowned, big hands cupping my face, gently turning it this way and that for his inspection. "You don't look okay. You look tired."

"I couldn't get to sleep last night. I'm bouncing back from the cold just fine, though. No more Queen of the Phlegm or any of that."

"You sure?" He gave me a dubious look.

"Screw you, bud. I'm glowing."

The big jerk gave me a sheepish look. "Sorry. Just been worried about you."

"Apparently my iron levels were a little low. I'm taking supplements now, eating more. I'll be back to normal in no time. And really, I feel fine. I feel great! Being up and around is awesome."

"Why couldn't you sleep?"

My mouth worked fine, but really my brain was too sleep-addled just yet to invent a plausible lie on demand. Worse, my face began to fire up. Crap. Out of all the questions in all the world, I particularly did not want to answer that one. Not even a little.

"Why?"

"I don't know, I just couldn't."

"Liz."

"Ben."

"Tell me why," he barked.

"Because the walls here are thin, okay? It was too noisy. Now enough with the questions. I'm hungry."

"Ha," shouted Mal triumphantly, hands on hips. "Your nightly fun-time party boy bullshit kept her awake."

"I'm on the other side of the fucking building," said Ben. "How the hell could I be keeping her awake?"

"But then, if it wasn't you . . ." Anne's brows slowly rose and she covered her mouth with her hand. "Oh dear. Sorry, Liz."

I nodded, unable to face her just yet.

"What," asked Mal, eyes full of confusion. "What are you two talking about?"

Jimmy snorted. A moment later, his brother did much the same. At least Ev and Lena managed to keep the bulk of their reaction on the inside. They were nice girls.

I'd never needed to know that my sister was a screamer. Never. That Mal was a screamer too just kind of confused me. If only you could have memories bleached from your brain. What an extraordinarily useful thing it would be.

"Pumpkin? Explain."

Anne pulled Mal in close and whispered in his ear. Then Mal started snickering.

"It's not funny," said Anne.

"It kind of is."

She shook her head, arms crossed over her chest.

"Lord of the Sex strikes again!"

"Shuddup."

Huge grin in place, Mal smacked a kiss on her lips.

"So you got caught up on sleep okay?" Ben asked, ignoring their carrying on.

"Yes. Thanks."

"We better get some breakfast into you. What do you feel like?"

"Hmm." My tummy grumbled audibly. Me no care. "I want the biggest omelet known to mankind."

"You got it."

His gaze fell to my waist, then his hand followed, tentatively covering my bump. It was still early days in Bean world. The bump might have been caused as much by bad posture as anything. But I knew she was in there, growing and doing her thing. Magic.

"You mind if I . . ." he asked.

"It's fine."

The palm of his hand warmed my skin, his calloused fingers softly tracing over me, tickling ever so slightly (Turning me on, of course. Gah.) The side of his thumb rubbed gently back and forth, the callus giving me goose bumps. Actually, I'm pretty certain he himself gave me goose bumps. It didn't even seem to matter what his hands were up to. And I had the worse feeling that I'd missed him this last week. His voice, his presence, all of him. I stared up at his face, spellbound. It came as naturally as breathing, feeling for Ben. Whatever he'd been up to while I was away didn't even seem to matter just then. How dumb was my heart?

Meanwhile, the silence was starting to make me nervous.

"Fifteen weeks," I said.

"Wow." He smiled and I smiled back at him, lost. Same as always.

"Guess I should get dressed."

"Nah," he said. "Don't worry. Come to my room and we'll order your omelet. You can fill me in on everything over late breakfast."

"Okay. I'd like that."

We turned to face the assembled crowd. Every eye was on us—apparently our little conversation had held them enthralled. I'd kind of forgotten we had an audience at all, caught up in the moment.

"Man," said David, his hand clapping down on Mal's shoulder. "C'mon."

"What?" Mal scowled.

"This is getting sorted out," announced Jimmy. "Now. Time to kiss and make up, you two idiots."

"Fuck off, Jimbo."

Ben let go of my hand, taking a step forward. "They're right. What's it going to take?"

With the air of one greatly wounded, Mal turned to Anne. She too nodded, giving him a small smile.

"What I did was wrong. I gave you my word and I should have kept it." Hands to his sides, Ben faced Mal. "We've been friends since we were kids. Never should've given you reason to doubt me. I'm sorry."

"And you got her pregnant," bit out Mal.

"Yeah. But I'm not saying sorry for that. Never giving my kid cause to think they're not wanted."

Mal's eyes narrowed as he appraised Ben anew.

"This ain't good for Liz," Ben said, "getting caught in the shit between us. She doesn't need the stress." With a deep breath, Ben held his chin high. "What's it going to take?"

"Three," said Mal.

"Not the face." David moved in closer to the pair. "Agreed?"

"Gotta keep him pretty for the pictures," said Jimmy.

"Fine." Mal flexed his wrists, curling his right hand into a fist. "Don't want to damage these precious hands anyway."

"Wait!" I rushed forward, comprehension finally dawning. "You are not talking about hitting him. Over my dead body."

The other women looked resigned, concerned, combinations of both. None of them would interfere, however. It was there in their eyes. Fuck them.

Ben turned, grabbing hold of my arm and setting me back a pace. "Stay over there. Just in case."

"Ben. No."

"We need it done with."

"You are not letting him hit you."

"Liz—"

"I'm serious!"

"Sweetheart, it's okay," he said, eyes gentle but face set. "Calm down. We've been friends a long time. You got to let us work this one out our own way."

Like hell. "Anne, help me!"

My sister just grimaced. "Maybe he's right. Maybe we need to stay out of it."

"If this was Mal, would you stay out of it?" The thought of Ben getting hurt, of Mal doing the hurting, and me being the cause . . . I basically wanted to vomit. "Mal, you lay one finger on him and I swear I am never talking to you again."

The idiot just rolled his eyes. "Please. I saw the sappy-ass way you just looked at him. He'll talk you 'round."

Then, before Ben was ready for it, Mal smashed his fist into the man's stomach. The breath whooshed out of Ben audibly and I winced. He bent forward, instinctively protecting himself. Without pause, Mal delivered the second blow, a sharp jab to Ben's side. Ben grunted, rearing back, and Mal slammed him once more in the belly. My own belly contracted in empathy. He'd done it, Mal had really done it.

The silence that followed was stunning. Ben's harsh breathing filled the room as Mal held his hand out for shaking. It was over.

I'd seen a couple of fights in my life. One particularly nasty one in a backstreet during my wild period. Then of course there was the night my pregnancy had been announced. At least the scent of blood didn't feature this time. Violence never fixed anything. Mal not waiting until Ben was ready, hitting him before he'd had a chance to brace for the blow, hurting the man I cared (too much) about. . . . Emotion tangled me up, turning me inside out. I didn't know whether to burst into tears or to start beating on things myself.

Stupid hormones. Stupider boys.

"All good?" asked Mal.

"Yeah. Nice one with that opening hit." Ben slowly straightened, pain flashing across his face. Then he shook his bandmate's hand. The guys slapped each other's backs and the women wore relieved smiles. These people were fucking insane.

"Float like a butterfly, sting like a bee." With his fists held high, Mal jumped around. "Lizzy, babe, c'mon. It's manly man's business. You wouldn't understand, kid. You just gotta go with it."

"You . . ." I searched my mind but there wasn't a word harsh enough, an insult vile enough. Violence it was. I'd wipe that smile off his face. Top lip raised in a snarl, I stalked toward him, my bitch-slapping hand at the ready.

Unfortunately, Ben was at the ready too.

"No you don't." He swung me up into his arms, cradling me against him. "It's over."

"Put me down."

"Time for breakfast, remember? Let's go."

I swore up a storm, the whole no foul language thing long forgotten. What can I say? It was a heated moment.

"Whoa," said Mal, eyes wide with surprise. "She's a fierce critter."

On the other side of the room, Ev opened the door and we made straight for it. Involuntarily on my part. "No. Ben—"

"What did you want in your omelet?"

"Put me down."

"And how about some juice? You want juice too?"

"Do not patronize me. I am not a child."

"Believe me, sweetheart, I know. Despite the tantrum you're throwing right now."

"This is not a tantrum! This is me being outraged at Mal hitting you."

The door closed shut behind us and we stood in yet another long hotel hallway. Red carpet this time, with groovy art deco mirrors lining the walls. Ben's long-ass legs got us as far away from Mal and Anne's suite as fast as they could manage. Outside another doorway he paused, carefully setting me down while keeping one arm around my waist—in case of any escape attempts, no doubt. He slid a card through the lock and pushed open the door, giving me an encouraging nudge in the desired direction.

Inside, he sealed the door shut, slumped back against it. Then he just kind of stared at me.

"What?" I grouched, crossing my arms.

The corner of his mouth crept up.

"It's not funny. I can't believe you let him hurt you."

With a hearty sigh, Ben raised his arms, lacing his fingers on top of his head. Still staring.

"That should not have happened," I said. "And it was my fault. You got hurt by one of your oldest friends because of me."

He blinked, the hint of a smile disappearing. "No. I let Mal take a couple of shots at me *because* he's one of my oldest friends. Shit, he's more than that. He's my brother. When shit went bad between Dave and me last year, he's the one that talked Dave around, smoothed it over. Now, I gave Mal my word on you, and I broke it. I deserved him being pissed at me, and between us we just sorted that out. End of story."

"I don't like it."

"You don't have to like it. This is between me and Mal."

"So what I think doesn't matter?"

"Not about this, no," he said, looking me right in the eye.

Assholes. I turned my back on him for a minute, pulling myself together. Everything inside of me was in flux, a crazy mess.

"Never had a woman try to protect me like that before," he said softly. "Mal was right, you're fierce."

I raised my chin, turning back to face him.

"Stubborn. Loyal."

I shrugged. "Hungry."

He laughed, pushing off from the door with one foot, coming toward me. Once more he placed a kiss on the top of my head. Without thought I leaned into him. Ben had somehow come to represent warmth and safety. A kind of home for Bean and me, despite my best efforts to keep a safe distance between us. But maybe home wasn't about the heart, exactly, but about something deeper. We'd made a child together, it made sense there'd be a link. No need for me to get all carried away.

I don't know.

My feelings for him hadn't particularly made me any wiser. They constantly pushed and pulled me in different, confusing directions. I didn't know if I'd ever figure it out. What I felt for him, however, and what I felt for Bean, were so extraordinarily big. I'd never known there was room in me for so much emotion. If I could just attach myself to him, that would be great. Perhaps he'd like a pet limpet.

Ha! It was all probably just another weirdo hormonal thing and in five minutes I'd be all whatever about him. A girl could hope.

"You okay?" he asked with a smile.

"Fine."

"Do me a favor?"

"What?"

"Stay out of fights. Keep our baby safe."

"Good point," I groaned. "I kind of lost it back there."

"Yeah, you kind of did."

"Sorry."

"I'm a big boy, Liz. You can trust me to look after myself, okay? I'm not going to be letting anyone else take a swing at me. I hit the gym just about every day with Jim. I'm no delicate little flower you need to protect."

"Okay."

He set his hands on my shoulders and gazed down. "And I understand. I do. Shit's complicated, but if anyone laid a finger on you, I'd lose it too. You're going to have to get over it and forgive Mal, though. I meant what I said. This isn't good. No more fighting within our family. I want it finished."

I gave him a nod. "I'll work on it. But there's no way I'm living with them anymore. For lots of reasons. Time to get my own room."

"Liz, you've just been sick enough to be on a week's bed rest. Anne said your blood pressure is still gonna be an issue for a while. I don't think now's the time to be alone. What if something happens?"

"What's my alternative? Jimmy and Lena need their alone time right now. I'm not going to inflict myself upon them."

Deep sigh. "Yeah, you're right. You better move in with me."

"With you?" I asked, surprised.

"Well, yeah." He spread his arms wide. "I get two-bedroom suites 'cause I like my space. Plenty of room for you."

"What about your nightly parties? I don't want to be a downer, but . . ."

"They'll go somewhere else. Fuck, Vaughan and Down Fourth can have 'em in their room for a change. Not a problem."

I slumped in relief. It also worked well to hide the excitement bolting through me. Me and Ben living together. Wow. What a notion. "Sounds great!"

"Cool." He clapped his hands, rubbed them together. "This'll work out great. We'll be meshing, working on being friends and all. Plus I won't have to worry about you being on your own."

"Friends. Awesome."

That word. I had to translate it to happy in my mind. Make it work. Ben and I would be friends. Friends friends friends.

He held up his big paw. "Give me five, friend."

I did so, smacking my palm against his with great zest. Firetruck, that hurt.

CHAPTER NINE

After Saint Louis came Washington, DC, followed by Philadelphia. It took until then for me to fully get my bounce back and to forgive Mal. Well, to begin to forgive Mal. As much as everyone else liked to rationalize it, the memory of him driving his fist into Ben's gut still felt too fresh. My bitch-slapping hand started to twitch every time he came near. I couldn't help it.

Ben and I living together had not been the astronomical step toward a bright and beautiful romantic future I might have secretly, stupidly hoped for.

But that was my problem, not his.

There'd definitely been no more hugging. As a roommate, he was very polite—and frequently absent. Yep, Ben was a busy boy. He'd emerge from his room grizzly and bed-headed at nine and we'd have breakfast together, which was nice. For an hour or so we'd chat over pancakes or eggs Benedict or whatever. Conversation usually revolved around my health and the movie I'd watched the night before. Then he'd disappear to "do band shit." I don't quite know what he did, but apparently it took him all day and well into the night. So I'd taken to sitting up in front of the TV, hoping to catch him when he came in at whatever time. Instead, I'd wake up tucked into my own bed, come morning.

All very friendly. I just needed to adjust. Still. And damn it, tonight I would. Tonight, my crush on him came to an end. It had to. The man really was hell on my heart and loins.

"Remind me again why we're here," said Anne, slipping her arm around my shoulders.

"To party."

"We're here to party?"

"How could you doubt it?" I smoothed the big, flowy black T-shirt down over my small bump of a belly.

"So long as we're not here to spy on Ben."

I scoffed. "As if I'd do that."

"'Cause you're so over him."

"Big-time. Huge. We're friends."

Anne made a humming noise. "Friends don't let friends stalk their friends."

"You and I aren't friends, we're sisters. Totally different." My jaw cracked on a particularly large yawn. Ugh. This growing a baby stuff really took it out of you. "You have to suck it up and support me no matter what crackpot crap I do."

"You two still sharing the suite but not the bedroom, huh?"

"Do you really want to know?" I asked, curious.

She sighed. "You're pregnant with his baby. I give up. Of all the males I might have chosen for you, he's not even remotely on the list. But at the end of the day, it's your choice, not mine."

I nodded, pleased.

"I just want you to know, you have options." Just like when we were kids, Anne twirled a lock of my hair around a finger and gave it a tug. I slapped at her hand, same as I'd always done. She grabbed my fingers and held on tight. "Mal and I have been talking. However you want to do this, we're happy to support you. Whether that's move in with us or whatever."

"I appreciate that."

"And on the off chance you and Ben can't work things out, you don't need to worry about money."

"Ben wouldn't leave me hanging like that, Anne."

"I'm just saying—"

"I know. But trust me, I don't need to worry about money."

"No. You don't."

"Yeah, I really don't," I said, turning to face her. "He put six figures in my account before the tour started."

"Huh." The whites of Anne's eyes were showing. "Good. This makes me think better of the bearded wonder."

"Mm." It was a step up from her calling him the Sperminator, at least.

We sat huddled together in a single large lounge chair, watching the postconcert party get going. When I'd moved into Ben's two-bedroom suite, the party had changed location to the room of Down Fourth's singer. He shared the smaller suite with his girlfriend, the band's drummer. She'd been more than welcoming, if a little surprised, when we knocked on the door.

I had the worst feeling that Anne was right, though, and I shouldn't have come. Not to this room, this tour, none of it. Also, apparently my mood currently registered around the shitty level. Shooty. No, that didn't work. Crappy. Yes, *crappy* made for a suitable non-sweary replacement.

"I hate that I have to be looked after, that all of a sudden I'm no longer me, I'm a condition, a baby-making machine." I leaned my head against Anne's with a *Poor me* sigh. "Should have stayed in Portland and worked in the bookstore. I don't belong here."

"Of course you belong here. Don't be a dolt."

I gave her a half smile. "I sound pathetic. Quick, slap me with a wet fish or something."

"If only I had one handy. This baby sure makes you an interesting person to be around. I never know what mood I'll get next."

"You have no idea. I need to get laid so bad . . . my dreams are just one endless stream of pornography."

"Oh-kay. So go on, talk to me about him. I'll try to be open-minded."

"There's not much to say."

"You two looked pretty cozy when he stormed the castle to rescue you from your evil sister and brother-in-law."

I raised my brows.

"Sorry," she said. "When he pushed his way in because he was worried about you—kudos to him for caring—you two looked like you were getting on well. I take it this is no longer the case, since you're clearly unhappy and we're lurking here, waiting for him to appear."

"We're very polite. We're always texting, he checks on me constantly, and if I need him he's there. But . . . I don't know. It's not like we're really saying anything. We share the same space but we're living at a distance. He does his thing, I do mine. He gets up and goes, comes back in the early hours after drinking here with these guys."

She frowned.

How to explain it? It was all such a mess. "Thing is, I can't get over him when I'm living with him. The proximity doesn't work. It just turns me into some perverted weirdo, hopped up on pregnancy hormones, sniffing his dirty laundry."

"You sniffed his dirty laundry?" Anne gave me a look of much judgment.

"It was only a shirt."

She cleared her throat. "Right. Okay."

"Anyway, it doesn't feel right, the way things are. I invaded his private space, taking up the offer of moving in. It was a bad move. So I've been thinking about either heading home or getting my own room."

"Don't leave. Move back in with me and Mal. I promise we'll keep the sex noises under control."

"No way. I still get these horrible flashbacks of that night and wake up crying, terrified that some sexed-up howler monkey is going to attack me." The sniggering—I couldn't contain it if I tried. So I didn't.

"Funny," she said drily.

"Thanks. I amuse me."

"I hate the thought of you being on your own."

"I know. But I'm going to be a single parent, Anne. I am on my own, it's a fact of life. Time I got used to it." I shrugged. "I know you and Mal want to do what you can, and I appreciate it. I do. Bean's lucky. She's going to have an awesome extended family with all of you guys."

"She really is."

I gave Anne's knee a friendly squeeze. "I'm glad we could talk about this. I've missed talking to you."

"Sorry I was so judgy. It was just hard, with all our plans for you to study and everything."

"Yeah, I know."

We just about sat in each other's laps we were so close. After the last few months, I think we needed it.

"I keep telling myself that he and I are just going to be friends," I said, letting it all out, dumping the whole sorry story on her. "There's a deeply stupid part of me that's still holding out hope, however, that doesn't quite want to accept it. I can't sit in his hotel room waiting for him to come home so we can have some magical moment together that'll fix everything and make it right. He and I are never going to be like that. I just have to accept it."

My sister just stared at me. "You have real feelings for him, don't you?"

I snorted. I don't know, it just seemed ridiculous that she was still in denial after everything.

"Sorry. I guess I just always thought this was some crush you'd get over," she said. "But it's not."

"No. But it's way past time for me to move on. You're right there. Hence we are here, waiting for him to make an appearance. I'll see him in action, schmoozing with sexy women, and hopefully realize the depth of my silliness. Then I'll tell him it's time for me to go big and get my own room or go home." I picked up my glass of lemonade from the coffee table and took a sip.

Anne cocked her head, studying me. "Are you in love with him?"

Good question.

"I just thought . . . maybe seeing him in action isn't what you need," she said. "Maybe taking a stand would work better."

"Demanding he love me? I don't think that would work."

"Hmm. But back to the original question. Do you love him?"

"I'm not sure I even know what love is."

"Does it hurt?"

Air was apparently in short supply. I stared at my sister, confused at the question and yet completely understanding. And that question—I didn't want to answer it. I needed to concentrate on my definites. Bean. Being a mom. Things like that.

"Well?" she asked.

"Yes." And god I hated it. The truth sucked.

Slowly Anne nodded, no smile on her face. "I'm sorry."

"Anyway." My smile felt so impossibly plastic. It was a wonder my face didn't crack. "When he gets here, I'll talk to him. In the meantime, party-party girl, that's me. And I've got a feeling this one's going to be an all-nighter."

"It's nearly midnight. I'm impressed you've managed to stay awake this long."

"You're only saying that because I've been asleep by eight o'clock every night this week."

She smiled.

"You wait. Later we'll go completely crazy and do shots of warm milk. It'll be awesome."

"Living on the edge."

"I know, right?" I turned to look over my shoulder at my new, ever-present shadow. "You can do the honors and pour, Sam."

"I'll look forward to that, Miss Rollins." The security man gave me an austere nod, never taking his eyes off the room. Damn it. He joked and smiled with the members of the band. I'd witnessed it with my own two eyes. Eventually I'd wear him down.

From out in the hall came the unmistakable wailing of He Who Shall Not Be Named. Stage Dive had finally arrived. Or some of them. Mal barreled into the room, searching for his mate, while Ben wandered in at a more sedate pace, chatting to a dude I didn't recognize. Ben's hair was slicked back, his beard neatly trimmed. I guessed he'd changed shirts after the show, because this one was a black button-down, neatly ironed. The cuffs were rolled up, the top few buttons undone.

He looked lovely. Hell, he looked like love. Harps, angels, all of it. God, I was a sap. I really had to get this under control, for my own sanity's sake if nothing else.

The crowd suddenly seemed at capacity. I guess a lot of people had been hanging out downstairs in the hotel bar, waiting for the important people to arrive.

The mad drummer went down on one knee before Anne, holding out a hand. With a grin, she placed her fingers in his.

"Who is this unearthly creature I see before me?" he asked. "You dazzle my eyes, mysterious stranger. I must know who you are immediately."

"I'm your wife."

"Thought you looked familiar." He kissed the back of her hand, turning to rest his spine against the bottom of the lounge chair, between her legs. "Fuck that was a long night. Adrian lined up an interview after the show. Next time the little butt-weasel does that, remind me to kill him."

"You got it."

"Work my shoulders please, Pumpkin," he asked, cracking his neck. "I hurt."

Anne started rubbing him down. "Book you a massage tomorrow?"

"You're the best." He gave me a pat on the knee. "Lizzy, you talking to me today?"

"I haven't decided yet," I said.

"Isn't much of it left, baby momma. Better make up your mind." He smirked. "Benny-boy know you're here?"

"I don't have to report my whereabouts to him," I sputtered.

Mal laughed. "No? This should be interesting."

"Tell him, Sam." I chugged down my lemonade.

"Miss Rollins is a fully grown, independent adult," the security man reported dutifully.

"Puh-lease," said Mal. "Fifty says he hauls her ass out of here within the next five minutes."

"You're on." Sam shook his hand.

Screw them both. If I had to choose, however, Sam would get the win. With no grace but with great purpose I wriggled and lifted, maneuvering my way up and out of the chair. "I'm going to the ladies' room."

"Oh now, c'mon. You can't hide from him," cried Mal. "That's not fair."

I just smiled.

"Benny-boy, look who's here! Why, it's sweet little Liz, and she's up way past her bedtime. Don't you think you should do something about that?"

The asshat. With swearing ruled out, I flipped Mal the bird. No way was he winning the bet. I'd talk to Ben when I was damn well good and ready. With all due haste, I ducked my head and made for the bathroom. The great thing about pregnancy is the way you basically always need to pee. It makes for such an awesome hobby. Sam took up guard duty outside as I opened the door and slipped in, shutting and locking it.

And wow, how about that. The bathroom was occupied.

"Hi." I raised a hand.

"Liz, hey." Vaughan laughed, one hand going down to cover his abundant essentials. "Guess I forgot to lock the door."

My face was on fire. "Guess so. Sorry to barge in."

"My bad. But good to see you."

"Good to see you too." And to see so very much of him. I stared, stunned. Whoa, the man was built. What this did to my already hormonally needy-in-the-sexwise charged state was a worry. "Yeah. Ha."

"Been wanting to catch up with you. How are you?" he asked, running a spare hand through his wet hair, all relaxed-like.

"Good."

"Heard you were sick," he said.

"It was just a cold. I'm fine now. Feeling great." And horny. Wildly horny. The boy didn't understand how close to being attacked he was.

"That sucks. Glad you're better."

"Thanks." As long as my eyes stayed on his face I was fine. It'd just been a while since I'd seen any downstairs action. No need for my cheeks to go thermonuclear. How uncool to get all fussed. Clearly the man himself had no such hesitation about nudity. "How's the tour been going?"

"Great. Really good."

"Excellent." I studied the floor. "Yeah. Should I leave?"

"No, stay. Fuck knows when we'll get another chance to talk alone."

"Ah, okay, sure. You maybe want to wrap a towel around your waist or put on some pants?"

"In a minute. I want to ask you a question first," he said, dimple flashing in his cheek. The man was seriously cute. Also, nice to know he was a natural redhead. I didn't mean to look, it just happened. A bare, unintended glimpse when I first walked in. A real live naked man smiling at me invitingly—my body liked the notion all too much. Crazy-ass hormones.

"Shoot," I invited, my face firing up yet again at the thought of his groin. Holy crap.

"You really pregnant?"

"Yes, I am." I flattened the oversize shirt again over my belly. Soon there'd be no chance of hiding it.

"Damn. And I take it the daddy's Ben, huh?"

My mouth stayed shut.

"Not so hard to figure out." He reached for a towel off the rack, wrapping it around slim hips. "There's tension between him and Mal, but no one's saying why. Then you come on tour."

I shrugged. Not my business to admit to anything on Ben's behalf. It was only on the part of my big mouth that Vaughan knew anything was afoot. Or abelly. I guess it should really be abelly.

"Dude definitely didn't like it last time we talked," he said.

"True." But who could explain why Ben said and did half the things he did when it came to me? I highly doubted even he had a clue.

"Then the parties move to here because you're sharing his room, all of a sudden. Even I could figure that one out, and I'm apparently not the most perceptive."

I narrowed my eyes, outraged on his behalf. "Who said that? I think you're great."

"Thanks." He grinned, hands on hips. It might have been my imagination, but I'm pretty sure his towel was sliding down. Man, if I could just stop looking. Me and my hand needed some alone time. Again.

"I think you're great too," Vaughan said, his eyes going soft as he stared at me. "Sucks that the situation's the way it is."

"Yeah." Or did it? How often did I get a pass from a very nice man with such enviable assets? "I mean, he and I aren't *together* together. I'm single. But yeah, definitely pregnant."

We both jumped at the sudden knocking. Then Ben's deep voice boomed out from the other side of the door, "Liz, you in there?"

Vaughan and I looked at each other, something uneasy stirring deep inside of me. God, was that guilt? I had no reason to feel guilt. None at all. Though the idea of explaining how I accidentally stumbled in on a wet, naked Vaughan could probably wait for later. Forever would also be fine.

"Be out in a minute," I called back.

"'kay."

"He treating you right?" asked Vaughan, his voice dropping in volume.

"I think he'll be a good father."

"Not what I'm asking." He took a step closer, studying my face intently. Outside, the music took a dramatic jump in volume. Good timing.

I didn't know what to say. Or think. "I, um, I'd appreciate you not saying anything about the baby to anyone yet."

"'Course."

"I better go."

"Sure," he said. "Ben's waiting."

"Right. Yes. Going." I fumbled behind me for the door handle, giving him a slightly dazed smile.

Vaughan stepped to the side, out of the line of sight. What a surprising encounter. Guess I'd finally started glowing. Of course, it might be the boobs. After I'd had the baby perhaps I'd consider implants, if this was the sort of attention they got me. Ha! Just joking. Mostly.

The minute I stepped outside, Ben was standing there, waiting, looming. Immediately my body went on high alert. I searched his face for his mood, read his body language (mildly impatient with a trace of don't-poke-the-bear cranky). There could be no denying that Vaughan was built and pretty. You'd have to be two days dead not to get turned on at the sight of him naked. But even then, Vaughan hadn't gotten to me like this. The moment I came into Ben Nicholson's orbit I was helpless, powerless to resist his pull. Foolish heart and vagina. The brain knew better but no one was listening.

People now filled the room and music was blasting out of the stereo. Ben bent, putting his mouth near my ear. "Anne said you wanted to talk. Let's head up to the room, yeah?"

I nodded.

"Everything okay?" he asked. And man, he'd asked me that question over and over again in so many different ways lately. I was tired of putting a smiley face on it.

"Let's talk upstairs."

He put an arm around me, safely guiding me out of the crowded room. People were dancing, drinking, who knows what. It was a regular rock 'n' roll hootenanny. We stayed silent, waiting for the elevator. When it arrived it was empty.

"Have a good night?" I asked, stepping inside.

"Explain something to me," he said, backing me up against the nearest wall.

"Ah, what?"

With muscular arms braced above my head, he narrowed his eyes on me. "I heard another voice in that bathroom. A man's voice."

I wasn't going to lie to him. I had no reason to. "Yes, I was talking to Vaughan."

"You were talking to Vaughan in the bathroom?" His head lowered, nose coming close to touching the tip of my own. The man had a raging fire in his dark eyes, I kid you not. Actual real live jealousy, burning bright.

"Are you serious?" I asked, deeply confused because I couldn't afford to be elated. Any minute now he'd do his usual thing and run. Just like in his truck that night. Just like in Vegas. I didn't really think I could handle it again. Not now. My life felt precarious enough as it was, so susceptible to sudden, extreme change.

"Very," he said, clearly cranky. "I already warned him off you."

"But you and I are just friends, remember?"

He blinked, outrage momentarily suspended by surprise.

"We already had this conversation and that's what you said you wanted," I said. "And now you're looking like you want to pee on my shoes to mark your territory." I shook my head. "What's going on here?"

"We need to talk."

"Yeah, good idea."

"Did he make a pass at you?"

"Not about that," I groaned. "Ben, I'm getting my own room. You do your thing and have your space, and I'll do the same. I think we'll get along a lot better long-term that way. That's what we decided, right? So that's what's happening. Decision made."

"Because of Vaughan?" he asked, his back teeth grinding.

"Vaughan has nothing to do with this. Because of us having a baby. Because of you and me and this crappy cycle we've got going on where I get my hopes up and then you run away or hide behind

the *friends* thing. It's completely doing my head in. It's not healthy."
I set my hands against his chest and pushed him back a step. "You
know, you pretend to be this easy come, easy go, laid-back kind
of guy. No ties or commitment, just living the rock 'n' roll lifestyle
to the limit and all that. And hey, that's just awesome, Ben. Good
for you. But if that's who you want to be, then don't go making a
separate set of rules for me. Because that's as hypocritical as fuck."

Whoops. Another dollar for the swear jar.

His jaw shifted angrily. Or his beard did. Whatever.

"Good night." The elevator doors slid open and I slid out, walking so fast I was damn near running. Time to get my stuff packed.
If there wasn't a spare room, I'd share with Anne and Mal for the
night, make other arrangements in the morning. Man, I was so
tired. Could have sworn my limbs weighed more than a mountain.
If I was glowing, it sure as hell didn't feel like it at this time of
night.

"I never wanted to be in a relationship," he yelled from back
down the shiny hotel hallway.

"Congratulations. You're not." I gave him the bird too, because
the bird was not swearing.

"Lizzy! Fuck. Wait."

I slid my key through the door lock and hustled my ass on in.
Not locking him out, though it was tempting. But hell, one of us
needed to be the adult. I charged on through the living room and
into my room, grabbing a suitcase from out of the closet. It was
already over half full. When you only ever stopped for two nights
at a time, there never seemed much point in unpacking. A few items
were hung up—a coat and a couple of dresses. The rest had gone
to the laundry service. There was just my makeup and junk in the
en suite, a couple of pairs of shoes strewn on the floor, and I was
good to go. Vacating the premises, ahoy!

"You're leaving," he said, standing in the bedroom doorway.

"Yep."

"Liz . . ."

"Hmm?" I turned, waiting for whatever nonsense he'd try to sell me on next. The big man just stood there, though, face set in harsh lines.

And he had nothing.

"Probably for the best," I said. "I'm not sure there's anything either of us could say right now that would help. Let's take some time to calm down and talk about it tomorrow, okay?" Yeah. Toothbrush, hairbrushes, and all that crap got thrown into my toiletries bag, which was then shoved into the corner of the suitcase. Next went my Converse, Birks, and fancy sandals with a heel. Then everything out of the cabinet. "You know, I think if we have our own space we might actually be able to give the being friends thing a good shot."

No comment.

Over went the top of the suitcase and I started zipping it up. Better call someone up to help me carry it, since I doubted Ben was in the mood to be helpful. If I'd been warned once about lifting heavy objects "in my condition," I'd been warned a hundred times. I'd mosey on down to reception and—

Ben's hand slipped around to cup my jaw, his lips pressing firmly against mine. My mouth had been partially open already; no big deal for him to slide his tongue in and rub it against mine. He kissed me determinedly, taking me over. Christ, I could feel that down in my toes. They curled up tight, along with my eager insides. The edges of his beard brushed against my face and his other hand grabbed my ass, pulling me in tight against him. Already the man was thickening, getting hard. It felt so superlatively, unbelievably good. All of it.

And wrong.

"W-what are you doing?"

His reply was the lash of his hot, wet tongue against the side of my neck. Every nerve-ending in the vicinity went up in flames, while I went up on my toes, leaning into him, getting closer. No. Bad me. This wasn't what we were supposed to be doing at all.

"Oh god. Maybe we should talk now."

The man's hands, they were so clever. Beneath the skirt of my jersey and up and into the back of my panties before I had a clue where they were even heading. Strong fingers kneaded my butt cheeks while his teeth sank into the base of my neck. He groaned as my breath stuttered, my lungs contracting sharply.

"I'm supposed to be going."

If I could just keep my legs shut I might yet win this battle. It seemed an insurmountable task, given the array of his arsenal. The size of his artillery. One hand dived down further, stroking between my legs, while the other held the back of my head. I was helpless, the battle lost. God, I sucked. All right, so I was too turned on to think straight and my hormones were in open rebellion. Any attempt at coherent, rational thought was mercilessly slain upon the altar of my lust. Damn it.

"B-Ben."

In a move proving he was indeed one of the greats of rock 'n' roll, he kicked my suitcase clear off the queen bed with one big, black boot while dipping me back into his waiting arm, while moving his hand around to the front of my panties to apply pressure to my clit in the most amazing way. Holy hell. Stars danced before my eyes, I was so ready to light up for him. Vegas had nothing on me.

Someone really needed to give him an award, though. Something to do with multitasking and hot sex moves and shit. Shoot.

My back hit the mattress and he climbed over me, situating himself between my legs. Fuck he was gorgeous. The strong, clean lines of his cheekbones and the moody-ass gonna-get-me-laid darkness of his eyes. I couldn't catch my breath, but it didn't matter. My breasts straining against his chest was its own reward. It was entirely possible I currently owned the hardest, happiest nipples in all of creation. They were so sensitive.

Who said pregnancy isn't fun?

He covered my mouth with his, kissing me stupid once more. Man, he tasted good. All the while he kept his weight on one elbow, putting no pressure on my belly. The things he could do with his free hand were delightful—running it up and down the outside of my thigh, slipping it up, up beneath my shirt to trace my ribs. But wait . . . I couldn't give up this easy. It was shameful. I'd been in the middle of making a point and everything.

"I was leaving. I was."

No answer from him. Instead, his hard cock rubbed back and forth between my legs, making my back bow. One pair of jeans and one pair of panties too many. That was the problem right there.

I gasped. "I don't think friends that are just friends are meant to do this."

Without comment he sat up, grabbing the back of his button-down shirt and pulling it off over his head. His chest was so pretty. So hard and big and stuff, it made my IQ drop to my shoe size. Everything about him did. The bearded sex machine turned me into a stuttering fool. Sad but true.

"Ben, I can't just spread for you the minute you decide you want some."

Sitting back on his heels, he grabbed both of my legs, holding them up against him. Off went my shoes, followed fast by my panties.

"Wait."

He didn't.

"Maybe I'm not interested in having sex with you." A blatant lie. But I was getting desperate for some kind of communication from him of the nonphysical sort. "Did you think of that?"

His gaze on mine, he held my underwear up to his nose.

"Oh my god, do not sniff my panties. Ben!"

A slow grin spread across his face.

"That's terrible. You don't see me going around doing stuff like that, do you? No." On account of me not wearing any pants, they couldn't catch on fire. Lucky.

He threw the innocent, soaked scrap of material aside.

"Anyway, my vagina is out of control. That proves nothing."

He placed a soft kiss against one of my fat ankles, giving it a good looking over.

"And don't look at my ankles. You know how I feel about them." I tried to retrieve my limbs, but he held on tight, wrapping both arms around them, holding them to his hot chest. "Why are you doing this?"

Slowly, he started one-handed massaging my toes. Nice, but beside the point.

"Say something."

"You said there wasn't anything I could say that would fix things," he mumbled, his warm, wet mouth kissing the side of my foot, his beard ticklish in just the right way. "Figured I'd just show you why you should stay."

"Sex?"

"Seems to be what you want right now."

I snorted. "You started it."

The bastard smirked. "Tell me more about your pussy being out of control. This interests me."

"No." Me and my idiot mouth. "Nothing to tell."

The lethal combination of his soft, warm lips and sleek beard was doing me in. The heat and strength of his body. Every time he touched me, I could have sworn there were sparkles inside of my skin. Little lights burning me up in the sweetest possible way. How the hell was a girl supposed to compete against that? The man had sexual super-powers and I was just me, dysfunctional at the best of times.

"Why do you want me to stay?" I asked, voice ever so slightly pleading. I didn't even know what for. Fingers wrapped around my ankles, rubbing gently. "Because of the baby?"

"No," he said. "Because of everything."

" 'Everything' being . . ."

His forehead went all wrinkly. "I don't know. I meant what I said. I never wanted to be in a relationship. But then you never wanted to be having a baby so young. Guess we're both just going to have to figure it out as we go along."

"Um, no." I shut my eyes tight. "Ben, we've been here before. You think you want something with me but then it's all too much and you run. And it's okay. It's okay for you to just concentrate on your music and living free and easy and to not want to be in a per-manent relationship. What's not okay is for you to get my hopes up again, because honestly the comedown really sucks."

And that was my professional psychology student opinion, right there.

"Liz."

"No. I can't do this again."

He fell silent.

Too much emotion ran through me, my body at odds with my sensibilities. Damn, this was hard. I drew back from him and started crawling off the bed. A nice long cry in a hot shower, that's what I needed. Plus to get off. This hotel had an excellent showerhead and I'd be making the most of it, yessiree. And maybe some ice cream too. It really was an excellent remedy for a broken heart.

"Wait." A strong arm stopped me, drawing me back against his body. I just went. The man had the muscles to put me where he wanted—he'd already demonstrated it on numerous occasions. Me liking being in his arms would just have to be ignored.

"Why?" I cried. "C'mon, Ben. Give me a legitimate reason. Why should I stay?"

"Because of this." One oversize hand splayed across my belly, his tanned skin a stark contrast to my own. "Because of us. We made a baby, Liz. You and me."

"Ben . . ."

"Shh. Relax. Give me a minute here."

Easy for him to say; he wasn't having yet another emotional breakdown. Fire-trucking hormones. That I wanted him so bad didn't help at all. Sexual frustration seemed to own me. But the risk of emotional damage was too damn high.

"Didn't realize you'd gotten so big." His fingers gently stroked my bump. "It's only been a week."

"Yeah," I sniffled. "I kind of popped."

His nose nuzzled my neck, lips placing gentle kisses. "Have you ever seen anything more amazing in your life? Our baby growing inside of you."

I nodded, covering his hand with my own. "I know."

"Then share it with me. I want to see you every day. I want to know how you two are doing, and be a part of things." Despite his soothing words, I couldn't help but tense up in his arms. "You're beautiful. Relax."

"You try relaxing with a huge boner rubbing against your back. I'm trying to break up with you—not that we're even together—and your penis is not helping."

Next came soft laughter, but he made no move to remove said hard-on from the area surrounding my buttocks.

"You're going to have to get over being jealous," I said. "Eventually I'll meet someone else. You can't go caveman every time a guy speaks to me. Baby or no, you don't have the right, Ben."

"Then give me the right."

"So you can get scared and bolt? No."

"Shit. Look, I can't get over you, Liz. That's the problem." He rested his chin on my shoulder. "You're the only girl I want."

I stilled. Well, apart from the frown. "It this about your erectile issue? Because you don't seem to be having much of a problem right now."

"I don't have an erectile issue. I have a *you* issue. My dick thinks you own it, apparently. But there's more to it than that. . . ."

"Cocks don't think. We went over that."

"We were wrong."

"Huh. So I have a pet penis. Okay, keep talking." Curiosity had definitely gotten the better of me. "What more?"

Heat flooded the side of my neck as he pressed his face there. "Can't fucking stand the thought of someone else touching you."

I rolled my eyes. Such a Neanderthal. And while both were interesting points, neither constituted an occasion for any actual change from our status as friends.

"It's not just about the baby." He grunted.

"I'm not so sure about that," I said, resting my head against his. Foolish of me, but it felt nice, cozying up to him. Besides, he'd grabbed me first.

"It's the truth."

"Prove it."

"Prove it? How the fuck am I supposed to do that?"

"I don't know."

"Christ. All right. I only used Sasha . . ." The rest was a mumbled mess. His warm mouth pressed against my neck, smothering the words.

"What did you say?"

More mumbling.

"Ben, speak clearly."

With a groan, he raised his head, leaning around to look me in the eyes. "I only used Sasha to get over you. Knew you couldn't be just a casual thing, and Mal kept asking what had happened in Vegas, if I'd gone out with you or what. Then he started saying you were seeing someone and he thought you were bringing them to the party."

"What?" I asked, screwing up my nose.

"Yeah."

"Why the hell would he do that?"

"Why do you think?"

"God that man is such a shit stirrer." Another coin for the swear jar. It'd be funding Bean's college education and first home at this rate. A gap year touring Europe, perhaps.

"Always has been, always will be. So I invited Sasha to that dinner to get him off my back. And I was missing you, and you wouldn't talk to me, and I thought you were bringing someone else."

I just shook my head.

"I don't know if it was just me trying to make you jealous or if a part of it was me trying to move on or what. She was a cool woman."

My chin jerked up. "You thought she was cool?"

"You didn't?"

"I didn't think she was that cool," I said in a voice without a trace of snobbery. Not even the merest hint.

"No?"

"I'm just saying, I thought she was a little bit know-it-all, really. Arrogant. And her hair was dumb. So . . . blue." Her hair was impossibly cool, but no way was I admitting to that.

The silence behind me was deafening.

"What?"

"Nothing," he said in a voice that implied anything but.

"Oh shut up." I sighed. "Fine, she was somewhat cool." At some point I'd started playing with his fingers, twining them with mine, touching and toying with them. This was the problem with Ben. For me, being intimate with him came far too easily.

"Anyway," he said. "That was all before I knew about the baby."

"That was a deeply crappy and immature thing to do to her."

"Yeah," he said solemnly.

"No wonder she was mad."

A nod.

Fingers caressed the side of my face tenderly.

"I'd have gone medieval on your man bits, if I was her," I said.

His brows descended in a fierce look.

I just shrugged. Reap what you sow, baby.

"Had to pay her off to keep quiet about you. Adrian and the lawyers sorted it out."

"No! The bitch."

"Hmm."

I huffed out a breath. "So we've established that we make each other behave like we're back in middle school. What does that prove?"

"That we need to figure this thing out between us."

"I thought that's what we've been trying to do."

A hand cupped my jaw. "I don't mean fight it. I'm done fighting it. I mean go slow and figure this thing out."

My forehead was a mass of wrinkles, I could feel it. I doubt my heart was much better.

"Sweetheart?"

"I don't trust you, Ben. I'm sorry. I wish I could feel differently. But I keep trying to do this with you, and thinking you want it too, and . . ."

"And I keep fucking it up."

"Yes."

I thought he'd let me go, run off back to the party to lick his wounds—or someone else maybe. But he didn't. Instead he settled on the bed with his back to the headboard, taking me with him, arranging me in his lap. I didn't fight him.

"Are you angry?" I asked, mystified.

"How do they say . . ." He made a low noise that was pure damn sex of the vocal chords, I tell you. "Lizzy, when you say you don't trust me it makes me feel like I want to tear shit up and go ballistic."

"That's an understandable if somewhat violent response."

"But with our history, shit's complicated," he said, rubbing his mouth and bristly beard against the back of my neck, sending shivers down my spine. Oh wow yeah. I needed to wear my hair up all the time. That felt divine.

"And as you said, we're having a baby," he said.

"True."

"But I'm not running away this time. Say what you want. Shred me. I'm staying."

"You are?"

"Yeah." Capable hands separated my legs, hot skin soothing up my thighs. Christ, I loved it when he touched me. So damn much.

"What are you doing?" I asked, ever so slightly breathy.

"Nothing."

The backs of his fingers ran up my inner thighs, tracing a path with his knuckles. I nearly cried when he stopped short of my pussy and turned back.

"I do not believe you."

Neatly, he folded up my skirt, exposing it all. A sound of pure sex vibrated out of his chest, traveling through into my spine. "Fuck, Liz. Look at you. Love your pussy. Missed it."

"Mm." My shoulders tensed, rising higher. "Ben . . ."

"It's okay."

"This feels dangerous."

"No. This feels right," he murmured, teeth nipping at my ear. "You got my dick on a leash. Might as well have the rest of me."

"What does that mean?"

"Means I've given up getting over you and I'm focusing on getting into you instead."

"Neither of these statements are reassuring me, Ben." I leaned my head back, twisting to the side so I could see his face. Seemed sincere. But then, I'd made that mistake a time or two before. "Explain in non–rock 'n' roll speech please."

"And you said Sasha had an attitude." The corner of his lips twitched. "Means I'm going to get you to trust me again."

Me? I had nothing.

Staring at me all the while, he stuck two fingers in his mouth to wet them. Then he ever so slowly traced them back and forth over my labia, making me gasp. Everything down there spasmed in glee. Lord help me. If the man ever guessed to what degree he owned me, I'd be doomed.

"Fuck, sweetheart. You really are out of control. I've barely touched you."

"It's the baby hormones. They're psycho."

He smiled. That smile—I didn't trust it. But holy hell was it beautiful. My heart and my loins went into bloom. A rush of heat and emotion crashed through me. It was entirely possible I was in love with the bearded jerk, god help me. "You really want me to trust you?" I asked.

He drew slow circles around my clit before sliding the tip of a finger back and forth through me. The man slowly played with me. Pure, exquisite torture.

"Yeah," he said. "I really do."

"You're serious about this? Us?"

"I am." Still not breaking eye contact, he slid a finger into me. "You're very wet."

"Yeah. You know, it's kind of hard to focus on relationship talk when you're fingering me."

"We can talk all you want later. Promise."

"'kay." I made a pitiful noise in my throat, my muscles tightening on his thick digit. My own hands were claws, digging into his rock-hard, jean-clad thighs.

"I mean, you got hot for me in Vegas. But this . . . Sweetheart, Christ, this is fucking awesome."

"I masturbate. A lot."

"Not anymore," he rumbled. "Looking after you is my job. Trust me, Lizzy. I won't let you down again."

The finger inside me sought a sweet spot and proceeded to massage it with expert ease. Just that simply, he turned me inside out. It was a mercy my nipples didn't poke holes through the fabric of my shirt. They sure as hell felt hard enough. My shoulders pushed back against his solid chest as the side of his thumb brushed back and forth across my clit. Lightning and shooting stars and all of the good stuff. The whole world went to white.

I throttled the scream in my throat. Or at least part of it. Oh boy and damn. I lay panting in his lap, my skin oversensitized, sweat beading on my forehead and back. How perfect.

He gently cupped my pussy with his hand. "I can still feel you throbbing."

I stretched and yawned, slowly coming back down to earth. All of the happy was mine.

"You really needed that."

"Yeah." I turned, cuddling against his chest. If I stayed sort of on my side, the bump was happy enough. And what a nice, big, comfortable man he was. Especially helpful when it came to orgasms too. His fingers were far superior to my own, I had to say.

"You going to sleep on me now?" he asked, incredulous.

I nodded, closing my eyes. Damn he smelled good. They should bottle his sweat. I'd buy it in bulk. Meanwhile his hard-on continued to press into my hip. Bad luck, bud. I was down and out for the count. No could do.

"You wanted to go slow," I said.

Disgruntled rumbling came from beneath me.

"You really want to be my boyfriend?" I asked, half opening one eye.

A hand smoothed down the fabric of my skirt and he shuffled us down the bed a little, getting comfortable.

"Boyfriend? Huh." His rough, deep voice rolled through me, lulling me further toward sleep. "Never been anyone's boyfriend before."

"No?"

"No."

Arms encircled me, the bristle of his beard brushing against my forehead as he settled back against the cushions.

"Your boyfriend," he mused.

"It's a big decision. You should take your time, think about it. Let me know when you're ready to talk about it again."

His forehead creased. "You sure are playing it cool."

And about time, frankly. Lord knows, chasing after the man hadn't gotten me anywhere. A girl could only beat her brains against a brick wall for so long before it was time to rethink things.

I shrugged and slid my hand up his side, getting closer. His skin was so smooth, his smattering of chest hair delightful to the touch. Everything about him was delightful really. In all likelihood, even his toenails would thrill me. Didn't mean I'd be making it too easy on him.

"Liz?"

"Hmm?"

"This boyfriend position . . . it come with perks?"

"Maybe."

"Do I get to sleep with you and shower with you?"

"Yes."

He made a happy noise. "What about touching? Do I get to feel you up when I like?"

"Within reason."

"Got to say, sweetheart, your body was always gorgeous. But it's seriously off-the-fucking-charts beautiful right now."

"Really?" I asked, raising my head to give him a curious look. "Mostly I just feel leaky and lumpy."

A large hand cupped an ass cheek, rubbing. "Fuck no. You're all soft curves and you're carrying my baby. Never thought that'd be a big turn-on—never thought about it at all. But, sweetheart, it is."

"Huh."

"What else is involved in this boyfriend shit?" he asked, his voice rumbling through his chest and into my ear.

"'This boyfriend shit'? Seriously?"

"Sorry. You know what I mean." He gave me a squeeze. "What else? C'mon."

"All right. Let me think." I trailed my fingers through his beard, sliding them back and forth through the soft whiskers. I could lie on him all night, happily, listening to his heart beating strong and steady within his chest. Feel the rhythmic rise and fall of his ribs with each breath. To lie there and know that this special man was alive and chose to be with me, here, right now. That sounded just like heaven.

"You know, I'm really not sure myself," I said in a quiet voice. "I've never had an official boyfriend before. But we have to be there for each other, and we have to talk. I don't see how it could work any other way."

"Hmm."

"And obviously, we'd be exclusive."

A grunt.

"If you decide it's what you want, then we take it slow and figure it out as we go, I guess."

"Yeah." He rubbed the heel of his hand gently up and down my back, smoothing out the tension.

"Ben, I don't want to take your freedom. I just want a place in your world. An important one."

He craned his neck, tipping my chin up to make me look at him at the same time. "Sweetheart, you've been important since day one. Only girl I kept coming back to. Didn't matter how far I ran, I couldn't get you off my mind. Never been this way about another woman."

"No?"

"No."

Fingers rubbed at my neck, working out the kinks. Silence fell between us for a while.

"I want to be your boyfriend, Liz."

I couldn't have held back the smile if I'd tried. "I'd like that."

He brushed the hair back from my face, gazing down at me. "Okay."

"Okay."

CHAPTER TEN

I slept well that night. Tattooed, bearded, bass-playing males easily outdid hotel pillows in terms of comfort. We slept in our underwear because of the whole taking it slow thing. I'd never spent the whole night with a man before, sexually active or no. But what could have been awkward, Ben made right. He fit himself into my life just like he belonged there.

My dreams were suitably pervy, though that was nothing new. The waking up with a man's head between my thighs, however, was a rather dramatic and welcome change. A hot, wet tongue dragged through the lips of my sex, startling the hell out of me. My hips bucked, eyes were suddenly wide open.

"Ben. What are you doing?" I gasped, the brain still in sleep mode.

"Licking my girlfriend's pussy," he said. "Perks, remember?"

Hands held my legs spread open, fingers digging into the flesh of my thighs. Then he did it again, the licking thing. I groaned and twisted, trying to get away, but not really, because holy shit. Nirvana.

"Go you," I happy-sighed.

The feeling of a man's beard brushing against your private parts cannot be adequately explained in words. It's a tactile delight. Soft and ticklish and amazing in all the ways. My muscles tensed, heels digging into the mattress. Where my panties had gotten to I had no idea. Nor any interest. What my boyfriend was up to, however, concerned me deeply. His tongue flicked back and forth over my clit, then his lips sucked at my labia. The man's oral skills were off the chart. Such attention to detail. And the enthusiasm—the man was starving and I was his meal. I shoved my pussy into his face, needing and getting everything he was giving.

But the raw energy between my hips, low in my spine—there wasn't enough me to contain it. The glorious sensation built and built, charging my whole being, lighting up my limbs. I came hard, calling his name. Pleasure tore me in two, my mind circling high. I was everything and nothing. Just floating around in the ether, enjoying the high.

But he wasn't finished.

He climbed up my body, shoving his boxer briefs down with a hand. Once, twice, three times he pumped his hard cock, spilling his hot seed on my breasts and belly. His forehead pressed against mine, warm breath on my lips.

"Hey," I mumbled, still trying to find my breath.

He kissed me, lips covering mine, tongue diving in. The rich taste filled my mouth as his fingers stroked over my belly, rubbing his cum into my skin.

"Morning," he whispered, still suspended above me on one elbow. Those perfect cheekbones, the wet curves of his lips, called to my fingers. I could happily touch him all day.

"Ben."

"Hmm?" Another kiss, this one softer, sweeter.

I lay beneath him, decimated. So many things I could say, that I wanted to say. But *slow* was the key word here. What he did to my heart and mind couldn't be described. The way he filled my heart to overflowing scared the crap out of me. "Good morning."

"No touching yourself," he ordered in a low, gruff voice. "Getting you off is my job now. You need me, call. Get to you as soon as I can, okay?"

"Uh-huh."

He kissed me some more, making my head spin. "Things moving slow enough for you?"

"Sure."

He smiled, and good god, all I could do was stare. Had there ever been a more beautiful man in existence? I think not. His focus on me was complete, making for such a heady feeling. Dark eyes never strayed from my face, as if he was memorizing me.

"We're doing good, Liz." His hand covered my bump, lips brushing over my cheek.

"Yeah." I had no words. Not when he was like this.

The edge of his lips picked up some. "C'mon. Shower time."

I was still in the bathroom, fixing my hair and applying some concealer and mascara to up my glow factor, when I heard Ben and Sam chatting in the living room. No way did I mean to listen in. It just sort of happened.

"With Mal the way he is, the band's already on tenterhooks," said Ben. "I'm just not sure we should add her to the mix."

Wait, were they talking about me? But I was basically already living and touring with everyone. That made no sense.

"I love Martha, but we all know what she's like," Ben continued.

"Things are more stable now. It might be good for her," said Sam. "Besides, she's not going to get her shit together out there on her own, acting like the party queen of New York and burning through money."

"I don't know."

Sam made a *humph* sound. "She still makes the papers now and then. From a security perspective, it'd be easier having everyone in the same orbit, if not under one roof. News will hit about the pregnancies eventually. Be good to keep everyone close. That's my only point."

"Sure your concern about Martha isn't more personal than that?"

"Don't know what you're talking about, Mr. Nicholson."

I wandered in, curious, interrupting the very manly staring competition under way. "Hi, guys. Problem?"

Ben shook his head. "What are sisters for if not to fuck with your life now and then, right?"

"Just think about it." Sam clapped him on the shoulder, heading for the door. "Later, Miss Rollins."

"Bye." I turned to my boyfriend, gave his T-shirt an affectionate tug, drawing him in closer for a kiss. "Anything we need to talk about?"

"No." He gave me a gentle smile and an even gentler kiss. Followed by a hearty slap on the ass. "Go do your girl thing. I'm meeting Jim for a run."

I made a swipe at his butt but missed by about a mile. "Yeah, you better run, buddy."

He laughed all the way out the door. I held the dumb smile on my face for even longer.

"I guess you're wondering why I called you all here today," began Lena, a bottle of spring water balanced on her belly. Neat trick.

It was around midday. All four of us, Lena, Evelyn, Anne, and I, sat gathered in Lena and Jimmy's luxurious suite, just hanging out. A range of swanky sandwiches, pastries, fruits, and cheeses were laid out on the coffee table before us. No cake pops, but there were macaroons and madeleines, which you have to admit are almost as good.

Ev wiped a stray bread crumb from the corner of her mouth. "I thought we were just having lunch."

"She wouldn't have made that announcement if we were just having lunch," said Anne, stirring extra sugar into a cup of sweet tea.

"True."

Lena sat in a damask lounge chair, peering out through her groovy horn-rim glasses at each of us in turn. The woman was a good month ahead of my sixteen weeks. God help me when I got that big. Ben could just roll me places.

Pregnancy. So not natural.

"No, we are not here just to eat," she continued. "Though eat we will, and then some. What we are here to do is to meddle in Lizzy's life, because we love and care for her. Also, because being on tour gets boring after a while so I figured what the hell."

"Oh good." I took another sip of my decaf—read warm, beige milk.

"Did you notice she has a hickey on her shoulder?" asked Ev, wiggling her eyebrows.

"Nothing to see here." I pulled up my shirt collar. "Move along please."

"She does seem especially glowy this morning." Awesome. Even my own sister was getting in on the act. No loyalty.

"I noticed that." Lena tugged at a stray thread on the hem of her maternity Stage Dive T-shirt. It had to be pirated, what with it proudly proclaiming in fancy lettering, JIMMY FERRIS, I'D TAP THAT. I couldn't imagine the man ever okaying the design in this lifetime. "And get this. When Ben stopped by to grab Jim to go work out earlier, the bearded dude was one happy, happy boy."

My brows descended. "No comment."

"About time," sighed Ev. "He's been so damn grumpy lately."

"Not anymore he isn't. She's got that boy walking on the sunshine."

"Thinking she used pussy magic on him?" asked Ev, eyeing me up in a dreadfully lewd fashion.

"That's my guess."

"You're not funny," I said, mostly unsmiling. "Anne, make them stop."

My sister tucked her bright-red hair neatly behind her ears and shook her head sadly. "Ah, hon. No can do. You're part of Stage Dive family now. Inner circle and all that. Best get used to it."

"Ben and I aren't married. We're not even together, exactly."

"Expound on 'exactly,'" said Anne, learning forward in her seat. "I haven't heard what happened last night after you two left the party to go talk."

"We talked. Nothing else to tell." Nothing else I was prepared to tell. The many changes were still too fresh. I hadn't quite turned all of the information over enough times in my head to make sense of it. Assuming I would in fact be able to make sense of it.

I was dubious.

My words were met with a chorus of boos and even some hissing. One individual who will remain unnamed (Lena) even went so far as to lob a Danish at my head. Pastries as projectiles . . . I never. Luckily I caught it before it could make contact. Cherry, yum.

"Okay, okay! Simmer down." Good lawd, these ladies. And I use the term *ladies* loosely. "The truth is I don't really know what's going on with us."

"Well, what do you think is going on with you two?" asked Anne, stealing half of my dessert. Girl was just lucky I loved her.

"Good question. Way I figure, there are several options." I paused to nibble. Oh such golden buttery flaky evil goodness—my third for the day. Seemed my self-control had gone weak in all sorts of interesting areas. I'd better watch it or my ass would be twice the size of my belly. On the other hand, golden buttery flaky evil goodness made me so-o-o happy, and really, isn't happiness what life is all about?

Bet they'd taste awesome with bacon on top.

"Continue," said Ev, clapping her hands together in a queenly fashion. "Tell us everything."

"Fine. One, I might be using him for sex," I confessed, a pronouncement met by several oohs and ahhs, and several sly grins. "I can't help it. The baby hormones have turned me into some sort of nympho and he's so beautiful and hot and I would like to point out that he started it. I did not go after him this time. And honestly, you have no idea how good that beard feels. The sensation of all that silky, bristly hair rubbing against your inner thighs and—"

"Whoa!" Anne covered her ears. "Stop."

"Sorry."

"Man. Wish that whole nympho thing had happened to me," said Lena. "I just got even more obsessed with pie. So unfair."

"Hmm."

"Lucky Jim's a breast man. He's like a kid at Christmas, playing with these cantaloupes. Can't keep his hands off them."

"They are damn impressive," I said, wiping my hands on a napkin. "Mine are annoying the hell out of me. I don't even usually bother with a bra, now that I suddenly have these apple-sized things hanging around. Not cool."

"What's option two in the you-and-Ben story?" asked Ev.

"Oh. Well, two, we might be going slow and trying to be boyfriend-girlfriend, but I don't know. He has a bad habit of changing his mind when it comes to me." I stared off into space, contemplating much but achieving little to no resolution. "Three, at the end of the day we're going to be parents, and that has to come first, whatever happens. So obviously, by putting this at three, I've been listing things in ascending order or something. Anyway, if he smashes my heart to smithereens yet again, we might well have a problem. Therefore, my question—seeing as you've all insisted on coming this far with me—is should I even be attempting anything beyond friendship with this man?"

"He smashed your heart to smithereens?" Ev's eyes got glossy. "That's terrible."

"I had . . . I have a lot of feelings for him. Each time he chose to not take things further with me, it hurt." I slumped back in my chair, relaxing, giving my full belly a chance to get with the digesting. "Ugh, boys suck. Such is life. What can you do?"

"Spoken like a true psychology student," said Ev with a smile.

"Thank you."

The blonde gave her ponytail a tug. A cute nervous trait. "I'm sorry you got hurt. I should probably never have given you his number. I knew he didn't date."

"Don't," I chided her. "I was a little obsessed with him, truth be told. One way or another I would have seen him again. He just gets to me. I didn't even think I had a type, but somehow he's it, from top to toe."

"He still should have thought of what he wanted, long before he came near you with his sperm." Anne's eyes narrowed in that deadly familiar way.

"Do you love him?" asked Lena, head tipping to the side.

I stared at the ceiling, my mind in a whirl. "Ah, like I said, I have feelings for him."

"Are those feelings love?"

"I don't want to answer that question."

"No?" Ev set her cup back on the table, setting her elbows on her knees.

I was surrounded. Encircled by well-meaning friends. Now I got it, why Anne was so taken with these girls. They were authentic, kind, and funny. And while it was nice, knowing their questions came from concern, I squirmed in my seat at the thought of airing mine and Ben's slightly soiled if not completely rank and feral laundry. I barely had a handle on the situation between us in my head, and by "barely" I mean not really at all.

"Because I'm not ready," I told the crystal chandelier hanging above our heads. Sunlight reflected on the walls, prisms splitting the white light into small slices of rainbows. Beautiful.

"No need to rush," said Anne, grabbing for my hand. "Slow."

"Slow," I agreed.

The suite's door pushed open and Jimmy and Ben strode in, both dripping sweat. Basketball shorts hung low on Ben's hips. He'd removed his T-shirt and was using it to mop his face.

"Hi, babe." Lena held a hand up and Jimmy grabbed it, leaning over the back of her chair to kiss her cheek.

"Cute T-shirt. How're my girls doing?" he asked, sliding a hand down to cover her belly.

"We're all good. Taking it easy, just like the doctor ordered."

"Girls?" Ev's eyes lit up like twin full moons.

"Oops. Secret's out," laughed Lena.

"A baby girl! That's so exciting."

No response from Lena, on account of her being busy trading spit with Jim. Whoa, they were really going for it. I wasn't so certain her obsession with pie was the only hormone enhancement.

"Hey." Ben kneeled beside my chair, sweaty shirt slung over one thick shoulder. His smile was all for me. It melted my insides, turning me to mush. What terrible power he had over me. The man should be ashamed of himself.

"Hi." I smiled. "Good workout?"

"Yeah, Dave even tagged along. It was fun."

Like a dinner bell had been rung, Ev jumped to her feet. Pavlov's dogs couldn't have been better trained. "Which means my hot husband's in the shower. Later guys."

And she was gone.

"Um, yeah. Meeting adjourned," Lena managed between kisses.

With a final evil-eyed look at my new boyfriend, Anne likewise got to her feet. "I should go see what mine's up to. Leaving him alone for long periods of time is dangerous. See you all on the flight to New York."

"Later." I waved.

"Am I going to have to let your sister take a swing at me too?" Ben grumbled in a gravelly voice.

"She'll come around."

"Thought letting Mal have his shots sorted all of this out."

"She worries about me." I tucked his long fringe aside, reveling in the freedom to touch as I liked. Sweaty or not, I'd take him and then some. "Give it time."

A scowl from the man.

"What? No." Jimmy barked tersely from the other side of the lounge chair.

"Just a little one," said Lena, stroking his face.

"I'm not growing a fucking beard. They itch."

"But—"

"Where the hell is this coming from, anyway?" Jimmy pierced me with a cranky look. "You been talking up beards or something?"

I gave him my best innocent face.

The broody lead singer shook his head. "You girls shouldn't be talking sex, for fuck's sake. We're all living on top of each other as it is."

"Liz just happened to mention the enhanced benefits of oral," said Lena, her face the picture of serenity. "You want me to be happy, don't you?"

"I keep you plenty happy," said Jim, rubbing the back of her neck.

"Of course you do, babe. I just thought you might want to think about growing one. You know, just to try something different."

Smirk in place, Ben took up the cause. Sort of. "Takes a real man to grow a beard. You're just not there yet, Jim. Don't feel bad."

"Go fuck yourself, sunshine." Jimmy hid a smile. "Both of you, out. I apparently have to prove my oral prowess to my girl, yet again."

"Sorry. My bad," said Lena, looking not the least bit sorry.

Ben snickered, rising to his feet, drawing me up by my hand on the way. Holding hands was nice. What was especially nice was how he didn't let go. Out we went, the suite's door locked soundly behind us.

"What've you been saying?" he asked, heading toward our own room. "Thought sex shit was private."

"Sorry. Girl talk. I got carried away."

"Hmm." His brows became one unhappy line.

"Are you really upset?" I asked, more than a smidgen worried. Relationships were so tricky. Me and my mouth needed to take more care and do no expounding on him or his facial hair's sexy-times goodness.

"Nuh. Worth it to see the pissed off look on Jim's face." He chuckled.

"Oh good."

"We've got two hours before the flight," he said, dark eyes looking me over. "Plenty of time for some serious slow."

My pulse took up residence between my thighs. The man had my pussy's number and he used it with zero hesitation. Boyfriend-wise he was all over the sex, and I have to say, I really did respect him for that.

"Figure we've got some more getting to know each other to do," he said.

"You do, huh?"

He swiped the key through the lock, pushing open the door. "I gave you a hand job last night and my mouth this morning. If slow means we're doing no penetration for a while, then sweetheart, I need you to take mercy on me. I'm in desperate need of your fist wrapped around my cock."

"I'd like that."

"Trust me, I've been thinking about it all day. You sitting naked on my lap, jerking me off while I play with your gorgeous, sensitive tits. Bet I can make you come just from that. What do you say we do some experimenting and find out?"

My body buzzed, my breathing speeding. I swear I nearly came just from listening to him talking dirty. The man had hidden talents. "Okay."

"That's my girl. Who knows, maybe you could even write a paper on it."

I burst out laughing. "I don't know about that."

He grinned down at me, already lifting my oversize T-shirt off over my head.

"Your pants don't fit?" he asked, inspecting the hairband looped through my jeans' buttonhole. The sole means by which I could keep them up, since the zipper was completely out. And these were my loose low-cuts.

"Not much fits since I popped."

"You need some maternity gear like Lena. Jim said she found some real cute shit," he said. "You're spilling out of the bra too. Not that I don't like the look, but that can't be good."

"You and Jim talk about girls' clothes?"

He gave me a dour look. "Jim was just giving me some hints, what with Lena being further along than you and everything."

"The clothes aren't an issue. I can make do for a little while longer."

"You don't need to 'make do for a little while longer.' I want you comfortable."

"Weren't we going to have sex?" I asked, crossing my arms over my bountiful boobs and checking out the room. For some reason I just didn't feel like looking at him right then.

"Have you touched that money I put in your account?"

"Not yet. I haven't needed to."

"Clearly you need to." He crossed his arms too. No fair—his were so much bigger than mine. The fact that they were muscular and covered in tattoos pleased me just then. To be fair, Ben didn't seem so happy himself. "What's going on here, Liz?"

"Nothing. Which is the problem. I thought we were fooling around."

He just looked at me.

"What?" I asked.

A long-suffering sigh. Then his fingers dealt with the band on my pants in less than two seconds, the denim pooling at my feet.

"Up," he ordered, lifting me off the ground.

At last, sex. I wrapped my legs and arms around him, refinding my happy. "Were you really thinking about me all day?"

"Yeah, I was. And you're sure as shit on my mind now." Lines covered his high forehead. "So tell me, what's this bullshit about you not touching that money? It's yours for buying what you need, and clearly you need stuff."

"It's for Bean."

"It's for both of you."

"I don't like taking your money."

A grunt of disapproval. "You didn't take it, I gave it to you."

"It feels the same."

"Fine. Okay." His hands cupped my ass, fingers massaging. "I don't want you feeling weird about this. And relationships are about compromise, right?"

"Ri-i-ght." Suspicion was my middle name.

"Tomorrow we go shopping and put all the shit you need on my card."

"That's not compromise!"

"You don't like touching that money I put in your account, so don't. In fact, you don't have to touch any of my money at all. I'll deal with it."

"Ben."

"Liz. Fact is, you're probably never going to have the kind of money I've got. Since the band started earning, pretty much all I've done is invest it. I'm not like Jim with the flashy suits or Mal with the massive beach house and parties. I don't need much, live pretty simply. Drive the same old truck. I've got one expense, but it's under control." Dark eyes drew me in. "You've made your point. There's nothing in me thinking you're into me for the money, okay? Now, I'm not having this discussion with you every time you need something. You and Bean are mine, and I look after what's mine."

I took a deep breath.

"We good?" he asked.

"I'll try."

"Do more than try. Rely on me. It's what I'm here for."

"That was a really sweet thing to say." My eyes misted up. Crazy-ass hormones. "I guess because I didn't grow up with much it just . . . it feels weird even having it there but not having worked for it. Like I stole it or something."

"Sweetheart, you didn't steal the money. You stole me. The money comes with me. Okay?"

"Okay." A tear trickled down my cheek. "I really like you, Ben. So damn much."

"Christ, what are you crying for? Come here, give me that mouth."

I did as told. After that, there was more coming than crying that day.

CHAPTER ELEVEN

Ben was gone again when I woke up the next morning, in New York. Due to the three scheduled concerts, we'd be in the city for nearly a week. The thing about being on tour was the endless possibilities for late mornings. I'd be part sloth by the time we got home. There'd been a band dinner the night before, despite Jimmy's complaint about everyone living on top of each other. I think his eternal bad mood secretly hid one hell of a soft inside. And yes, that was my professional opinion. I'd caught him stroking his chin while giving Lena a thoughtful look, more than once. Wouldn't surprise me if we had another beard on board in the near future.

With my sloth side in mind, I met Anne at the gym and we took up residence on a pair of exercise bikes for half an hour. The last gyno I saw a few days back had said light exercise was fine and dandy. Despite the occasional fetish for some weird food, and Lena's pastry party yesterday, I hadn't been indulging too much. Lots of salad and vegetables and the occasional trip to the dark side of decadent desserts. Total denial didn't suit me. At the end of the day, a healthy Bean and happy me was more important than the size of my butt.

The menfolk had gone off for a sound check, followed by various TV appearances before they hit the stage. Maternity shopping could fall by the wayside for a while, no biggie. A reporter from some big-name music magazine had taken to tagging along with the band, adding to the busy. Apparently an in-depth Stage Dive on Tour: The Real Story Behind the Public Facade article was in the making. Ben had seemed singularly unimpressed with the whole thing. But then, little moved him. He tended to take the bulk of things in his stride.

Which was great.

I could, I know, become rather strung out at times. Overthink things a little. Though with the gene pool Anne and I came from, it was probably a wonder we hadn't both become crazy cat ladies at the age of eighteen or something. Not that I was making excuses or suggesting that passing on blame for a person's personal behavior was a go. But for me, I think Ben's aura of calm and direct was a good thing. People with low self-esteem fear love. (Yep. Psychology degree rears its head again.) They doubt another person's ability to appreciate them, because they don't see the worth in themselves. I knew I deserved good things. Or at the very least, I wouldn't settle for less than a good thing.

In my rolled-down yoga pants, tank top slightly too small to contain the boobs and belly, and sweaty ponytail, I wandered back into our suite. Charcoal gray with features of slate this time. Awesome view of Manhattan. Very nice.

What was waiting inside for me, not so much.

"You are fucking kidding me," the stranger snarled, glaring at my baby belly.

I put a hand to my middle, stopping cold.

The woman was tall, brunette, slick beyond belief. Around thirty maybe. It was hard to tell, the way her sneer warped her model-like face and cherry red lips. Guess she was Ben's hookup in New York or something. How awkward. Also, how the hell had she gotten in here?

"And you would be?" I asked, with an edge to my voice.

"If you think you're getting a fucking dime out of him without a paternity test you are dreaming. And even then, he will fight you for custody."

Interesting. She seemed to believe she knew a hell of a lot about my boyfriend without actually knowing anything at all.

"Your name, please?" I asked.

"You're not the first little cunt to try this shit with one of them, and you sure as hell won't be the last." The woman, henceforth known as "the bitch," stared down at me from her stiletto-aided superior height. "Why Adrian didn't let me know I have no idea."

She was pals with Adrian? Not a good sign. Everything I'd seen and heard about the band's manager led me to believe he was one of the great douches of our time.

"Was Ben expecting you?" He sure as hell hadn't mentioned any visitors to me.

"I'm welcome here."

"Yeah? How did you get in, just out of interest?"

"Security knows me." A defiant flip of the hair. Christ, the woman was just like every mean girl I had ever encountered in high school. Amazing how some people just stopped developing beyond a certain age and got stuck.

Outside I did my best to look calm and cool, but inside I was one riled-up, unhappy camper. What the hell was she doing in our room? I guess Ben hadn't had a chance to break it off with this chick. Awesome. "Would you like a juice? I'm dying for a juice."

"Let me guess: you're some trailer trash little gold-digging whore who thought getting backstage and sucking one of the guys' dicks would get you somewhere."

Guess she didn't want a drink. But also, "You don't get pregnant by sucking dick. I'm not majoring in biology or anything, but pretty damn sure of that one."

The bitch just stared at me. Okay, so this was really not going well.

"Sorry," I said. Not sorry. "Didn't mean to interrupt your righteous rant. Please keep going. I honestly can't wait to hear what you have to say next."

Beautiful face scrunched up all cat-asslike, the woman actually had the audacity to stalk toward me, her hands curled into fists. The girl was out of her god damn head. My heart beat double time, every protective instinct in me rising up in alarm. Do violence on me and my Bean? I think not. Happily, the bar had a wide assortment of weapons at the ready. My personal favorite being a bottle of Chivas. I hefted it from one hand to the other. Three quarters full. It was weighty enough. No way was I playing nice with this piece of work.

"Martha," shouted Sam the security man, saving the day. Don't know when he'd snuck in, but I was mighty damn glad to see him. Given half the chance, I'd cover his craggy face in kisses. "Lay one fucking hand on her and your brother will never forgive you. I guarantee it."

The bitch froze.

"Hey, Sam. You want some Chivas?" I asked, offering the black-suited muscle man the bottle.

"Perfect. I'll take that, shall I, Miss Rollins?" He set the bottle back in its place among the fine selection of booze.

"So you're Ben's sister," I said, sucking down my apple juice once more. "Interesting."

Sam put his cell to his ear, eyes looking somewhat worried for once. The bulky bodyguard had never shown the slightest hint of fear before that I'd seen. What a turn for the bizarre my day had taken. And what an almighty bitch on wheels Ben's sister was. I sent up a quick prayer that those particular genes skipped a generation or three. No wonder Dave had traded up for Ev. Yikes.

"No way can he be swallowing whatever shit she's peddling," spat Martha.

"Mr. Nicholson," said Sam into the cell. "Your sister has come to visit."

"Let me talk to him." Martha stuck out her hand.

The look Sam gave her. Whoa. It even made Martha pause again. Whatever the history was, there, I bet it was one hell of a tale.

"Yes, Miss Rollins and her have met," reported Sam into the cell. "I just interrupted them exchanging words. The situation was somewhat volatile."

He quieted, listening to whatever Ben was saying. Then he turned to me. "Miss Rollins, he'd like to know if you're okay."

"Best of health, Sam. All good." I grinned. It'd been a good six or so years since I'd gotten into any fights. The bulk of us grew up and cut out such nonsense. If Martha was hell-bent on meeting my protective mothering instincts, however, then so be it.

Ben and Sam chatted on. Mostly the conversation on Sam's side consisted of yes, sirs and so on. "Sir," said Sam eventually, "I wonder if it might help resolve the situation if I had a quiet talk with your sister?" One final "Yes, sir" and he disconnected the call.

"Miss Rollins, would you be so good as to give Martha and I a moment alone?"

"Sure, Sam." I wandered into my bedroom, juice in hand. My ear was pressed up against the closed door within two one-hundredths of a second. Listening in to others' conversations is a terrible flaw, I know. No way, however, could I miss this.

"What the hell is wrong with you?" Sam began, his voice low and deadly. "I watched you fuck up shit with your brother and Dave for years. To the point where you had to be sent to the other side of the country so you'd stop causing trouble."

"Who is she?"

"She's the girl your brother thinks the fucking world of, and she's carrying his kid. He was planning on introducing you to her tomorrow, after giving you a heads-up about the situation," said Sam. "He was hoping you could help her get some maternity clothes, since you know the city."

The bitch scoffed. "You must be joking."

"No. See here's the sad thing. Your brother actually believes in you, thinks you've just made a couple of mistakes but that you've learned from them and have grown up. He doesn't get what a bitter, self-centered bitch you are."

Apparently she had nothing to say to this.

"But then, love fucks with how people see things. And your brother, he does love you, despite all the shit you've pulled over the years."

"I only want to protect him," she said, voice trembling with fury. "She's conning him, she's got to be. Ben's never been the type to settle down, you know that as well as I do. He's basically a professional millionaire slacker. He can barely see beyond the next jam session and bottle of beer."

"People change."

"Well, if he's so into her then no way is he thinking clearly. He's soft, Sam. He's not like us. We see the world as it really is. People are just out to use the guys, they always have been. And this girl is no different, I can tell just by looking at her."

Like hell she could.

Sam swore fervently. "You're right that we see things as they really are. What are you really afraid of, Martha? Worried that if your brother's actually in a relationship for once, got a woman and a kid to look after, he won't be inclined to keep propping up your expensive lifestyle?"

Silence.

"You're the user here, Martha. You always were."

"Fuck you. He's my brother."

"Yeah, your brother, not your bank account. You might want to learn the difference between the two one day."

No way. Holy hell. So that's the expense Ben talked about last night—keeping his sister in the lifestyle she'd apparently become accustomed to while living with the band. The only real family he had was bleeding him dry. What an utter bitch. No matter what he'd said, I highly doubted that anything involving this money-sucking leech was under control. Man, did I want another chance to swing a nice hard object at her pretty little skull. But it was his money and family, not mine. Therefore, none of my business really. Not that I stopped listening or dreaming of ways to make this woman disappear. Odd, caring for Bean and Ben really brought out the violent side of me. I swear I was a pacifist usually.

"That girl—"

"Loves your brother. And he loves her. I've never seen him like this with anyone, and she's good for him. He's spending less time alone, talking more, interacting. He's happy, Martha."

"Please. What the hell would you know? You're just the hired help."

"Don't be naive. If you were really that stupid we wouldn't even be having this conversation."

"He can't be that hung up on her. I didn't see a ring on her finger."

"It'll happen. They're just both too thrown by the baby to get around to making shit official yet," said Sam, the hammering of my heart nearly drowning him out. "You do one thing to cause trouble for them and I will make sure you are never accepted back among the band ever again. Your exclusion will be permanent."

"They're my family," she said in a horrified tone.

"Then start acting like it. Stop taking your brother's money and stand on your own two feet. Treat Lizzy and all of the women with some respect."

No reply.

"You're never getting Dave back. Those days are gone. Accept it. If you don't want to lose your brother too, you'll take my advice."

A moment later the front door slammed shut.

Then the knocking on my bedroom door slammed through my head. Ouches. Eavesdropping was a dangerous pastime.

"You can come out now, Miss Rollins."

I emerged, sipping the last of my juice, doing my best to appear blasé about all the drama-rama.

Amusement shone in Sam's eyes. "It's rude to listen in on other people's conversations."

"I don't know what you're talking about," I said, my nose sky-high.

"Of course you don't."

I lowered my nose back to where it belonged before I got a crick in my neck. "You really think I make him happy?"

The black-suited dude smiled. It was the smallest of things. There and gone in an instant. "You're the psychology student. Think about it. Each of the guys plays a role in the band. Not just an instrument, but a piece of the puzzle that makes them work. Dave's the sensitive poet, Mal's the loudmouth clown, and Jimmy's the brooding bastard. But Ben, he just goes on with the work, doing his thing. He's the only one I don't have to flip out about if he goes out in public. No interest in the limelight. The guy just pretty much blends, you know?"

"Yeah. I guess so."

"The other guys all bought mansions and shit, but not him. He just kept moving, living in hotels, playing his music." Sam looked at me down the length of his busted nose. Lord knows how many times it'd been broken. "You're giving him a place to belong, things to plan for, a life outside of all of this. Idiot didn't even realize he needed it, but he does. You're grounding him. No one else has given him that in a long time."

"You're kind of a philosopher, Sam."

"Nuh." Another millisecond smile. "I just use my eyes. It's what I'm paid to do."

I smiled back at him. Mine lasted longer.

"Martha comes back, call me. I don't think she'll cause any more trouble, but with her . . ."

"You got it."

Something woke me at around one in the morning. The light from an e-reader, strangely enough.

"Ben?" I yawned, rolling over to hit warm, hard flesh. "Hey. When did you get in?"

"Not long ago." He pushed my hair out of my face, proceeding to rub my neck. "Didn't mean to wake you. Want me to go read out in the living room?"

"No." I mooshed my face against his ribs, breathing in hot male. Divine. Even the soft, soap-scented hairs under his arms worked for me. As for the treasure trail leading from his belly button down into his boxer briefs . . . heaven. Impossible to keep my fingers away from it.

"You are such a cuddler." He chuckled.

"Is that a problem?" The thought that my limpetlike attachment to him might be annoying hadn't crossed my mind.

"Nope. I like having you close. Means I can keep you out of trouble."

I set my chin on his chest. "And what does that mean?"

"Heard about your showdown with Martha today. Were you really going to brain her with a bottle of twenty-five-year-old Scotch whisky?"

"If she'd come any closer to me and Bean with her hand raised, you betcha. Apparently I have a violent streak these days, which is a worry. But I'm not willing to stand by while me or mine get hurt."

"Hmm."

"I did not initiate it, Ben."

"I know." The corners of his gorgeous lips turned down. "I'm so fucking sorry that happened, sweetheart. Had no idea she'd react like that. I mean . . . I knew she'd think the worst. She's seen enough of the crap people have tried to pull with the band over the years. Just thought I'd be here to control shit."

I hid my face against his side. There weren't a great many polite ways to tell someone that their only real family was an asshole of the worst sort.

"Was hoping you and her would be friends," he added.

Not fire-trucking likely.

"What were you reading?" I asked, taking the safer option.

"Jim gave it to me. Loaded it up with baby books."

"He did?"

"Yeah." Ben smiled and raised the e-reader up to his face. "Did you know that contractions are like waves from the deepest sea, rolling pure natural energy through you? You must embrace them and open like a flower to the morning sun so your child can be born."

"That sounds like some fantastic crap."

"Yeah, don't know if this book's so worthwhile. Might try another."

"I haven't done a huge amount of research yet into the actual delivery process. But mostly I'm imagining pain, drugs, and yelling random abuse at anyone nearby."

A snort. "Also, babies need a shit-ton of stuff," he went on. "We better get cracking on that. Jim lined up a specialist for him and

Lena, who'll work with them on decorating the nursery and putting in everything they need."

"Wow."

"Yeah. Might be worth thinking about, since we're still on tour for a while."

I rubbed my chin against his pec, thinking deep thoughts. "That all sounds great, but we've only just decided to try the girlfriend and boyfriend thing. We have no idea if we'll be living in my apartment or where."

"True." He tossed aside the e-reader and curved his hand around my hip. "Was thinking, some of the books said yoga was great through maternity and preparing to give birth and all. I remember you saying you liked doing it but didn't have a lot of time or money when you were studying. So—and don't get pissy at me here, 'cause you don't have to do if you don't want—but I thought it might be nice if you and Lena had a specialist instructor along, to work with you whenever you felt like it."

My mouth fell open. "You did?"

"Jim said Lena would be into it, and I thought you might enjoy it. But it's your call," he continued. "Oh, and Jim said to especially point out that in no way is this me worrying about the size of your ass or something, 'cause it's not. I think your ass is awesome. If it gets bigger, that just means there's more of it for me to play with. I just wanted to do something good for you, and I know being on tour gets a little bit boring sometimes. And I thought—"

I alleviated his concerns by straddling the man and kissing him good and hard. And then I kissed him good and hard some more because he'd thought of me. No matter that he'd been off doing his thing, totally unrelated to me. At some stage of the day I'd been on his mind. I mattered to him. Proof of this was just about the sweetest thing ever.

Breathing heavy, my boyfriend gave me a slow grin. "You like the idea."

"I love the idea. Thank you."

"Tomorrow I'll take you shopping myself, okay? Promise."

"Okay." My chest filled to overflowing with warm and fuzzy feelings. Every last little bit of emotion inspired by him. We were going to make it. We were. Him, me, and Bean would be the best family ever. Our baby girl would never doubt she was loved and looked after.

"I really am sorry about my sister today, sweetheart," he said. "No fucking way should you have had to deal with that shit."

"I don't want to talk about her right now," I said, climbing down his long body.

"No?"

"Nope. I'm hungry." I buried my face in his neck, breathing in the scent of him. God help me, Sam was right. I was in love with this man. I could put off saying the words and deny it all I liked. The truth, however, wasn't going anywhere. Slow. If we just took it slow, this could really work.

"What do you feel like? I'll order you up some room service."

"You."

"Me?" His voice dropped by at least an octave.

I kissed first one flat brown nipple then the other, taking turns flicking my tongue across each. "Mm-hm."

With the aid of my feet, I pushed down the sheet, shuffling slowly lower and lower. The line of each rib and the curve of each muscle. The indent of his belly button and those lines on either side, leading out to his hips. Soon enough I was face-to-face with his hard-on, which was straining the black cotton of his boxer briefs. I swear the man's eyes were on fire, watching me do my thing.

Nothing was said. But then, nothing needed saying.

A large candy skull tattoo decorated his left side, the detail and colors amazing. Lines from an old Led Zep song covered his right. The man was a walking work of art.

He ever so helpfully raised his hips so I could slide his underwear halfway down his muscular thighs. I'd never really stopped and reflected, really gotten up close and personal in this manner with his cock. A damn shame. He was thick and long and ridged with veins, the wide, flat head just calling to my tongue. For now, though, I ran the flat of my thumb over the silken skin, feeling out the ridge and indent where the sweet spot sat.

Ben inhaled hard when I massaged it, his rib cage standing out. Man, he was beautiful. His vibrant eyes and the lines of those cheekbones. His perfect mouth and that beard. Whoa, that beard. The things it could do. If the man ever shaved it, I wasn't putting out till it grew back.

"What are you thinking about?" he asked, voice barely above a rumble.

I tightened my grip on his dick, enjoying the feel of him so smooth and hot against my palm. I pumped him once, twice. "Nothing."

"You know, you act real nice, but you've got a bad girl streak in you. I like it."

"I don't know what you're talking about." Nice and slow I bent over, dragging my tongue across the flat head of his cock. Mm, salty pre-cum. Yummy.

"Playing with me like this, for starters."

"You don't like this?" I traced the ridge of his dick with the tip of my tongue before digging in deep to his sweet spot. The head fit into my mouth just fine—all the better to suck at him.

"Fuck," he hissed, hips bucking, forcing himself further in.

I drew on him hard, sucking and slurping his thick cock, making a meal of him. There'd been no lie in me, I really was hungry. And pleasing my boyfriend was number one on the menu. I took him in as deep as I could go, trying to get my jaw slack. This would really require practice, given his size. Somehow, I doubt he'd mind.

On my hips above him, wearing only a thin tank top and panties, I gave him my all. If my technique was messy or somewhat technically lacking, Ben never mentioned it. I dragged my tongue back and forth up the length of him, tracing the veins and teasing the ridge. Then I opened wide and took him as deep as I could. Probably wasn't much, but what I could take I made count. It was definitely one of those occasions were suction equaled love. Lots of love. The salty taste on my tongue and his moaning and the words of praise filling my ears confirmed this.

Giving head to Ben was great.

The big, hairy man was completely at my mercy. His hips started churning, obviously unable to hold back much longer, and I drew on him hard. He shouted, hands tangled in my hair, tugging just the right amount to wake up my scalp. That slight sting worked for me, big-time. He held me in place to take all of his cum. I swallowed as fast as I could, cleaning up the rest with tongue and fingers. He was mine, and taking care of him was definitely its own reward.

Cheeks pinked and rib cage working hard, he stared down at me in awe. I don't know that what I'd done was so remarkable, but it was nice to be appreciated. The man certainly brought out my will to please. He looked cute right after he came. All dazed and befuddled, his face slack, at peace.

I climbed back up him, lying on my side on his chest. Immediately his arms came around me, holding on tight.

"Sorry I grabbed your hair, held you down," he said, still breathing heavy. "Never done that before."

"It was fine."

"It'll never happen again. Don't know what the fuck came over me."

"Hey," I said, getting up on one elbow to look him in the face.

Some serious panicky eyes there. "Ben, I liked it. I like that you were so into it, that I could do that to you, make you lose control a little."

He just stared.

I gave him a smile and carefully rolled off. "I'm getting water. You need some?"

A nod. "You really didn't mind?"

"I like being soft with you. I do. But I think getting a little rough with you now and then is fun too. I know we're kind of limited with what we can do with baby on board." I gave my belly a pat. "After, though?"

Another nod, this one downright enthusiastic, to the point where I was worried he might give himself whiplash. Seemed my man really did like to play.

"Great," I said.

After all, what was the point of having a gorgeous, hulking big boyfriend if you weren't willing to play with him? It was all just another healthy exploration of the bounds of our relationship. Us meshing in bed gave me good feelings. It gave me hope.

"I'll look forward to it." I gave him a wink.

I so had this girlfriend thing down. Go, me.

CHAPTER TWELVE

"Lizzy!" Mal skipped over to me, dragging Anne by the hand.

"Hey, you two." I sat, kicking my heels, down in the hotel café. My iced chocolate loaded with ice cream and syrup had long since disappeared from the glass in front of me. Not that I was cranky at being left waiting. All good. He hadn't forgotten me, he'd just gotten held up with something. I trusted him.

"What're you doing hanging down here on your own?" asked Anne.

"Ben's taking me maternity clothes shopping."

"When?"

I gave her a half smile. "Soon."

"Shouldn't you have Sam or one of his goons with you?" asked Mal, tucking his long blond hair behind an ear.

"No need. Ben'll be here soon."

"When?"

"Soon."

"You keep saying that." Mal frowned. "Give me specifics."

My cell buzzed in my bag. "This'll probably be him."

But it wasn't. Weirdly enough, my ex-roommate Christy's name flashed up on the screen. We hadn't talked since the nightclub abandonment issue.

"Hello?"

"I'm really sorry. Is it true?" came at me in an almighty rush.

"Is what true?" I asked.

"That you're pregnant?" she said. "I didn't mean to give them the photo, but then Imelda said it would be okay. That everyone deserved their fifteen minutes of fame. They said they were just doing a piece about life on campus. I didn't think you'd mind. I had no idea they were going to use it like that."

"Who is 'they'?" I asked, my insides twisting as the dread rose and rose.

"A reporter from *The Daily*."

"Check *The Daily*," I said to Anne. She whipped out her cell and got busy. "Christy, what photo did you give them?"

She paused, gulped. "Well, they just asked if they could use my pics from Facebook. I hadn't really thought that much about what was on there. I was kind of hoping they'd use the one of the two of us at Crater Lake. You remember I always loved that shot. But they wound up using that one from the Hawaiian luau at one of the sororities last year. When you were talking to those guys from Economics. I'm really sorry."

I knew the picture. All the girls had been in bikinis and grass skirts or sarongs. I'd worn cutoff jeans, covering more than most because that's how I'd felt comfortable. Each to their own and all. Everyone was sinking red Solo cups of beer, decorated with those dumb little umbrellas and chunks of pineapple. An interesting taste sensation. A member of the football team had worn a bright yellow mankini on a dare. It'd been hilarious. Good music. A good night. So I'd had a few drinks at a party while talking to a couple of guys, one of whom had thrown his arm around me for the shot. We were all grinning big, just enjoying the party. Why the hell would that excite a reporter?

Anne's brows drew tight and she showed me her cell.

College dropout pregnant with Stage Dive baby. Reportedly continuing living the high life with her numerous male friends. Grave concerns for the fetus's health. Vicious tug-of-war over custody anticipated. Demands for millions of dollars in alimony expected. A person close to the band reports they are horrified. Ben Nicholson as yet refusing to comment.

With numb fingers I hung up on a still babbling Christy.

Reportedly. Anticipated. Expected. It was all so brutally worded, the worst inferred to perfection by the photo. Assholes. They didn't have a clue who I was. Worse, they didn't even care. Whatever lies would sell. Thank god I didn't have a juvenile record for them to go poking around at, closed or open. Still, if they asked certain people about what I was up to during that misspent year of my youth . . . Nightmarish thoughts flooded my mind. If Ben and I did split, if something happened and things turned bad, would it be enough for him to claim full custody of Bean?

Christ.

And what about when I went for a job? Who the hell was going to trust their kid to a psychologist with a background like mine?

People were talking but I couldn't quite make out the words. It was like being underwater, the noises distant gibberish. The bubbles in my ears made hearing anything impossible.

Hands held my face, tipping it up. Then he was looking down at me, dark eyes intent. "Sweetheart?"

The bubbles burst, reality intruding, pushing the shock aside. "Ben?"

"Let's go up to the suite."

"Yes," I said, taking Ben's hand and letting him lead me, shelter me with his body.

There was yelling behind us. A sudden scuffle and the clicking of cameras. Security closed in. Everything happened so fast. I guess the paparazzi had been following Ben, figuring he'd lead them to me—knocked-up party girl, money-hungry whore extraordinaire in a bikini top.

Mal and Anne followed close behind, piling into the elevator. Soft pan flute music filled the air. No one said anything. Worse yet, no one even looked that surprised. Apart from me, that is. The whites of my eyes and pale face were perfectly reflected in the shiny metal doors. They slid open and Anne grabbed at my arm.

"Let me talk to her."

"Later," said Ben. "Right now she needs to lie down and chill out before she falls down."

"I'm not going to fall down." But I held on tight to his hand just in case. "I'm fine."

Anne let me go without further comment. Just as well. I couldn't dump all of this on her. She was still in blushing bride, newly married mode. No way should I be messing with that. Lately she'd taken on more than her share of big-sisterly duties, accompanying me on doctors' visits, staying behind with me in Portland.

The suite seemed eerily quiet after all of the commotion downstairs. All of the noise and thoughts continued rattling around in my head, however. Out beyond the floor-to-ceiling windows the city carried on. Christ, this was really happening.

"Come and sit down." He led me to the suede couch.

I disentangled my hand from his, shaking with some emotion. I just wasn't sure which, yet. "No. I . . . I don't want to sit."

Ben collapsed on the couch, crossing his legs, ankle to knee. His arms spread out along the back of the couch, watching me pace back and forth. So many words were crammed inside me, fighting to get out. If I could just think straight. No point taking it personally, the journalists and photographers were just doing their jobs. Didn't make them any less of a bunch of gossip-mongering asshats, but there you go.

"I feel so . . . so powerless."

"I know," he said.

"They basically made me out to be some alcoholic who has orgies every night of the week ending in *Y*." I rubbed my hands against the sides of my jeans. Still staying up by virtue of a hairband. Though pants weren't much of a problem in the scale of things right now.

"You're not," he said, so certain.

"My *numerous* male friends," I sneered.

"It's bullshit."

"Why does it always come down to sex with women in the media? How many people have you slept with?" I asked, hands on hips. "Well?"

His tongue played behind his cheek. "I, ah, I didn't really keep count."

"They didn't infer you were some kind of slut, and you've probably slept with dozens more people than me."

He gave a careful nod.

"Hundreds?" I hazarded.

He cleared his throat, turning away and scratching at his beard.

"Right. Not that it matters. And yet I'm the slut because I'm the woman. Like it's anyone's fucking business how many either of us has slept with or if I enjoy going out for a beer occasionally. I'm not getting behind the wheel of a car and driving drunk. I'm having a few drinks with friends at a party and organizing to get home safely. And if I'm taking someone home, that is none of their business. Those hypocritical motherfuckers, condemning me for these things. What consenting adults do in private should not be entertainment for the world at large. Nor is it in any way a viable judge of a person's character."

"Liz."

"Mother-fire-truckers." I gave my belly a pat of apology. "Sorry, baby."

"Liz."

"That double standard between men and women drives me insane."

"Yeah, I'm getting that." One side of his mouth tipped up. "You want me to sue for defamation? I can get the lawyers onto it now, if you want. See what we can do. But they probably can't do much. The press had a field day with Jimmy, and we could never get a retraction on even the most out-there stuff they wrote. But if that's what you want . . ."

With a sigh, I went back to pacing. "It's out there. No matter what, it's out there now."

A slow nod. "Yeah, sweetheart. It is."

"I just . . . I never thought this would impact on my future this way. I knew studying would have to take a backseat for a few years to motherhood." I pulled my blond hair back off my face, giving it a fierce tug. "I knew Bean would have to come first, that's the reality of it. But I thought one day . . ."

"You will get to finish your study and practice psychology. Don't you dare give into this shit." Ben sat forward, elbows on his knees. "There will always be some fucknut out there saying something, trying to bring you down just to make a buck or because they can. Because their own lives are shit. You cannot let them win."

"They're saying it to a potential audience of billions on the Internet, Ben."

"I do not care," he said, eyes blazing with anger. "You will not let these shitheads win. You're better than that. Stronger."

I stared at him, amazed. "You really believe that?"

"I know it. From the minute word got out you were pregnant, you weren't looking for someone to blame. You were pulling yourself together, planning ahead for your baby."

I stood taller, just looking at him. It was as if I could feel myself being stronger just because he believed it.

"Well?" he asked.

"To be honest, I was kind of upset with your penis and testes for a while. I may have called your sperm some bad names."

He chuckled. "Yeah? How you feel about my reproductive organs now?"

A sudden urge to burn up the panicky energy raced through me. "I feel that I'd very much like to fire-truck you."

Once more he sat back, arms spread out along the back of the couch. Such a slow, filthy smile on his handsome face. "Just so happens, I'd very much like to be fire-trucked by you."

"Child-appropriate dirty talk. There's something very wrong with that." I wandered over to him, kicking off my flats. Next came unhooking my hairband waist rigging so I could push down my jeans. My top and bra disappeared in a flash, leaving my panties for lucky last.

And all the while Ben sat there, taking me in, mouth slightly open in appreciation. "Fuck, you're pretty. And I love it when you get all riled up and righteous."

"My bearded beauty."

He laughed, hands reaching for my hips. "At your service, sweetheart."

"I'll hold you to that." I straddled his lap, bare-ass naked and perfectly content to be so. This was trust, giving him all of me, no holding back. "No more slow."

His nostrils flared as he inhaled hard. "Whatever you want."

"You. Just you."

Our mouths met, kisses hard and soft, sweet and greedy. Everything all at once. Perfect. I slid my hands up beneath his T-shirt, pulling it up over his head. How annoying, leaving his mouth for even a moment. But for skin on skin, these sacrifices must be made. And holy hell, Ben's skin. All of the art of his tattoos and the hard of his muscles. His hands covered my breasts, ever so gently massaging.

"More or less?" he asked.

"A little more." Fingers toyed with my nipples, turning me right the hell on. "That's it."

I rubbed my bare pussy against the ridge in his jeans. Who even invented clothes? What an idiot. My hormones ran rife, my skin alive with sensation. Calloused fingers slid down to my round belly, spreading out over it.

"You're fucking beautiful, carrying our baby."

"Glad you think so."

"Ah, sweetheart. You got no idea. You drive me out of my fucking mind."

A hand tangled in my hair, holding me in place for his mouth. He kissed me till my head spun. His tongue exploring my mouth, teasing and tantalizing. I could happily kiss him forever. If only my insides didn't feel so empty and needy. A thumb toyed with my clit, sliding back and forth through the ample wetness, raising my awareness of just how turned on I was. Like I needed reminding. Him in me now was the only beat running through my brain. The abrasive rub of his jeans felt . . . interesting good. For sure I'd left a hell of a wet patch to testify to that. But I seriously needed to get at what lay beneath, and I needed it now.

I raised up as high as I could on my knees, hands tugging at his belt buckle. "Off!"

"Where's the manners, sweetheart? What kind of example you setting, hmm?"

I groaned. "Please, Ben, will you take your pants off for me? It's kind of important."

"Sure thing, Liz. Thanks for asking so nicely." He wriggled down a little, dealing with his belt and jeans button and zipper far more effectively than I ever could. The thick head of his cock prodded at my slick opening. "Easy. It's been a while since we did this."

"I don't think we're going to have any problems this time." Wet as I was, my only fears were for staining the suede couch. No way, however, was I stopping. Expensive furniture be damned.

Slowly, I lowered myself onto him. The swollen lips of my pussy parting, my body opening, letting the thick length of him go deep where he belonged.

"Oh god, that feels good," I moaned.

"Yeah."

Teeth grazed my neck, nipping, sending a thrill racing down my spine. Finally, I sat on his bare thighs, the waist and zip of his jeans lightly scratching my ass. Next time we'd make it to the bedroom. Get all naked and go for it. Next time. Because there had to be more and it needed to be soon.

I threaded a hand through the longer hair on top of his head, fucking up his too-cool rock star do, tugging just a little. He opened his mouth wide, nipping at my lips, smiling. Two could tease.

"You want to play, Lizzy?"

"With you? Always."

"You're killin' me."

Despite my dare, he settled for licking my bottom lip, sucking on it. Then the strong hands beneath my ass took the lead, gently lifted me up, before letting me slide back down. We both moaned then. Holy hell, it all felt so good. His cock was a thing of pure man magic. Don't get me wrong, though, only this man would do. He made every piece of me light up with sensation, loving it. Loving him.

No matter his teasing, with his strength, he was so careful with me. Delicate even. No one had ever done that, made me feel like I was precious. Only him.

I got in on the action, raising and lowering myself with his help, riding him harder. Careful was all good and well, but a girl knows what she needs. I needed him. He filled my body in every way, gave me what I needed in a way my own nimble fingers never could. Also, emotionally, he left my hand way behind. No way could I wrap me up warm and safe like this. Fingers dug into my ass, his thick cock powering into my body. I wrapped my arms around his neck, holding on. His beard brushed against my cheek, then his mouth pressed into the corner of my lips.

"You're so fucking close, I can feel you," he said, breath hot on my skin.

"Ben," I panted. I'd be embarrassed at being so easy to please, but psycho baby hormones, etcetera. I needed it bad with him, no excuses. "I need to come."

"Get to it, sweetheart. Show me how it's done."

His slid further down, giving me more room to rise and fall on his lap, moving me into a better position without putting pressure on my belly. With one hand on his shoulder and the other between my legs, I got busy. Thighs working hard, keeping the sweet slide of him going in and out of me.

"Fuck me," he muttered. "Hottest thing ever."

His language truly was appalling during sex. Later, after I'd come, I'd definitely have stern words with him about it. In the meantime . . .

"Harder," I ordered/begged. One or the other. With all the panting it was a little hard to tell.

The grin on Ben's lips was its own reward. "That's my bad girl."

The hands on my hips slammed me down onto his cock. I centered my efforts around my clit. Close. So damn close. Felt like my body was about to go *bang*. Energy gathered at the base of my spine, all around where we were joined. I wanted that peak as bad as I never wanted it to end. Then his cock moved over something wonderful inside of me and I gasped. Bright light blinded me, my whole body tensing before releasing completely. My head fell forward onto his shoulder, all of me shaking and shuddering.

Ben held me down hard, his hips bucking, driving himself in as deep as could be. Amazing.

Then, I kind of died. Or did a very good impersonation of it, collapsing on top of him, totally limp. Maybe I'd just have a snooze right there, with him still lodged inside of me. Not an ounce of inclination to move. Hopefully there'd be no leakage of shared body fluids. Have to admit though, I didn't really care.

Hands soothed down my back, tracing each and every ridge of my spine, massaging my ass, stroking my thighs. It went on and on. Him just touching every part of me he could reach. Soothing or claiming me, I don't know. But I loved it. The scent of us lingering in the air, our sweaty bodies all but glued together. If I stayed sort of on my side there was plenty of room for the swell of my belly.

"Comfortable?" he asked. "Warm enough?"

I nodded.

"I'm sorry they came at you like this, saying that shit about you."

"It's okay." I sighed. "You're worth it to me."

"Sweetheart." He kissed the top of my head, the side of my face.

Nothing needed to be said, not right then. One day soon, I'd tell him. If he couldn't feel it, however, with me basically trying to climb beneath his skin, to get as close as I could to him . . . well then, the man was a dumbass. My feelings for Ben Nicholson were huge. Epic. As far as his were concerned, with his hands traveling over me, treasuring me, they had to be good and real. They had to be.

Soon enough we were going to be a family. Already we were each other's home.

Turned out Ben did get a somewhat hefty bill for the cleaning of the suede couch. The man swore it was worth every cent, bless him.

CHAPTER THIRTEEN

"Hell of a fucking coincidence," said Jim, adding more baked salmon and broccoli to Lena's plate.

"Thanks, babe." She dove right in.

It was beautiful, the way he way he paid such keen attention to her. The woman was clearly his world. Lena had no sooner looked at something than he was serving it up. She shifted in her seat and he ran for more cushions. A queen couldn't have been treated better. The love in her eyes and the soft smiles every time she looked at him made my heart ache. It was an intense love, so open and honest. Every love, every relationship, was different. And no way could anyone who wasn't on the inside understand how that couple worked. Let people judge. People didn't know shit. Shoot. At any rate, I didn't need to be the center of Ben's world. But I knew me. I did need to be up there, vying for top position with his music, having his trust.

One day Ben and I would get there. Without a doubt.

Each of the Stage Dive couples was pretty much variations of the same. Maybe that's the way musicians and artists loved, how they committed. All or nothing. They were in touch with their passions, so those passions tended to run large through their lives.

We'd all attended the concert tonight to hear the first performance of one of the band's new songs. Not a slow love song, though there'd been a lot of love in it. More of a hot, raw, rock 'n' roll, doing-my-girl-makes-me-pretty-damn-happy kind of thing. A little awkward when you knew the guy and girl in question. David did like to write songs about his wife, and damn he did it well. The crowd had gone wild.

Yesterday we'd had a day off. Given that the news of my whorish money-making scheme had hit the papers just the day before, Ben and I had stayed in. It'd been nice. We'd slept until ten and had a late breakfast in bed. I'd even bravely dealt with all the missed calls from my mom. There'd been some yelling and tears on her part. A fair amount of *what would the neighbors think*. Thing was, my mom checked out of my life a long time ago, to Anne's and my detriment. That I permitted her back in at all was sort of a miracle. Her opinion on my life was not required. I let her carry on for five minutes exactly and then told her I had to go and hung up. My life currently held enough drama without her getting involved. I didn't want to hurt her, but nor would I allow myself to be hurt by her. The end.

Ben and I watched movies and caught up on some sexing. In the afternoon a plethora of boxes and bags from places like A Pea in the Pod, Neiman Marcus, and some boutique called Veronique arrived. All the maternity wear and then some. I didn't dare ask what it cost. Ben gave me the Look. What with now being in a relationship and having my own Look, signifying a line which should not be crossed, I respected his need to support me and Bean and wisely let it go. At seventeen weeks, I looked rockin' good that night in my maternity jeans and black tunic, both of which actually fit for a change.

But back to the dinner conversation.

"Marty can definitely be rabid when she puts her mind to it," said Mal, his arm slung around the back of Anne's chair. "Wouldn't have thought she'd sic the press on someone, but like Jim said, hell of a coincidence, timingwise, for the story to break the day after her visit."

We sat gathered around a big mahogany dining table in David and Ev's suite, sharing an extravagant dinner. The chefs in these places knew their stuff. Foodgasms galore.

"I don't buy it." David sat back, fingers pinching his lips. "She knows that'd only lead to them being all over Ben too. For all her faults, she loves her brother. No way she'd do anything again to directly fuck with him."

"She didn't do it." Ben remained adamant. And rather peeved, if the furrows on his forehead and sliver-thin lips were any indication.

I put my hand on his leg, gave him a small smile. Frankly, I wouldn't put anything past the crazy-ass bitch. Right now, though, Ben needed me on his side. With next to no evidence, I'd be cautious but I wouldn't damn her just yet. Nor would I be letting her near me, however. "What does it even matter who did it? It's done."

My sister gave me a long, assessing look.

"It was bound to come out sooner or later, especially with us on tour," said Anne, taking my back. "God knows how many different people have seen her coming in and out of Ben's suite, or just seen them together in general. And she's showing now. It wouldn't take much to put two and two together. There'd be big money up for grabs for a story like that. Especially once they had the right pic to sell it."

"Exactly. I doubt the girl will be throwing me a baby shower anytime soon. But let's not assume the worst until we know more."

Ben gave my hand a squeeze of appreciation.

"Pumpkin's right. It was bound to get out. Fact is, we'll probably never know who the helpful little shithead was who ratted

Lizzy out." Mal swirled a glass of red wine before downing it in one fell swoop. "Let's just enjoy our night off."

Various nods and murmurs of agreement. Thank goodness.

"Hear Down Fourth are breaking up after the tour," said Ben, one hand holding mine and the other holding a beer.

"No shit?" Jim hand-fed Lena a chocolate-covered strawberry.

"Keep that up I'll be as big as a house," she said after swallowing it down.

"Making babies takes a lot of energy."

"Lead singer got offered a solo deal and their drummer's moving on to Ninety-Nine," continued Ben.

"Hard on Vaughan and Conn," said David.

"Nature of the business. Some bands are just pit stops on the way to other things. Surprising, though. They've been together a long time." Mal beat out a rhythm with thumb and forefinger on the table. "Vaughan's actually a damn good guitarist with not a bad voice. Heard him messing around the other night. Think he just got stuck playing bass for them. Might be a chance for him to trade up."

"Nothing wrong with bass," said Ben, giving the drummer a foul look.

"Be fair, Benny-boy. There's nothing right with it, either." Mal grinned. "Is it true bass players can't count past four?"

"Says the dickhead that can barely hold two sticks."

"Enough," said David, raising his chin. "The girls wanted a nice dinner, with no arguing for a change."

"A noble dream," chuckled Mal. "Seriously though, bands breaking up happens all the time. Takes a fair amount to put up with the same people day in, day out."

"This your way of saying you're out?" asked Jim, smirk in place.

"Damn, man," said Ben with a straight face. "We'll miss you and shit."

"Wait, what was your name again?" asked David, scratching his head.

Mal gave them all the bird. "Ha-ha. You useless fuckers. You'd be lost without me."

David lobbed a bread roll at the drummer's head.

"No," shouted Ev. "No food fights. We're behaving like adults for once. Stop it."

"Way to be the fun police, child bride," chided Mal, setting a profiterole back on his plate.

A waiter in a fancy suit stepped into the room, carrying a silver platter with a single white-frosted cupcake sitting in the middle. He stopped beside Lena and with great pomp and pageantry offered her the dessert.

"What is this?" she asked Jimmy, pointing at the cake like it was toxic. "We talked about this."

"Yeah, and I disagreed."

"You don't get to disagree." A distinct little line appeared above her nose. "You asked, I said no. End of discussion."

Clear blue eyes unimpressed, the man sat back in his seat, propping his ankle on his knee. "Sure I do. Put on the ring, Lena."

Crap, he was right. I don't know how I'd missed it. But there was an almighty chunk of bling sitting in pride of place on top of the cupcake. Holy hell, it would have made Liz Taylor weep with envy.

Lena narrowed her eyes on the man. "I said no. I still say no."

"No worries, babe. You don't want to get married, we won't get married. But you're still wearing the ring."

"Why? Why is this so important to you?" she asked, mouth drawn in frustration. Or maybe she too was slightly astounded by the size of the rock. And I'd thought Anne's and Ev's rings were huge. This one bordered on accidental-eye-gouging ridiculousness.

"'Cause you're mine, and I'm yours. And I want that clear to everyone." Jimmy sat forward, staring her down. "I love you, Lena. Put on the fucking ring."

"Put on the fucking ring," she mumbled, doing an apt impersonation of the man. In a discreet show of emotion, the very pregnant brunette sniffed. "Honestly. You didn't even say 'please.'"

Jimmy rolled his eyes. "Please."

"Fine," she grouched, plucking the rock out of the cake and sucking off the icing. Then she slid the massive diamond onto her ring finger. "I'll wear the stupid thing. But we are not getting married. I don't care what you say. We've barely known each other half a year."

"Whatever you want, Lena."

She snorted. "Yeah right."

There was a stunned sort of silence around the table as Jimmy sucked down some mineral water and Lena got on with eating the little cake. Like nothing had happened.

Finally, David Ferris cleared his throat. "Did you two actually just get engaged?"

Lena shrugged.

"Yeah. Pretty much," said Jimmy.

Barely holding back a laugh, Ben raised his beer. "Congratulations, guys."

I, David, Mal, and Anne likewise raised drinks in salute. With a gasp, Ev clasped her hands to her mouth, eyes glossy with emotion.

"Don't make a big deal out of it," said Lena. "It's just a ring. The way I'm retaining fluid, it won't even fit me by next week."

Jimmy rolled up the cuffs on his fitted white shirt. "No worries. I got you a nice matching chain necklace for you to wear it on."

"You do think of everything."

"Anything for you, Lena."

She gave him a dry look.

"What about you two?" asked Mal, tipping his freshly refilled glass of wine in Ben's and my direction.

"You're the only one left now," said David, his amused gaze on Ben.

My boyfriend shifted in his seat, letting go of my hand. He licked his lips and fussed some more, clearly uncomfortable with all of the attention. Fair enough. We'd been dating for like two of the seventeen weeks I'd been pregnant. We'd known each other for only a few months before the miraculous conception. Now was definitely not the time to put on the pressure and rush into marriage.

"Don't know if I'm really the marrying kind," he said with a deep, not so humorous laugh.

Shit.

Every eye in the place apart from his turned to me, waiting on my reaction. Of all the things for him to say, the hundred and one ways to put off the question. God, laughing at it alone would have done the trick. I kept my gaze down, concentrating on my mostly empty plate. My stomach clenched, a weird, wiggling, vaguely nauseous sensation rising up inside. Meanwhile, you couldn't have found a more profound silence in a church.

The ringing of Ben's cell broke the quiet. He answered it with a manly grunt. Did I even want to marry someone who answered the phone with a grunt? I don't know. And apparently I'd never need to decide. He wasn't the marrying kind. All of a sudden the safety I'd found with him felt precarious indeed. The ledge that was our relationship had begun crumbling beneath my feet.

"Yeah . . . sure, send her in." He turned to me, sounding relieved to change the subject. "Ah, Martha's here. She wants to apologize to you for the other day."

I just looked at him.

"That's all right, isn't it?" he asked, obviously referring to his sister. Sadly, I was still stuck back on his awesome announcement.

The door opened and the woman herself walked in, head held high and a big black patent leather handbag slung over one shoulder. A brief flash of pain crossed her face at the sight of David, her nose wrinkled at Ev.

Ben pushed back out of his chair and stood, going to her side.

"Make it good," he ordered in a low voice.

As if I had any interest in an apology, good or otherwise, from this woman.

Ben's words twirled around and around inside my head. We'd never even talked marriage, not really. I guess the fairy tales had been playing out in the back of my head, though, the usual fantasies of tulle, silk, and eternal love. The odd dove or two. Cake.

Yeah. Not so much, apparently. I needed to leave right now. Go be alone for a while until I had things figured out again, now that my bright shiny future had been flushed down the toilet.

Martha retrieved a couple of papers from her handbag and shoved them in my general direction. "You want me to believe you're not just using my brother and this child to make some money? Prove it to me. Sign this."

The whites of Ben's eyes were huge, massive. "Martha—"

"What is that?" I asked, the noise of my voice coming from far, far away.

"It's the contract he had drawn up, covering shared custody and a more than fair payment for maintenance—upon proof of paternity, of course," she answered.

"Of course."

"Shouldn't be a big deal for you to sign." She took another step forward, still holding out the papers. "Your own sister signed a prenup. Did you know that?"

"It's what Anne wanted. You've got no fucking business talking about that, Marty." Mal slowly got to his feet, a hand on my sister's shoulder. "And I am very unhappy at Adrian for discussing that shit with you."

"He didn't." The snake of a woman sneered. "But his new little secretary is very chatty. Not the brightest, though, unfortunately for her."

"Get the fuck out of here," said David. "Now, Martha."

"Doesn't concern you," she said without sparing him a glance. Still looking at me, she continued, "You want to prove to me that you love my brother? That you have his best interests at heart? Sign it."

I just stared at the papers, perplexed.

"Martha!" David kicked back his chair.

"When?" I asked Ben, doing my best to meet his eyes, but not quite managing. I stared off over his thick shoulder at the lights of the city below. It was all just too raw, too painful. "You agreed we'd handle this between us not twenty-four hours after you found out I was pregnant. So when exactly did you ask for this contract to be drawn up?"

He stared at me, unmoving.

"Let me guess. You had it drawn up 'just in case'?"

"Lizzy." His Adam's apple bobbed.

"Did you think I wouldn't understand your need to protect yourself?"

"You didn't like the idea when I first brought it up."

"I barely had a chance to get used to the idea," I cried. "Christ, Ben. Most people would be a little wary at the mention of having lawyers sicced on them, don't you think?"

"What's it matter?" he asked, jaw shifting angrily. "I haven't asked you to sign it."

"Don't play stupid with her, Ben," Martha sneered. "Adrian sent you a copy weeks ago. His little secretary said he asked her to double check that you still had it last week. He was wondering what the holdup is."

Ben glared furiously at Martha, but he didn't deny it.

"Just in case." I wrapped my arms around myself, holding on tight. "Why are we even doing this? I mean really. You lied to me, Ben. You're just waiting for this to fall to apart, aren't you? You're not the marrying kind? Honestly, I don't even know that you're the relationship kind. In a lot of ways you've avoided commitment at every step. I was just too stupid to see."

"Check it out, Ben," said Martha, voice low and hypnotic. "This is what happens when you threaten their money. The claws come out and you find out what they were up to all along." She turned on me. "So go on then. Storm out and lawyer up all you want—but everyone here has seen you for what you really are now."

"God, you . . ." There weren't words bad enough for this sort of bitch. I snatched the contract from her hands, slapping it down on the table. It was surprisingly slim, only three or so pages. "Pen!"

Martha hunted through her handbag for one.

"Don't," Ben said, pushing the word out through gritted teeth.

I grabbed the pen Martha was offering. Funny, there was none of the triumph or venom remaining on her face now. If anything, her gaze seemed confused, cautious. Like I could care. This had nothing do with her anymore.

I moved my dinner plate aside and flipped through the papers, finding the big, juicy number meant to buy me off. Fuck's sake, he'd already put half a million into my bank account. How ridiculous. Without hesitation I scribbled out the number and wrote in a big fat zero. Then I read through it, doing a check on the custody and other assorted details. As promised, Bean would be shared evenly between the two of us. Any disputes would be sorted out in family court, in the event of mediation failing. Good. It all seemed standard.

There. Signed and done.

If they needed anything else they could catch up with me later. At a mutually beneficial time when I wasn't about to have a messy emotional breakdown, possibly involving puking my guts up.

His sister snatched up the contract, hurriedly examining it.

"I'd appreciate it if you'd give me an hour to remove my belongings from the room before returning to it," I told Ben, not even bothering with the pretense of facing him this time.

"We need to talk," he said. "Liz."

"You signed it," Martha said. "You even crossed out the money." The look on his bitch of a sister's face would have been hilarious had I not been in the middle of getting my heart broken. Her brows might never return to normal, they'd risen so high on her perfect forehead.

"I don't give a fuck about the contract," Ben snarled, grabbing hold of my arm.

"If you didn't give a fuck about the contract, then it wouldn't exist." I tugged my arm from his grasp. "You sure as hell wouldn't be carrying a copy of it around with you."

"Sweetheart—"

"No. Never again. I'm an never . . . ever . . . going through this with you again." I sucked in a sharp breath. "Don't feel too bad about it, Ben. You did warn me, after all. I was just stupid enough to believe that maybe I could matter to you as much as you do to me. My bad."

Still, Martha stared at the papers, stunned.

"You do matter to me," he said, breathing hard.

"But not enough. Not enough to be honest with me. Not enough to talk to me about this, about your fears . . . God, did you really think I would be like her?" I pointed a thumb at his abomination of a sister. "That I would cheat? Lie? Use you for money time and again, messing with your life?"

"I love my brother," Martha shouted.

"You shut your god damn mouth!" Tears poured down my face. I was beyond caring, really. Beyond everything. I rested my hand on my belly, feeling that strange stirring sensation within again. Bean apparently didn't care for shouting. I lowered my voice accordingly. "I will deal with you when I am good and ready."

Martha shut it, face still stunned.

"I was never trying to change you," I said, finding my last ounce of bravery and staring Ben in the face. "I just wanted some of your time, your attention. I wanted to be a part of what you love."

Dark eyes gave me nothing but grief.

"You've got another six or so weeks on tour. I don't want to hear from you during that time," I said, turning away. "I'll make sure any medical updates are forwarded to you. Otherwise . . . I just . . . I need a break. From all of this."

"You're going back to Portland?" he asked, obviously unhappy. His man-feelings had been hurt. Too bad.

"Yes."

As expected, Anne opened her mouth, rising to her feet. She'd have my back, of course she would. But I halted her with a hand. "Later."

She nodded.

I turned toward Martha, tamping down the need to beat her with the nearest solid object. "I don't have much family, and sadly, your brother seems all too willing to tolerate your borderline personality disorder. But you will *never* treat my child in a way that is anything less than loving and supportive. Is that understood?"

Numbly, she nodded.

"Good."

Anne took my hand. Solidarity among sisters, etcetera, and thank god for it. I really needed her right then. Together, with Mal behind us, we left.

CHAPTER FOURTEEN

"Are you sure?" my sister asked, not for the first time. Not even for the hundredth, for that matter.

"I'm sure."

"I don't like you being sure."

"I get that." I sat on the bed in her suite's spare bedroom, watching as she meticulously packed my case. My underwear had basically been alphabetized. "And I love you for it."

She sighed, refolding one of my maternity tops for the third time. "I love you too. I'm just sorry it ended this way. He seemed so into you. I really thought he'd get his act together."

"I guess some people are just wandering souls. They really are better off alone. They need their freedom more than they need love and companionship. Better to find out now than to keep persevering at a relationship that's ultimately doomed because he's unable to trust and commit." I gave her the same brave, what-can-you-do smile I'd been wearing for the last twenty-four hours. My cheeks hurt. Much more and I'd have to ice my face.

"You're so full of shit," she sighed.

I smiled some more.

"Stop trying to appear so cool about it. I know full well the asshole has ripped your beating heart right out of your chest and stomped all over it with his huge black boots."

"Nice visual."

"I hate him. Next time we have a band dinner, I'm stabbing him with a fork."

"You are not stabbing him with a fork," I said, patting her hand. "You're going to be perfectly polite and carry on with business as usual."

Eyes narrowed, she gave me a stubborn look.

"For Mal's sake," I said. "I'll go home and get the nursery sorted. It'll be fine, Anne. Really."

"Let me come with you."

"No." I shook my head determinedly. "Absolutely not. You've never been to Europe. You've been looking forward to this trip for months. It's only six weeks. I'll manage. Besides, honestly, I need the space right now."

Her shoulders slumped in defeat. "You promise you'll call me if you need me."

I held up my hand. "I solemnly swear."

"Hmm."

"Killer and I are just going to hang out, take it easy."

"He's definitely going to be relieved to get out of the pet hotel. That's one silver lining at least. The last few times I've called, he's flat-out refused to speak to me."

"He's a dog, Anne. He can't talk."

More frowning. "But he used to make these little yipping noises and bark at me. You know what I mean. I'm worried this has given him abandonment issues. He's a very sensitive animal. He's like Mal, deep down, in a way."

"He's a lunatic who chases his own tail until he falls over," I said. "Actually, he kind of is like Mal, you're right."

"True." Anne nodded with a thoughtful look.

"Well, I promise to apply all of my psychology skills to resolving his issues before you return." In my experience, Killer's happiness could be bought with a pack of Canadian bacon and the destruction of one of Mal's Converse. I'd already stolen a reasonably new-looking shoe out of Mal's closet for just this purpose. The dog would be back to his usual tail-wagging, gleeful, psycho self in no time.

My own abandonment issues might take a little longer to resolve.

Tomorrow, Stage Dive moved on to Montreal, then Europe. Slightly sooner, in secret, I'd return to Oregon. Everyone was going to the concert tonight for the first performance of yet another song. I guess it was a new tradition to have everyone there. Nice. Seemed David was in fine writing form these days—touring agreed with him. While they were gone, I'd make my sneaky exit. Anne didn't know, she thought I was leaving in the morning. But she'd understand. There'd been enough drama. A big emotional good-bye wouldn't help anyone. Certainly not me. Staying in the same city as Ben, even for the last twenty-four hours, was grating on me. I ached to have his whole world behind me. I wasn't being naive and pretending my grief wouldn't be boarding that plane right along with me. It was more a feeling that I couldn't even begin to move on until I could see this city recede into nothing through the little airline window. It would be all the closure I'd get.

Besides, the town of Seaside on the Oregon coast was beautiful this time of year. It also wouldn't be where the press would expect me to turn up. I'd drive out there in the Mustang and get a room, something overlooking the ocean. A pretty view to help me pull myself together, to get over my disappointment and get myself in the right frame of mind for single motherhood. Me and Bean would be fine. Killer too, for that matter.

"You're just going to go to sleep?" Anne asked, zipping up my case and lugging it off the bed.

"Yeah. I'll take a shower and then crash. Thanks for helping me pack," I said. "You better get going. The guys will be taking to the stage soon. And you know what traffic is like in New York."

She dropped a kiss on top of my head. Then went crazy with both hands, messing up my hair like we were all of fourteen again or something.

"God, grow up, would you?" I groused, pushing my long locks back off my face.

"'Night." She grinned. Marriage to Mal had apparently given her the childhood she'd missed out on the first time around, what with our parents' selfishness. It was nice, if occasionally somewhat annoying. I really needed to remember to give her a wedgie in retribution, next time I saw her.

"'Night."

She walked out with a final wave.

I sat perfectly still, waiting for the click of the outer door closing. Then, just to be certain, I waited another ten minutes. And . . . yes. Operation Make a Run for It was a go.

I slipped on my black flats and stuffed my blond hair up under a plain black baseball cap, raising the handle on my case. Done. My one-way ticket home had been booked earlier, during a particularly long stint in the john. It seemed the only place some concerned soul wouldn't interrupt me every two minutes: Was I hungry? Nope. What about a drink? Nuh. How about a rehashing of the god-awful events of the night before, followed by a good long cry on concerned soul's shoulder, with excessive hugging thrown in? No way. But thanks for asking.

I loved the girls. Honest to god I did. But right then I needed space from everyone.

I peeked my head out. Nada. Not a sign of security in sight. To be expected, given I'd promised to stay in my room and you could only access the floor with the special key. Down I went in the shiny elevator. Across the bright, busy ground floor I all but ran, towing my case behind me. My plane left in a little over two hours. Even with the hellish New York traffic, it should be plenty of time to reach the airport and get through security.

Outside, the night air was warm, alive with light and color. New York really was the city that never slept.

"Can I help you, miss?" a nice doorman asked me, holding out a gloved hand for my case.

"Yes, thank you. I'd like a cab to JFK, please."

"Of course, miss." He held up a hand, summoning a taxi like magic.

In no time at all my case was in the trunk and I was safely buckled in the back. That was when things went kind of wrong.

The car door opened and a large, smelly male slid in beside me. It's a reality of these types of men, not often discussed. In the same way that cowboys stink of horse and cow crap, after a concert, rock stars reek of sweat—and lots of it. Kind of bursts the bubble somewhat, doesn't it? But the stink alone narrowed down the cab-stealing stranger's identity.

"Hey, Liz."

"Vaughan?"

"How's it going?"

I blinked. And then I blinked again, because he was still there, messing with my escape plan, damn it. "What are you doing here?"

Without so much as an as-you-please, he directed the cab driver to the stadium where Stage Dive was playing. The hundred-dollar bill he passed along with the instructions meant he got the driver's attention. Not little old me.

"Any particular reason you're hijacking my cab?" I asked.

"It was going to be Conn, but then, you haven't really met him. We figured it'd freak you out less if it was me."

"Right . . . right." I nodded. "Doesn't really answer the question."

"Well, all of the other guys are busy playing, so it had to be one of us." He slicked back his sweat-dampened hair with a hand and flashed me a smile. "Need you to see something."

"What?"

"You'll see." He chuckled.

I chuckled along with him. "Wow. Yeah. I'm really going to miss you after I kill you and throw your body off the Brooklyn Bridge."

"C'mon, don't be like that. You don't like what you see, I'll make sure you still get to the airport with plenty of time to make your flight."

"How do you know about that?" I leaned an elbow on the window ledge, trying to keep my cool. Not really succeeding. Outside the city lights sped by.

"Same way I was waiting for you to make your escape," he said. "Sam."

"Ah." Trust the superspy security guy to be a step ahead of me. Jerk.

"Anyway, they figured I'd have a better chance at sweet talking you into coming along."

"Did they now?" I showed him my teeth. It could have been misconstrued as a smile, but as previously noted, Vaughan was no dummy.

"Liz, please. If I didn't think it'd be worth your while, no fucking chance I'd have let them talk me into this. I got no desire to have you hate me."

I sighed determinedly. "Look," I said, putting on my best laying-down-the-law voice, "all I want right now is to get all of this behind me as fast as I possibly can. I'm sick of being here. I'm sick of the band, and rock 'n' roll, and most of all I'm sick of smiling through it all. I do think you're sweet, and kudos to you for trying whatever you're trying. But I am officially over it. I am so past over it."

"Huh," he said, sitting back in his seat and smiling out the window at the Manhattan lights. "I guess I'm the opposite, aren't I? It's all over for you and you can't wait to get away. It's all over for me too, and I just keep trying to squeeze out another few seconds from my fifteen minutes of fame. Your strategy does sound better. Figures, what with your psychiatry degree and all."

"Psychology," I corrected absently. I'd forgotten I wasn't the only one who was dealing with a breakup of sorts. "I heard you guys were finishing, but it's hardly all over for you, is it? I've seen you up onstage. You've got it going on just fine."

Vaughan smiled sadly. "You've never really seen the rock 'n' roll life, have you?" he asked. "You just got vaulted into the penthouse without getting a taste of the industry. For every Stage Dive there's a hundred Down Fourths. A thousand. We had one or two hits. We backed up a major band. If we'd held on to that and managed to score a major label contract, who knows? Maybe it all would have happened. Rock superstars, platinum albums, and the cover of *Rolling Stone*. But we couldn't keep it together. Too many egos and pissy little arguments, to the point we're barely fucking talking to each other. Luke's off to bigger and better things, sure. But for the rest of us it's back to square one. At the end of the day, the last ten years don't mean shit. I'm tired, Liz. Tired of sleeping in shitty hotels and always traveling and playing shows, trying to make enough to pay for just a little more studio time. I want to go home and see my family, wake up and actually know what town I'm in. I want to see if there's a better way to do this that doesn't cost me my sanity and fuck with my liver every night of the week."

"You're right, I never thought of any of it like that."

He scrubbed at his face with his hands, gave me that same sad smile again. "I love the music. Always have, always will. But maybe the constant push to get big enough to play stadiums isn't for me."

"Maybe not."

"Maybe I'll find a girl like you who isn't already pregnant and is all over finding me bare-ass naked. A girl who won't even think about asking me to cover up."

I laughed, covering my face with my hands. "I really hope you find her, Vaughan. You're a great guy. You deserve the best."

"Thanks. Anyway, enough of my shit. Come with me to the concert," he said, his voice quiet. "Maybe it can be the last crazy thing you do with a rock star. Maybe it can be the last crazy thing I do as a rock star." He smiled, but his eyes looked sad.

Resigned.

Slowly, also resigned, I breathed in through my nose and out through my mouth. "I better not miss that flight, Vaughan."

"You come along with me and don't like what you see or hear . . . the minute you say so, I'll get you out of there and it's a Stage Dive limo straight to the airport. Deal?"

"You know, you should get out of rock 'n' roll and do psychology," I grumbled. "Deal."

Backstage hadn't changed any. Lots of busy people and equipment on the go.

With no fuss we made our way through security, one of Sam's men appearing at my back. No one questioned us further once he was there. Vaughan took control of my luggage—more in case I tried to make a run for it than to be helpful, I think. I'd never imagined being in this position again—access to all areas, escorted down hallways and up stairs to the side of the stage. I wasn't a girlfriend anymore. I wasn't anything.

So what the hell was this all about?

The band were playing "Last Back," a hit off the previous album. Anne, Ev, and Lena were over on the other side of the stage, weirdly enough. I was pretty much on my own, apart from some sound guys and Pam, the tour photographer. She was a nice woman, married to Tyler, one of the favored sound engineers. They'd both been with the band for ages.

When Anne saw me, she cocked her head curiously, giving me a wave.

I waved back but stayed put.

The song came to an earsplitting crescendo, finishing with a staccato frenzy of belted chords. At point-blank range the noise shuddered up through my ankles and quivered my spine. The fans went wild.

"Ladies and gentlemen," purred Jimmy, in full leading-man mode, standing front and center on the stage. Clad in black pants with a black button-down shirt, the cuffs rolled back to reveal some of his ink. "Got something special for you tonight."

Lots of screaming from out in the stadium. I covered my ears, but too late. Holy hell. Inside my belly, the squirmy sensation came again.
Huh.

"Benny-boy, our bass player here, has a little something he'd like to say."

And I'd been trying so hard not to look at him. My face felt brittle, my eyes hot and hard. He handed over his favorite bass, the Gibson Thunderbird, to a roadie. His gaze strayed over to me as he walked up to the microphone. He knew I was there. Even in the darkness outside the footlights, he saw me.

Jimmy gave his shoulder a squeeze and then stepped back. Ben moved a hand up to cradle the microphone, but his eyes stayed on mine, his face sideways to the crowd. I shouldn't have come. Sweat poured out of my palms, from within my clenched fists. Far more than the night air could account for.

It would be okay. This was nothing special, surely. Just some weird variation on a rock star good-bye. These guys, they always did things big. Maybe there'd be a sorry-it-all-went-to-shit song just for me. How sweet.

Ben wore the typical black boots, blue jeans, and a faded gray T-shirt with some band name on it. His usual uniform. Man, if only he'd stop staring at me. It was like he held me immobile. I couldn't move, couldn't breathe.

"Hey," he said, his voice filling the night air, magnified however many thousand times. Once again the crowd went wild. Some started chanting his name, screaming out I love yous and the like. Who the hell could ever compete with this? The mass adulation. The worship of a crowd of this magnitude. I'd never stood a chance.

"Know there's been a lot of shit in the papers lately, gossip about my becoming a father." The long dark hair on top of his head had escaped whatever styling product they'd used. It fell around his face, strands catching on his beard. "I wanted to set things straight tonight."

More mania from the crowd. General confusion from me. This all could have been done without my presence. Easily. Hell, he could have held a press conference tomorrow, when I'd be on the other side of the country, licking my wounds and rebuilding my life. Why this? My emotions had been through the mill enough already.

I turned to leave but Vaughan caught my arm, halting me.

"Give it one more minute," he said.

"Oh for fuck's sake." I turned, not so barely holding in my temper. Not even sorry I'd sworn. Fucking Ben fucking Nicholson. Well he could just fuck right off, couldn't he? Yes he fucking could. Not a single fucking fire truck needed to be involved in the entire process.

I looked back to find him staring straight back at me, dark eyes searing into me, despite the distance. One fucking minute, that's all he had. And I'm pretty damn certain by the set of my lips he knew it too.

"I love you, Lizzy," he said.

Everything stopped. It was like the world held its breath. I know I did, stunned.

"I was a fucking idiot not to say it to you sooner." His hand tightened on the microphone, the lines of tension embedded deep in his face. "Shit was just changing so fast and I . . . I got scared."

Talk about making a public statement. Holy hell. The beat of silence dissolved, and the screaming and cat-whistling of the crowd came close to drowning out his words. As for me, I could barely believe my ears.

"You can have my time, and you can have my attention," he said, words slow and deliberate. "Sweetheart, you can have whatever the fuck you want, I promise. Whatever you need. No more holding back, no more fear. And if you still feel you have to get on that plane tonight, then we're doing it together."

I sucked in a deep breath, what with my body urgently needing it and all. White dots receded and I saw him clearly once again, standing before me, offering everything. I swayed slightly, the squirming sensation inside stronger this time, more definite. Vaughan and the security guy each grabbed an arm, keeping me upright.

Ben bolted across the stage toward me, grabbing me carefully around the waist and shifting me onto the stage, beneath the heat of the bright lights. I could hear the crowd screaming, but they sounded distant, otherworldly.

"What's wrong?" asked Ben, eyes panicked.

"She's moving," I said, one hand on his shoulder and the other on my belly. "She's moving, Ben. I felt her move. Our baby."

He buried his face in my hair, keeping me close, taking my weight.

"I didn't know what it was before, but it's her. Isn't that amazing?"

"Yeah, that's wild."

"Your voice was so loud, she must have heard it and recognized it." I smiled at him in amazement.

He swept me off my feet, holding me high and striding toward the center of the stage. "That's great, Liz. It really is. But, sweetheart, I need to know if you heard me too."

Slowly, I nodded, putting my palm to his face, against the bristle of his beard. "I heard you."

"What do you say?"

I took a moment, thinking it through. Big, life-changing decisions deserve at least a second of contemplation. "We don't have to get on that plane."

"Okay," he exhaled hard, smiling.

"And I love you too."

His smile stretched his beard wide. "I know I'm going to fuck up now and then, but just stick with me, okay? I don't want to do shit without you. I don't want to be places where you're not. That's not who I am anymore."

"We'll work it out."

"Yeah. We will." He covered my lips with his, kissing me stupid.

"Everybody," Ben said into the microphone, his voice once more filling the stadium. "This is my girl, Liz. Say hi. We're going to be having a baby."

And that was that.

EPILOGUE

"Get! It! Out!"

"Okay, sweetheart," said Ben, holding my sweaty, straining hand. "Just breathe."

"Don't you *sweetheart* me. It was your penis that did this."

Dr. Peer, the obstetrician, looked at me over the rim of her face mask thingy, eyes singularly unimpressed with the drama. Asshole. She wasn't the one lying on a bed with her legs up in stirrups, vagina exposed for the whole fucking world to see, was she? No. No, she wasn't. I was. And this whole labor thing had been going on for twenty-one fucking hours now, so really something needed to be done sooner rather than later. At fifteen hours I'd given in and asked for an epidural. Best thing ever. But now my high was fading. My happy was long gone.

"You can do this, I know you can," said the amazing maternity nurse, Amy.

"Have you done it?" I snarled.

"Well . . . no."

I let my eyes do the talking.

The woman took a step back.

"Easy," said Anne, bravely holding on to my other hand.

"Liz, your baby's head seems to be lodged in the birth canal," said Dr. Peer. "She isn't showing any signs of distress yet. So we can continue on as we're doing, and hopefully push her out the old-fashioned way, or you could let us help things along with a suction extraction."

"I read about those." My eyes stayed on the blip-blip-blip of the baby heart monitor screen beside me.

"Is it dangerous?" asked Ben.

"With any procedure there's a risk, but it's very minimal. Generally the child's head will just display a small bump, something like a blood blister, on the crown of her head for a couple of days. Nothing more."

"What do you want to do, sweetheart? Keep going a little longer?" He picked up a wet cloth and wiped my sweat-soaked face with it.

"I'm so tired," I cried. "Why is your head so big? If your head wasn't so big this wouldn't be happening."

"Sorry," he mumbled. At around fourteen hours, Ben had stopped trying to defend himself. Probably for the best. I wasn't to be reasoned with.

"I feel very bad for me." I cried some more.

"Another contraction coming soon," Anne announced, watching the monitor.

"Miss Rollins, why don't we set up for the extraction, just in case?" asked the ever-calm Dr. Peer.

"Okay." Some weeping.

"Oh my fucking god," said the voice of about the last person on earth I had any interest in dealing with just then. "What is the holdup in here? Do you have any idea how boring it is, waiting around for this kid to appear?"

"Martha, you cannot be in here," said Ben through gritted teeth, giving his sister a foul look.

"Get out, bitch," said Anne, ever so eloquently.

The woman swanned on over to my bedside, avoiding the sight of my girl bits so proudly on display, with a look of distaste on her perfect face. "Liz. Christ you're a mess."

Ben cracked his jaw. "Martha—"

She placed a hand on her brother's arm, gave him a look. "Relax. I have an important role here that everyone can agree I am well placed to perform. I'm here to take the abuse. Figure by now you must be running out of energy for it. And given I could hear her screams from the waiting room . . ."

"Contraction coming," warned Anne again.

"Get that uptight fucking bitch out of my sight," I said.

"Is that the best you've got?" Martha yawned oh so delicately. "I thought you'd be getting to be a seriously cranky little girl by now."

"You are the worst person to be in here."

"Oh please," she said, sitting down beside me and patting my shoulder. "You were handing out worse abuse to Ben and Anne, and they're saints compared to me. Let it all out."

"God you suck."

"You know, I've been sitting out there for hours, putting up with the stinky diapers and crying from Jimmy's little twin angel girls. And if your kid is anything like them, count me out for baby-sitting." Hand on hip, she faced me down.

"As if I'd allow my child anywhere near you unchaperoned," I snarled.

"Cute names, though. Lori and Jean. Much nicer than what you've got picked out. I really do pity that child during her school years."

"Fuck I hate you!" I screamed, every inch of me straining, bearing down with my very last reserves of energy, giving it my all.

"Tell me something I don't know!"

"You know the reason you thought I'd never sign that contract?"

I raged. "Because you have the miserable condition of believing the rest of the world is as money-grubbing and selfish as you are. It's called projection."

"That's more like it," she said. "Cutting and all too true. I think you'll make a pretty good psychiatrist after all."

"Psychologist!"

"Whatever," she shrugged. "You can put it in whatever fancy college terms you want, but you haven't got anything I haven't heard before."

"Sam's in love with you, you dumbass undeserving bitch," I growled.

Her face blanked. "What?"

"If you weren't so clueless and self-obsessed you'd have noticed it years ago."

"Push," said Anne, fingers tightening on my hand.

"C'mon, sweetheart," said Ben. "You can do it."

Dr. Peer and Amy waited between my spread legs for any development. Everyone in the fucking room singing the same tune: *push*.

But it was Martha that did her best to get in my face, having apparently recovered from her surprise. "Enough dicking around, Liz. Get that kid out of you. Now."

"I'm trying!"

"Try harder, you slacker! Push!" she screamed right back at me. "Come on!"

"Argh!" My poor innocent vulva opened dreadfully, horribly, unnaturally wide. And then plop, the rest of my baby's body slid out into the waiting arms of Dr. Peer. A moment later, a truly annoyed little cry filled the air, tiny baby fists flailing.

My baby. Oh wow.

I sagged back in relief, just trying to catch my breath. Anne was crying. Ben was watching our newborn child with open won-der. Martha was giving me a smug smile. Cow.

"Knew you just needed the right motivation," she said, inspect-ing her perfect manicure. "Hate-fueled anger has its place, you know."

"Clue-less," I singsonged back at her, as much as my complete lack of energy would allow. We both smiled. I don't really know why.

The pediatrician did a quick check of our baby while the after-birth was swiftly delivered and everything dealt with. Oh wow yeah. Never again. Never ever. Probably.

"Ladies, I present to you Gibson Thunderbird Rollins-Nicholson." Ben carefully handed my swaddled, screaming baby into my arms.

"Hey, baby. It's okay." Oh my god. The warmth inside of me, the pure love filling me up to overflowing. He quieted down, the shrill noise turning into tiny I'm-quite-put-out whimpers. A tiny nose and mouth, and two china blue eyes staring back at me. A shock of dark blond hair. "Look at you. You're wonderful."

"Isn't he?" said Ben, letting Gibson wrap a tiny finger around one of his sizably larger ones.

"He's a he," I stated, somewhat startled. "Wow."

"Wondered when you were going to clue in to that."

"And I was so sure you'd be a girl." I shook my head.

"He's perfect." Anne gazed at him with absolute adoration.

Strangely enough, so did Martha. I'd never even imagined see-ing her face so soft and smitten.

"We're naming him after your favorite bass?" I asked.

"If you don't mind." Ben leaned forward, placing a kiss on my forehead. "Good work, sweetheart. You kicked ass."

"Sorry I was so hellacious."

He laughed. "Never mind."

"Gibson Thunderbird Rollins-Nicholson." I stroked a finger across his soft, sweet little cheek. "You are loved."

"Truer words were never spoken," said Anne, giving my shoulder a squeeze. "We'll give you two guys some time alone."

"Right. Later. Nice baby." Martha followed my sister, brows drawn down and a thoughtful look on her face.

The good doctor and nurse had likewise made themselves scarce. Thank goodness for the quiet. To think, after all those months of being careful with my language, all he'd heard upon entering the world was profanity. Oh well. Win some, lose some.

"I love you," said Ben, nuzzling my face.

"I love you too." I turned, kissing the tip of his nose. "We're a family now."

He smiled. "Lizzy, you've been my family since the day I met you. My best friend. My lover. You going to make it official now and be my wife too?"

Gibson started to cry, little head trying to turn this way and that—seeking out something to suck, most likely. God, he was amazing. So beautiful.

"Here." Ben helped me rearrange him, opening the neckline on my gown to give my bubba access. "Guess I'm going to have to share those for a while."

"A noble sacrifice."

One hand rubbing his son's back, and the other smoothing back my messy hair, Ben stared down at me. "You didn't answer my question. Will you marry me?"

I smiled through the happy tears. "Oh yeah. I'd really like that."

Read the rest of the Stage Dive series!

Book one

Lick

Waking up in Vegas was never meant to be like this . . .

Evelyn Thomas's plans for celebrating her twenty-first birthday in Las Vegas were big. *Huge.* But she sure as hell never meant to wake up on the bathroom floor with a hangover to rival the black plague, a very attractive, half-naked tattooed man next to her, and a diamond on her finger large enough to scare King Kong. Now if she could just remember how it all happened . . .

One thing is for certain, being married to rock 'n' roll's favourite son is sure to be a wild ride.

Book two in the Stage Dive series

Play

Mal Ericson, drummer for the world famous rock band Stage Dive, needs to clean up his image fast — at least for a little while. Having a good girl on his arm should do the job just fine. Mal doesn't plan on this temporary fix becoming permanent, but he didn't count on finding the one right girl.

Anne Rollins never thought she would ever meet the rock god who she'd plastered on her bedroom walls as a teenager — especially not under these circumstances. Anne has money problems. Big ones. But being paid to play the pretend girlfriend to a wild, life-of-the-party drummer couldn't end well. No matter how hot he is. Or could it?

Book three in the Stage Dive series

Lead

Can rock 'n' roll's most notorious bad boy be tamed by love?

As the lead singer of Stage Dive, Jimmy is used to getting whatever he wants, whenever he wants it – now he's caught up in a life of hard partying and fast women. When a PR disaster serves as a wake-up call and lands him in rehab, he finds himself with Lena, a new assistant hired to keep him out of trouble.

Lena's not willing to take any crap from her sexy boss and is determined to keep their relationship completely professional, despite their sizzling chemistry. But when Jimmy pushes her too far, he just might lose the best thing that's ever happened to him. Can he convince his stubborn assistant to risk it all and let her heart take the lead?